Vaquero Padre

VAQUERO PADRE

PAUL COLT

THORNDIKE PRESS
A part of Gale, a Cengage Company

Copyright © 2022 by Paul Colt.
Maps © 2022 Matthew Hampton, Cascade Cartography.
All scripture quotations, unless otherwise noted, are taken from The Catholic Public Domain Version (CPDV).
Thorndike Press, a part of Gale, a Cengage Company.

LIBRARY OF CONGRESS CIP DATA ON FILE.
CATALOGUING IN PUBLICATION FOR THIS BOOK
IS AVAILABLE FROM THE LIBRARY OF CONGRESS.

ISBN-13: 978-1-4328-9470-2 (softcover alk. paper)

Published in 2023 by arrangement with Paul Colt

Printed in the USA
1 2 3 4 5   27 26 25 24 23

This book is dedicated to the clergy of every faith tradition, who enrich the lives of their flocks with love of God and neighbor. They unselfishly serve a vocation to better the human condition, nourishing our spiritual and temporal needs, while leading all to the way, the truth, and the light.

PROLOGUE

Hala
Tyrol, Germany
1663

The infirmary is small, set apart from the student dormitories for confinement of the sick. It is overwarm, shrouded in shadow pierced only by points of candlelight. The boy Eusebio, eighteen, lies in sweat-soaked sheets, his frail frame near transparent with fever. The black-robed physician rises from the boy's bedside and closes his bag. He meets concern in reverend headmaster's eyes. Eyes closed, he shakes his shaggy white mane. Sorrow sags the headmaster's shoulders. So promising a student. So young to be so afflicted. He goes to the bedside, traces a cross on the boy's fevered forehead, and offers his blessing. Time enough for Last Rights before long.

"Come," the physician says. "He must rest." The headmaster follows him out of the room and down a narrow winding stairway, creaking with age on steps shuffled smooth with the wear of thousands of feet.

I remember nothing for much of that night, as at the time I was delirious with fever. I know I prayed. Later I recalled praying for the aid of my patron. *San Francisco Xavier intercede for me, for should I survive this disease, I shall see it as a sign to follow you to mission.* A shroud of peace settled over me at that, from the top of my head to the tips of my toes. Serenity becalmed my spirit. I remember donning comfort, like a garment it enfolded the essence of my soul. Within, a soft voice spoke to me.

Eusebio, my son, rest. You have some way to go. Look to your patron to guide you. I will be with you and you will be my instrument.

At that the fever must have broken for I fell into deep sleep. I heard no more. I dreamed no more until I awoke to the light of day. In the window the song of a lark floated on a gentle breeze. At the sound of the song, I remembered. The voice. I crossed myself. *In nomine Patris, et Felii, et Spiritu Sancti. You have some way to go,* but where? *Look to your patron to guide you.*

My patron, Blessed San Francisco Xavier, missionary to the Indies. The Indies. *Some way to go.* In the footsteps of San Francisco? His mission to Cathay remained unfinished. Could it be? A sickly boy, given such purpose? I nearly laughed at the absurdity. *I will be with you and you will be my instrument.*

I crossed myself again. Could it be? It could. Could I? I must try. With that my journey began.

CHAPTER ONE

Jesuit College of Ingolstadt
Bavaria, Germany
1665

Two years later, at age twenty, I took the cassock of the Company of Jesus, as we Jesuits are known, determined to pick up the footsteps of my most holy patron. In confirmation of my mission, I took the name Francisco to my own, Eusebio Francisco Kino. After four years of novitiate, I entered college to complete my formation and training for priesthood.

The life of a missionary to foreign lands can be physically and spiritually demanding. For this I imposed upon myself a rigorous regimen of prayer, study, work, and denial. I took little sleep. When I did, I trained my body to sleep on the floor without comfort of a mattress. My ablutions were done in cold water. I divided my days by thirds devoted to prayer, study, and works of mercy.

I rose in the small hours of night to pray, before attending holy mass at dawn. It was in the dark of a starlit night I came to a comprehension that would ever after influence the direction of my spiritual journey. In prayer, I contemplated the great celestial movements of the heavens. The sheer vastness of those lights washed over me. In my studies, I'd taken a practical interest in astronomy. The missionary is called to unfamiliar lands, where the sun, the moon, and the stars become essential to navigation. They serve a practical need. I became fascinated by the order and precision of the great celestial movements. I saw divine design in the cyclical order of the universe down to the smallest manifestations of life on the earth. I saw God, visible in the whole of his creation. In further contemplation, I encountered the first principle of spirituality professed by our founder, Ignatius Loyola. God present to us in all things.

The lark that spoke to me on my sick bed too carried the miracle of creation along with all the wondrous creatures that crawl the earth, swim the sea, or soar in the air. Even the tiniest of seeds held the potential of a beautiful flower, a mighty tree, or its fruit. I wondered in awe at the power to unlock all these potentials and bring them to fruition. In all this, the hand of God is manifest.

By these reflections, I saw myself as a seed, a potential as yet unlocked. This journey I am called to will lead to potentials chosen for me. A journey my Lord has set out for me will unlock them. And thus, I threw myself into my prayers, studies, and works of charity.

My courses of study began to reveal my own potentialities. My interest in astronomy complemented a proficiency in mathematics. Mathematics, so difficult for many of my brother seminarians, came to me easily. In charity I found I could assist others in their studies. In that I began to understand the relationship between potentialities and talents. We are given talents, to each his own and in his own measure. For these, I found guidance in scripture.

Matthew 25: 14-30 teaches us the Kingdom of Heaven is like a master who went on a journey. Before departing, he distributed a wealth of talents to his servants. To one five, to another two, and to the last one. On his return, the master reckoned accounts with his servants. The one who had been given five talents traded with them and earned five more. The master rewarded him a good and faithful servant. The servant with two talents earned two more and in turn was rewarded a good and faithful servant. The servant with a single talent buried his in the ground. When he settled his account with his master, the single talent he had was taken from him.

Talents are given to be given away. I did not yet fully realize my own potentialities, but I determined to find these talents and give all to any who might be in need of them. Mathematics and astronomy, where might they lead? Very naturally both lend themselves to navigational arts and from there to cartography. Fascinated, I became a student of both. I knew Cathay to be a closed society. I also knew the most proficient of scientists could be found admissible. It struck me as irony science may afford gateway to spiritual endeavor. The Lord indeed works in mysterious ways.

Cathay. I was convinced. My patron's path led to Cathay. For that, I knew I should need more than scientific gifts; language would also be needed and so I began to search for a course of study to that end. I became frustrated in this, for owing to the remote and closed nature of Mandarin society, I was unable to locate a source of instruction. It would prove unnecessary. I should have known the meaning of my frustration. I did not. Such is the nature of human frailty. Had I thought of it, I might have discerned my journey would have no need of the language of Cathay. The Lord's purpose for me would lead in a different direction.

Seminary introduced me to a fellow pilgrim who would become friend, companion, and spiritual confidant in our early shared ministry. Matías Goni was a jovial Italian, come to the Company of Jesus from humble circumstances; but armed with a keen intellect and an abiding love of the Gospel and Holy Mother Church. Matías and I fashioned a close bond out of disparate talents. While my strengths tended to mathematics and sciences, Goni took to letters, philosophy, and a deeper appreciation for theology. It first became apparent to me in our course of scriptural study.

We were engaged in studying the letters of Saint Paul, Apostle to the Gentiles. Perhaps better said, Matías was engaged. I struggled. I consider my thinking orderly, linear, and logical, likely the influence of mathematics and science. In my reading of Paul, I was confounded by his tortured logic and contorted argument. I had great difficulty making sense of the inspired writings of the great apostle and missionary. How was I to bear his message to those I might be called to serve, when his words came incomprehensible to me? I expressed my frustration to Matías and asked his help in instruction. He smiled.

"Eusebio, Paul can be difficult, but the truth is there in his message if only we parse it out."

"Parse it out? Why can't he simply say what he means? Why must the subject of conversion struggle so to understand a message of saving grace?"

"There are two reasons for this, one practical, the other spiritual."

"Now even you, my friend, speak in riddles."

"Ever the pragmatic, Eusebio. Consider the practical construction of Paul's messages. Paul thinks in Hebrew, writes in Greek, and we translate his words to our own tongue. What possible difficulty might arise from that?"

"And we in turn must express his words in the language of those whose conversion we seek. It would seem we are condemned to struggle with the meaning of his messages in both comprehension and communication."

"Hardly condemned, my friend. God's

word is there for those who seek it. In seeking we find. Paul offers a path on our spiritual search for truth."

From that I learned. It didn't improve my understanding of Paul. It improved my understanding of my lack of understanding. In prayerful seeking, I was able to pass the course. I also came to know my friend Goni for the priestly father he would be to his flock.

Chapter Two

Cosari
Pimeria Alta
1672

Black Thorn watched the girl Rain leave the village on the path to the olas kih of the moon, a hut thatched over bent poles in the manner of a Pima dwelling. There she would spend the first days of her womanhood. Soon she would be purified for her maidenhead dance. Black Thorn noticed his childhood friend blossom to womanhood in the last passing summers. It gave him strong feelings for his own budding manhood. Soon Rain would dance, announcing her eligibility for marriage. Filled with unfamiliar thoughts and feelings, he set off on a run up the mountain trail to a favored plateau rock. There he would seek a vision from his spirit guide.

The trail climbed and twisted through thickets and rocks leading to a place in touch with the sky. Sweat slicked his chest, staining his breechclout at the thong fastening it about his waist. His lungs and the muscles of his thighs and calves burned with exertion as he reached the summit. A broad flat rock overlooked the village below with its cluster of low round olas kih lodges. He sat cross-legged and lifted his eyes to the clear blue sky.

His thought returned to the girl woman Rain. She would dance. He tried to picture her clothed in a woven skirt, adorned in paint and shells, feathers in her hair. After her dance, the corners of her eyes and mouth would be tattooed, signifying her eligibility to suitors. She would have suitors. Who would be among them? He could think of more than a few, Coxi and Yellow Feather among them. Many said in his summers Coxi would be chief, he would be Cacique. She might choose such a man for her husband. Given her many choices should Black Thorn offer himself? Would he be acceptable to her father, Raven's Wing, when others might offer greater honor? No one would be given to her acceptance who was not first approved by her father. Then who might she choose? Might she choose him? What if he offered himself and she chose another? He would be humiliated before his family and the whole of his clan. What to do? These choices lay in the future. The question Black Thorn placed before his spirit guide was should he offer himself for the favor of Rain. He closed his eyes, feeling brother sun ride the sky.

He awoke to the cry of a hawk riding wind currents above, the sky reddening in the west. The hawk swooped down over the village, arcing in a graceful circle around the olas kih of Rain's family. Black Thorn recognized the hawk for a powerful spirit guide. After her dance, emboldened by the heart of the hawk, he would offer himself to Raven's Wing.

The people gathered the evening Rain returned from her purification. They would see her dance the celebration of her womanhood. The unmarried young men stood with all the other villagers near the central fire. A smaller fire was set nearby for the maiden. She would dance. The young men would watch her. The villagers would watch the young men, amusing themselves in speculations about who her suitors might be.

Night fell still, save for snapping and popping fires. Showers of sparks lit the darkness like clouds of fireflies. Black Thorn waited anxiously. He watched the other young men, gauging their interest in Rain. As expected, Yellow Feather and Coxi were among them. Rain would have her choice. Which one might it be?

She emerged from the family olas kih, a shadow floating in darkness on the measured steps of a dancer. Black Thorn strained to see her. She stepped into the circle of light at her fire, her eyes cast down modestly at being the center of so much attention. She wore her long black hair gathered loosely at her copper shoulders with a single strand of shells for a crown. Somewhere in the darkness a drum took up a steady rhythmic beat. She moved with the grace of a willow. The beads of her skirt swayed, matching her hips. Her skin glistened, alive in the firelight. Streaks of ochre and blue paint accented her movements, slowly at first, building ever so gently in power and strength. Her dark eyes caught the firelight searching, first the fathoms of sky, then daring the shadows cast by silent young men watching her.

A lump gathered in Black Thorn's throat so struck was he by her beauty. His childhood playmate come out from its cocoon like a beautiful butterfly. He glanced at Yellow Feather. He saw nothing to betray his interest. Coxi's chest rose and fell with the beat of the drum, matching the yearning Black Thorn felt in his belly. Rain would have choices. The drum drew him back to her spell. She wove the mystery of her maidenhood in soft waves and curves. Black Thorn felt parched with need. Come what may, he must try.

Black Thorn did not sleep well that night. Visions of Rain danced in his dreams. He awoke before first light and took his morning run. He returned to the village with the sun at his shoulder. He started for the olas kih of Raven's Wing only to come to an abrupt stop, frozen by the sight of Coxi already speaking with Rain's father. His heart dropped in his chest. His rival had reached her father's ear before him. Tall and proud, soon to be Cacique, Black Thorn saw his dream blow away on the morning breeze. He turned back to his family olas kih, unable to watch what might happen.

He filled a bowl from his mother's bean pot in its place beside the embers of the family fire and sat down to eat. Despondent, the weight of his shattered dream hung heavy on his heart. What next? He could not say. All seemed lost. Even the savory stew of his mother's bavi beans tasted bitter on his tongue. As he scraped the last of his bowl, Coxi passed by. Curious, he saw no sign of the jubilation one might expect from a successful suitor. He walked shoulders bent, his features dark with anger or humiliation who could say. Could it be? Certainly Raven's Wing would have accepted him as a suitor. Could Rain have refused him? He leaped to his feet and ran.

He found Raven's Wing at the family olas kih. He loosed a tongue, tight with hope, fear, excitement, and a stir of emotion for which he had no experience. Raven's Wing folded his arms expectantly.

"Black Thorn wishes to wed your daughter Rain, should you judge me worthy."

Raven's Wing looked into the young man's heart and nodded. "Rain, you have a suitor."

She stepped out of the olas kih. Her eyes met Black Thorn's. She said nothing as was the custom. She did not turn her back in rejection.

Raven's Wing nodded. "Then come to our lodge, my son."

Black Thorn let out a whoop and ran to gather his sleeping mat. Four days he would lodge with Raven's Wing and his family after which Rain would be his bride.

CHAPTER THREE

Cathedral of Our Lady
Munich, Germany
1672

At long last the days of our formation came to a close. Matías and I were ordained to the deaconate for the final year of our training in preparation for ordination to priesthood. Ordination marked an important passage on my faith journey. The end of the beginning and the beginning of a quest to the purpose of my ministry. I believed that purpose lay in the east, in the footsteps of my patron the most reverenced San Francisco Xavier, to the shores of Cathay. I said as much to Matías as the day of our ordination approached. He shook his head with a small smile and a twinkle in his eye.

"Eusebio, you may plot a course as is your nature, but God has a plan."

"But why, why cannot it be? I can feel it. I have known it in my bones since the day I rose from my sick bed. God is calling me to this. I'm to be his instrument."

"As are we all. Perhaps you shall indeed have your dream. Then again, your path may lay in some direction you are not yet given to know. As an obedient servant, you have to expect the possibility another need awaits your ministry."

I had to accept the possibility. Still my calling to the east felt strong. The journey could only begin by the acceptance of Holy Orders.

On the day of our ordination, we were taken to the Cathedral of Our Lady in Munich. There we were presented to the archbishop for the sacrament of Holy Orders to priesthood. The cathedral is one of breathtaking beauty. More than two hundred years old, it is massive with towers and ceilings approaching the heavens. The altars and artistic adornments, the statues and window depictions of sacred scripture passages and holy saints all make a fitting house of worship for the Lord. Music filled the whole cathedral on this joyous day of celebration.

The solemn rite of ordination is performed, as it should be, during the liturgy of the most Holy Sacrifice of the Mass immediately following the Word of the Gospel.

At the proper time, we were each called forward and presented to the archbishop by our spiritual directors. The candidates are found worthy and welcome, whereupon the archbishop set forth our instruction.

"You are about to enter into a most sacred and holy office. You will continue the work of Christ Jesus in this world, teacher and shepherd, tending the flock of the faithful. You have completed preparation for this holy work. Now accept the sacred mantle of responsibility and mold your life and your being into that of the Good Shepherd . . ."

A good shepherd. I pondered the meaning of that in prayer. I am called to tend a flock. A flock I must first seek out. That is the mission for this journey. My thoughts at that moment could go no farther as we were called to our promises and vows. We pledged ourselves to faithfully discharge the duties of priesthood, to minister the Word of the Gospel, teach the faith, celebrate the sacred mysteries in sacraments, care for those entrusted to us, and grow through prayer into communion with Christ the High Priest. We pledged obedience to the Company of Jesus and the rule of Saint Ignatius Loyola. With these promises and vows we prostrated ourselves on the floor of the sanctuary where the whole of the assembly prayed for us, singing the Litany of All Saints. There the spirit of the Good Shepherd filled me with desire to shepherd my flock wherever I might find that flock. I confess I added a small prayer that it be for Cathay.

Consecrated in the most Holy Spirit, we followed the ancient rituals of ordination, the imposition of hands, the prayer of ordination and investiture. At the anointing of hands, I beheld my hands as those of a stranger. Soft hands, hands of an academic, hands anointed to God's work, prepared to administer the sacraments and celebration of the most Holy Sacrifice of the Mass. From these hands would flow the blessing of Eucharist in succession unbroken from the Lord's breaking of bread at his last supper. These hands would surely change over the rigors of the journey ahead. In what way, I could not say. It began as it should with the breaking of bread and blessing the cup, the banquet of God's gifts. We exchanged the kiss of peace. Ordained, we celebrated our first mass.

Having had years of preparation for the priesthood and having received the Holy Orders of ordination, I felt my journey to the Orient imminent. What I learned is that all my preparation prepared me only for more preparation. We busied our time in waiting with further study and works of mercy and charity. More given to action than patience, I confess I chafed at waiting. Waiting for what? My thirst to win souls for Christ burned within me, unsated. Time it seemed went wasted. I prayed. I beseeched. I waited. Matías counseled.

"Patience, Eusebio. Our time comes in due course. When, we are not given to know."

My friend was right, of course, though I am afraid I profited little from his counsel.

Cosari
Pimeria Alta
1677

Black Thorn sat outside his olas kih. Alone in the dark of night, head bowed, he prayed. His lodge belonged to the work of women this night. Rain's time had come. She would give birth. In this Black Thorn had no part. Willow, the mother of Yellow Feather's wife, assisted as she did in most clan births. The pains came on near sunset. The night was now well advanced. Women and babies made birth in their own time. Anxious waiting chafed, banishing the veil of sleep. Rain made guttural sounds with each passing

28

pain. Slow during moonrise, more frequent now as it followed the dark trail of the sun.

Black Thorn may have dozed, awakened by a lark's twitter, greeting a blue sky, pinking in the east. The cry came full throated from the olas kih. Not the cry of his Rain. This cry came of a son, testing his voice. Black Thorn stood. He waited long, but only a short time. Willow brought him the tiny bundle wrapped in a soft robe. He lifted the robe. Round red face, matted thatch of black hair glistened in first light; Black Thorn welcomed his son.

He lifted his eyes to the sun-capped hills above. There a hawk soared. Much as he'd seen his spirit guide the evening it circled Rain for his bride. The hawk spiraled down, swooping low over the village, flaring wings and tail, haloed in rising sun it cried shrill greeting to Black Thorn and his son. He lifted the boy to the sky, offering brother hawk proof his prophesy fulfilled. The hawk darted away, having claimed its own.

Black Thorn carried his son back to the shelter of his olas kih. Inside, the lodge was dim and warm. Rain lay on her robes. A tired smile lit her face at the sight of her husband and child. Black Thorn knelt beside her and handed the bundle to her breast.

"He is Hawk."

She nodded. "It is good."

The following spring Yellow Feather's wife, Sweet Grass, delivered a girl child they named Fawn.

Jesuit College
Bavaria, Germany
1678

Curious I made haste to the office of our Provincial Superior. The summons came as a surprise. Along the way I examined my conscience, but could discern no transgression that might give rise to some disciplinary reason for the call. I bounded the marble steps two at a time, nonetheless. Brother Felix greeted me with a nod in reception. Great carved double doors opened to Father Provincial's office.

"Father Kino to see you Reverend Father."

"Send him in."

Brother Felix stepped aside. I entered the spacious office lined with bookshelves sufficient to house a library that might be the envy of any of the university colleges.

"You sent for me, Reverend Father."

"I did Eusebio. Come." He motioned me forward. "Have a seat."

He said it kindly. I relaxed still curious as

I approached his massive desk across thick carpet. Stained glass windows at his Excellency's back bathed the room a rosy glow. I took a seat in a beautifully carved chair set before the desk, cushioned in red velvet.

"How may I be of service?"

He smiled. "Well said. An assignment has come for you."

"Cathay!" I confess I blurted in my excitement.

Reverend Father Provincial smiled. My desires were well known to those in authority. "Cathay, I'm afraid it is not."

"*Oh,* I only thought . . ." Disappointment. I sought unsuccessfully to hide it.

"We plan, my son. God acts."

I heard Matías's voice. "Of course, Reverend Father. What then?"

"King Carlos II of Spain has reached out to the Holy Father, requesting support for a missionary venture to New Spain. Our Society of Jesus has been chosen to provide spiritual guidance for the mission. Knowing your desire to mission, our Superiors agreed you would be an excellent choice to become a member of this royal service."

"I am humbled by this calling, but where is this New Spain?"

Reverend Father Provincial rose from his desk and led the way to a corner of his office. There he lit a candle to illuminate a globe. "We are here. You will first travel to Spain where you will obtain His Majesty's passage to New Spain in the New World. He turned the globe across a long sea passage. It may not be your Cathay, Eusebio, but it promises a rich harvest of souls."

I left Reverend Father Provincial's office, my head spinning. I marveled at the thought. Such a strange land. So far from my known world. God had indeed set forth a plan I could never have anticipated. The journey would take me halfway around the world in the opposite direction of my presumed calling. Even then the journey to mission would only just begin. Where might the journey lead? What service might I be called to? I had no notion. I could but take comfort, God would provide.

As I departed Reverend Father Provincial's offices, who should I encounter but Matías matching the confusion and haste from which I'd only recently and partially recovered.

"What brings you here, Matías?" I said it trying not to betray a knowing expression from which he might take relief.

"I've been summoned to see Reverend Father Provincial. And you?"

"I have already seen him."

"And what does it mean?"

"It is not my place to break such as might be your news, for I know only my own."

"You make it sound ominous."

I shrugged. "Don't delay. We can talk when you have been given to know."

He rolled his eyes and hurried along. I smiled to myself. Goni's company would smooth the road we might travel together. I waited for him to share his news with me.

"New Spain," Goni said as we left the prefecture by a long-covered archway dappled in late afternoon sun.

"It's a long way from Cathay."

"It is. Did you really think you might realize your dream?"

"I prayed."

"Well, we have your answer."

"As you said, we have God's answer."

"Yes. And you know we might have guessed."

"New Spain?"

"No not that. All the time you planned to spend studying Mandarin would have been wasted."

CHAPTER FOUR

Genoa, Italy
June 5, 1678

[Then the Lord] sent them in pairs before his face into every city and place where he was to arrive. (Luke 10:1)

We traveled southwest by carriage to the port city of Genoa in northern Italy. There Goni and I would join confreres in the Company of Jesus who were similarly assigned to missions in New Spain. The road into Genoa spilled out of the hills into a city sprawling along hillsides leading down to the sea. The city clustered, crescent shaped, around the seaport town center. Stone and stucco buildings with steep tiled roofs crowded together along a warren of narrow streets. Here and there markets bustled, busy with the commerce of daily life. We were received at a monastery near the docks where we would be housed until we sailed. We were shown to our cells and thereupon celebrated safe completion of this first stage of our journey by a prayerful visit to chapel.

We took our supper at the table of Father Abbott Anjolli in the monastery's austere refectory. There we were served simple fare, potage, dark bread, and watered wine. Father Abbott inquired after our journey to this New Spain. We recounted our plan to sail from Genoa to Cádiz and thereon to New Spain. He listened thoughtfully.

"My brothers and I shall keep you in our prayers," he said at length. "The journey you propose is perilous indeed. Weather on the high seas can be severe. Even the sheltered voyage from here to Cádiz, sails waters infested with pirates."

This last brought a start to Matías's eyes. I endeavored to put him at ease.

"Our mission is from the Lord. He will see us safely to his intended purpose."

"Whatever that may be," Father Abbott said with his blessing.

Port of Genoa
June 12, 1678
She rode at anchor offshore. *His Majesty's Ship San Crystobal.* A glorious Spanish galleon, her three decks rose above the hold.

Gunports lined the first two decks amidships to her bow. Her aft decks climbed in ornately carved rich wood gleaming in gilt edge. Three tall masts carried square-rigged spars to a bright blue sky. We stood in a black-robed gaggle, awaiting passage to board.

"Is she not magnificent, Matías?"

"She floats."

"Are you apprehensive, my friend?"

"Only my stomach."

I clapped him on the shoulder. "Think of the adventure. Think of the journey it takes us to. Our humble part in the great and glorious work of salvation."

"I do think on higher purpose. It is only my breakfast that rests uncertain."

A dinghy bobbing in light sea chop came to the dock to fetch us. It did little to instill confidence in Goni's misgivings. We climbed down a salt stained, rickety wooden ladder affixed to the side of the dock. Timing a step down to the small boat proved a task demanding of some attention. Once settled in the boat two crewmen rowed us out to what would be our new home on this leg of our journey. Standing, rocking in the skiff beside the ship, we were greeted with a rope ladder inviting us to climb aboard. My poor companion faced the prospect of the ladder, chalk white in pure terror.

"Have no fear, Matías. Follow me." My declaration proved full of false bravado as I discovered the rope ladder rose and fell with the swell of the ship and the similarly unsynchronized motion of the dinghy. At the dock we had only one moving part to negotiate. Here we had two. Still, I managed to secure a foothold and started up, trailing a reassuring smile over a shoulder for poor Matías. I next discovered a cassock makes an apparel choice ill-suited to rope ladders. Thus, I paused mid-climb to tuck the hem of mine into my pantaloons belt. I hoped Matías took note before beginning his climb. I reached the deck rail where I was met by the captain who assisted me aboard. As I climbed over the rail, I chanced a look down into the anguished face of my terrified companion gauging a lunge to a rope that might plunge him into the sea. I must confess, I could not bear to watch.

"Capitán Diego Santiago, at your service, Padre," he said with a deep bow, doffing a stylish wide-brimmed hat with a crimson plume to go with a dark blue coat cuffed in the gilt emblems of his rank. A crimson sash, cream-colored britches, and polished knee-high boots completed an elegant effect. He turned up tips of a full mustache to a neatly trimmed goatee. His dark eyes fairly crackled with the air of command.

"Eusebio Francisco Kino," I said releasing my cassock. It was at that moment I noticed the docks at the shoreline rise and fall with the ship. Poor Goni. A successful boarding was not likely to improve his seafaring experience.

"If you will excuse me, Padre, let me assist your compadre."

I took the opportunity to look over the ship topside. Decks of oak gleamed in the sun. I made her one hundred forty cubits in length, fifty at the beam. Three masts rigged for square sheet stood foredeck, with the main amidships and mizzenmast aft. Crew quarters were housed in the forecastle; officers and passengers were housed aftcastle. A cargo hold and two gunnery decks bristled below the main deck. The lower gunnery deck mounted sixteen, thirty-two pound culverin. The upper gunnery deck stationed twelve lighter demiculverin. The presence of such formidable weaponry harkened back to Father Abbott's warning concerning the dangers of brigands on the high seas. I calculated the presence of so much firepower would do little to comfort my anxious companion.

At that, Capitán Santiago helped Matías

over the rail. I was drawn to pity for the ashen appearance of my friend's color.

"Matías, are you all right?"

With that he turned away and bent over the rail, relieving himself of his disquieting breakfast. Thankfully he disposed of it aft of the dinghy bobbing below. It was an inauspicious introduction to captain and crew. Unfortunately, it foretold an undignified position he would occupy for much of our early voyage.

Settled into our cabin I returned to the rail on the aftcastle outside our stateroom to watch the crew prepare to weigh anchor and set sail. Down the gangway to the portside, Capitán Santiago climbed the stairs leading to the bridge. He waved.

"Come along, Padre, if you care to watch, the view is much better from up here."

I smiled and made haste to follow. On the bridge, I was struck by the massive ship's wheel and soon taken by a curious instrument I would come to know intimately. At that moment however the main deck below commanded attention. Sailors scampered up rope ladders into the rigging like so many nimble monkeys. They unfurled the sheet as others manned a powerfully built winch, turned to draw a heavy linked chain, hoisting the anchor.

"Set sail," the capitán called. His command echoed by the first mate, rang across the deck to crew stationed at each mast. Sail billowed in the breeze as the anchor broke the surface of the waves.

Santiago glanced to the seaman manning the wheel, "Quarter to port."

The bow swung to port in response to the wheel. Sail filled. She began to move, taking up a southerly course, holding the coastline to starboard. Wind filled my nostrils, reminiscent of the Holy Spirit filling the apostles at Pentecost. Our journey commenced.

CHAPTER FIVE

Mediterranean Sea
June 17, 1678

Poor Goni passed his first five days at sea at the rail. He could partake of only water and small bits of bread. I became concerned for him. As I found my sea legs, I prayed my companion soon would too. By the fifth day, he began to show improvement. We marked it a blessing for this was to be but the first leg of a long sea journey, the beginning calmed by the shelter of our passage.

Capitán Santiago proved an affable man, patient and tolerant of my curiosities. The intricacies of navigation fascinated me in my academic pursuits. On land, we had maps and roads to follow; but here in open water, navigational arts took on a far more scientific bent. Here I found practical application of the tools and knowledge I had only known in the abstract. When I showed interest, the capitán graciously invited me to observe.

"On this voyage, Padre, we have only to keep the coastline to starboard. We follow it from Genoa to Cádiz."

"But what of the passage to New Spain? We cross open sea, no?"

"We do. For that we have the stars and our compass," he said indicating the instrument I'd noticed on my first day on the bridge. It stood suspended in a small cabinet allowing it to remain level amid the motion of the ship. My academic understanding of the instrument hadn't reckoned accounting for the motion aboard ship. The capitán invited me to closer examination. The compass face showed four points of direction, north, south, east, and west. A magnetic needle pointed north by natural attraction. The points of direction were subdivided north by northwest, north, north by northeast, east, and so on. By these directional variants, course could be plotted and steered in reference to north, similar to ancient instruments used to plot direction in reference to the North Star. While celestial plotting offered greater accuracy, problems of weather and visibility of the celestial bodies at sea increased the risk of reading errors.

Capitán Santiago's grasp of navigational

arts and the quality of his tools favored my confidence in the surety of crossing. In times to come, my own grasp of navigation would further my mission and more than once, save my life and those of my companions.

Six days out from the port of Cádiz, Matías enjoyed much improved humor. We stood at the rail, taking the air and the scent of the sea. Green waves stretched forth southeast to the horizon. Standing at the bridge rail with wind in our robes we had only to enjoy the gifts of wind and God's golden sun on the waves.

"The color of vigor replaces pallor on you check, Matías. You must be feeling better."

"Aye. For a time there, I didn't know if I should fear death or failure to succumb."

"That bad?"

"You have no conception, Eusebio."

"Well, I'm pleased the worst seems to be past."

"Corsairs!"

The alarm sounded by the lookout high above in the main mast crow's nest. Capitán Santiago hastened to the rail. He extended his glass and swept the sea south and aft.

"Ottoman corsairs by the strike of the green scimitar and skull." He said more to himself than to our benefit. "Gunners to station!" He barked the command.

I could make out nothing with my untrained eye. "What does it mean?"

"Pirates, Padre. Ottoman pirates. These waters are infested with them," the capitán said.

"What do they want?"

"Plunder and Christians, Padre."

"Plunder I understand. Why Christians?"

He collapsed his glass. "Christians feed the Ottoman slave trade. Pray we can hold them off. You and Father Goni would make fine prizes. You wouldn't enjoy it."

With that, he was gone to see to his battle stations.

"Oh, dear," Matías said crossing himself.

I turned to the horizon. Where moments before I saw nothing, now I could make out a white speck. I watched it grow.

"What do you see, Eusebio?"

"There," I pointed.

"I don't see anything."

"Watch. You will."

"Is that a sail?"

"It is."

The *San Crystobal* lumbered along under full sail. Magnificent as she stood at anchor, the galleon lacked speed and maneuverability. The corsair sloop gained on us with maddening speed. A sleek sloop, three masts at full sheet. She gained on us, setting a course far enough off our portside to deny us effective use of our guns while keeping open water behind them. By the time I could make out her colors, I clearly saw the skull and white scimitar on a green field. She cut low in the water. Her hull bristled with gunports above and oar ports below, though at her wind speed she had no need of oarsmen. Turbaned heads clotted her deck. As they raced by, they shook curved swords, shouting taunts, indistinct in the wind over the waves in the distance.

"They seem to be passing. Perhaps they mean us no harm," Matías said.

Santiago bounded up the steps to the bridge to this last. "They mean to cross us. Their guns to our bow. If they can volley sufficient damage, they'll attempt to board."

The capitán set his glass on his adversary. Well ahead of us now the sloop sliced to starboard and trimmed her sails as she glided toward attack position.

"Hard to starboard!" Santiago's order brooked no question.

Slowly *San Crystobal* began to come about. The sloop came into view off the port bow. Balls of fire burst from her gunports. Blooms of black powder smoke spread over the surface of the sea. Rumble and whine announced the balls. The port bow rail shattered to matchsticks. A ball screamed overhead, crashing into the sea off the aft starboard quarterdeck. *San Crystobal* came about three-quarter broadside. When the Ottomen realized their peril, they set sail, preparing to recast the fight.

"Fire!"

Port guns erupted in a rolling thunder along the gun deck, shaking the decking on which we stood. I might have been thrown to the deck with the pitch had I not grasped the rail. I managed to keep my feet, Goni's too as he crashed against me. Acrid black smoke billowed up all along the port rails burning the eyes before dissipating in the wind. The corsair must have taken a thirty-two pounder amidships for bow and stern twisted in a most unnatural way. A volley of light culverin raked her masts and rigging. She lay dead in the water unable to flee.

"Another volley, capitán?" The gunnery officer cried from somewhere below.

"Save the powder and shot. She's taking on water. That nest of vipers shall bother no one any longer."

Alarmed at the looming loss of life, I spoke up. "Capitán, there seem to be survivors waving from the deck. Should we not lower boats and assist them?"

"Assist them, Padre?" He arched his brow in disapproval. "And have our throats slit for the pleasure of our own stupidity. You don't know these animals."

"I know they are infidels, but they too are God's children."

"Not any God you and I revere." With a curt nod he departed to see to our damage.

CHAPTER SIX

Cádiz, Spain
June 25, 1678

Sunday, we dropped anchor in the port of Cádiz. Matías and I celebrated the Holy Sacrifice of the Mass at dawn with Capitán Santiago and crew in thanksgiving for safe passage. The sea was calm that morning, scattered clouds with a light breeze to freshen first light of a new day. We took our breakfast with the capitán who wished us safe voyage on our passage to New Spain. Once again, we negotiated the rope ladder descending to the longboat that would ferry us to shore. This time Matías, now a seasoned mariner, descended the ladder without incident and I too with the hem of my cassock safely tucked away.

The bustling docks of Cádiz were eerily quiet early on a Sunday morning. We had only to scan the rooftops climbing the hillside from the docks to find the cathedral spire of our intended destination. We arrived at the time of Solemn High Mass being said by the bishop. We took places at the back of a magnificent church washed in golden light and fragrant incense. One day perhaps New Spain would celebrate a house of the Lord so grand as this; but in my heart I knew it must spring from the humble roots of a mission not yet set upon the soil of an unknown land. Humble roots. Funny to think that, for as yet I had no understanding of the conditions they would come to represent.

With Mass concluded we sought audience with the bishop at his residence where we were welcomed with warmth and generous hospitality. Seated in a most comfortable parlor to his rectory he broke bad news gently.

"I'm sorry to tell you the fleet for this season has sailed."

"Sailed?" I said.

"Without us," Goni echoed.

The bishop smiled kindly. "It would seem so."

"But what are we to do?" Matías wrung his hands.

"Wait for the next sailing."

"When might that be?" I asked.

"Not until next year, I'm afraid."

"Next year! What are we to do until then? Where will we live?"

"Your Company of Jesus has a provincial house in Seville. I am sure you will be welcome there. We can assist you in passage."

And so, after two days reacquiring our land legs, we departed by carriage for Seville.

Seville

The city overwhelmed the senses. A mass of humanity wedged in intricate narrow warrens punctuated by broad plazas, merchant bazaars, and towering spires of beautiful churches dotting the city. Wealth and nobility dwelt in the upper city, apart from the teeming, impoverished masses of the lower city. Commerce attracted French and Dutch merchants, bankers, and investors to the Spanish upper classes. The needs of the poor fell to the church, served by her monasteries and clergy. There among the city's needy we were delivered to the front gates of Loyola House, a community dedicated to the society's blessed founder Ignatius.

The gates opened to a dusty courtyard leading to a second set of doors at the entrance to a large brown stone building at once austere and imposing. Here we were greeted by the porter and shown to the offices of Father Rector Goetz. A kindly soul, Father Rector listened patiently to our plight.

"And so," I said in conclusion, "we are at a loss as to what to do."

"You are not the first to face this predicament. Passage to New Spain can be problematic. Commercial passage is very expensive, usually prohibitively so. Passage on slave ships, while less expensive, cannot be condoned for the immorality of the practice. That leaves the movements of His Majesty's fleet, which are subject to the purposes of the court, not those of an ecclesiastical schedule."

"So where does that leave us?"

"You are welcome to stay here with us until you are able to resolve the matter of your passage."

"That is most kind of your Reverend Father Rector. Is there some ministry we may assist you in?"

"The poor are always in need. If you but look, the Lord will provide his opportunity for you. Others who have experienced similar delays have used the time to learn useful language. How is your Spanish?"

Matías and I exchanged glances and nods.

"That is a most excellent suggestion, Father. Perhaps you might direct us to a suitable tutor."

"I shall see to it. And now brother porter will show you to rooms. Vespers ring at four o'clock. Supper follows at six."

He gave us his blessing and with that we joined the community of Loyola House.

In the days that followed we immersed ourselves in the study of Spanish with the assistance of a novice of Spanish descent. He was most eager to take time from his own studies to further ours. Father Rector of course was also quite correct where it concerned the needs of the poor. We took to the streets, Matías and I, to make use of our new Spanish language in finding our way around the city. In these explorations we further sought some meaningful call to ministry. Everywhere we walked we encountered the great gulf between opulent wealth and abject poverty.

The walled and gilt gates to the estates of the upper city set the aristocracy apart from the masses of humanity seething beyond the bazaars in the lower city. We spent little time in the upper city. Wherewithal to meet need could be found there, but unlocking it from the clutches of those who held it seemed beyond the means of two humble priests.

The bazaar markets struck us as more fertile grounds for opportunity. Here the gentry and those who served them came to bargain, barter, and shop. The working poor toiled at their occupations selling produce, services, and crafts from cramped stalls thronged with crowds. Odors of cooking food, waste, and humanity hung in fetid hot air. The poorest of the poor could be found here too, living the life of Lazarus at the rich man's gate. We saw the image of that scriptural passage played out in thousands of faces. The need so large, the window of mercy so small, one seemingly lacked the means to make even the smallest difference in the other.

So small. Matías saw him first. A street urchin of perhaps five years old. Dressed in rags with dirt-smudged cheeks and sunken eyes, large black pools filled with hunger, fear, pleading. I saw the child Jesus in those eyes. It spoke to my heart. An Ignatian encountered Jesus in a most personal way. Our founder made a spiritual principle of it.

Goni knelt.

"Where do you live?"

The boy stared blankly as though the question had no meaning. I prayed it might be the state of our fledgling Spanish. My heart knew differently.

"Your parents?"

He shook his head. An orphan.

"Are you hungry?"

He nodded.

I glanced around. I purchased an ear of roasted corn from a street vendor and gave it to the lad. He devoured it. Within moments another boy stood at my side. Slightly older, his eyes no less desperate.

"Are you hungry too?"

"Sí, Padre."

I bought another ear of corn.

"Do you have a name?" Matías asked the little one.

"Pablo."

"Do you know this boy?"

"Juan is my brother."

Matías stood. "What are we to do?"

Now it was I who had no answer.

"They are orphans, living on the street."

"They are," I said. In that moment of uncertainty, I heard the words of Ignatius Loyola, beloved founder of the Society of Jesus, who asked, *"What have I done for Christ in this world? What am I doing now? And above all, what should I do?"*

"It seems our ministry has found us."

CHAPTER SEVEN

Loyola House

We took them home with us. Reverend Father Rector greeted us with an arched brow.

"What have we here?"

"Orphans," I said.

"What do you propose to do with them?"

"We don't know as yet," I said.

"We couldn't simply leave them to the streets."

"Do you know how many there are like these? Thousands. This house could not possibly care for so many."

"But these are just two," Goni said. "And small at that."

"If you think they are two, just wait until morning."

I sensed Father Rector was about to take exception to our two little guests and our newly found ministry.

"Reverend Father, you yourself said if we

55

looked the Lord would lead us to a ministry. It seems He has."

"Perhaps so. We shall see what your ministry has grown to by morning. I suggest you give some thought to how you plan to support your ministry. Regrettably, the need far exceeds the means of this humble house and community."

I winced.

By morning, our gates opened to the gathering of a dozen more orphans. Word, it seemed, spread quickly through the lower city. Two ears of roast corn had opened a crack in a dike holding back an ocean of need.

"What are we to do now?" Goni said, wringing his hands.

"Support our mission as Reverend Father Rector suggested."

"How do you propose to do that?"

"I don't know yet. I pray the Lord who gave us this mission may have some plan for how we are to fulfill it. You stay here and see what you can do for the boys, while I go in search of some form of support."

"I'll do as you say, Eusebio; but if I am to take care of the boys, what am I to do with the girls?"

"Girls?"

"Three this morning. It appears girls also become orphaned."

With that, I set off for the upper city.

Upper City

I collected a following passing through the bazaar to the upper city. It only reinforced for me the urgency of my errand. Urgent though it may be, I had no plan. I climbed the broad avenue of luxury past one locked gate after another. I rounded a bend in the road and came upon an open gate attended by a liveried servant clad in purple vest and pantaloons. He eyed me with suspicion.

"Good morning," I smiled.

"Padre."

"I wonder, would your master be about?"

"Is he expecting you?"

Here I put my trust in providence.

"I believe he is."

He may not know it yet, but I believed at that moment his gate opened to me for a reason.

"Who may I say is calling?" He eyed the children who'd followed me from the bazaar.

"Eusebio Kino of the Company of Jesus."

"Wait here. I shall announce your presence to Conde de la Vega."

A count no less. For a mercy we have

57

found wealth. I offered a prayer of thanksgiving and petition as the servant disappeared across a broad sun-soaked plaza beyond the gate. Presently the servant returned in obvious ill humor.

"My master does not know you and is not expecting you."

"Perhaps he has only forgotten. I come in the work of the Lord."

"That is your affair. My master is not to be disturbed."

I must confess I was disheartened at being summarily dismissed without so much as an opportunity to make my appeal. As I turned to go, I met the expectant gazes of the children. The face of their need left me utterly empty-handed.

The clatter of a carriage intruded on my quandary. A beautiful ornate coach emblazoned with the gilt crest of Casa y/Vega, emerged from the villa, drawn by a magnificently matched team four-in-hand. The driver and footmen wore purple livery, matching that of the gatekeeper. As the carriage passed, a side curtain parted for a glimpse at me and my impoverished entourage.

"Driver, stop please."

The voice from within carried authority and the musical notes of an angel. The driver drew a halt. The coach curtain parted to a truly angelic apparition. Porcelain complexion, ebony hair, thickly lashed green eyes, ruby lips.

"Padre, I am Condesa Maria Rosa de la Vega. I understand you sought audience with my husband. May I ask why?"

"My Lady," I bowed. "These children, along with many others, are in need of an orphanage. I hoped I might appeal to the Count's charity to support us in our mission."

Her eyes softened as she looked on the children.

"They need food, shelter, and schooling just as your own children need these things."

She cut suddenly sad eyes to me. "We are childless, Padre."

"I am sorry to hear that, Your Grace. Perhaps in this ministry you are not."

She knit her brow in thought, her attention drawn back to the children.

"Should you find it in your heart, we are at Loyola House in the lower city."

"Driver."

With that the carriage clattered away. I held out my arms to our little circle of hope and started back down to the lower city.

CHAPTER EIGHT

Loyola House

For the next two days I trod the avenues of the upper city in hope of finding some meaningful benefactor. All I achieved for these efforts was a growing number of orphans threatening to overspill the Loyola House courtyard. I returned from the upper city the second day to find a dispirited Matías and a resolute Reverend Father Rector insisting we could not continue to turn our community into an orphanage. Our circumstances looked grim as night fell. The refectory offered our confreres only coarse bread and water at our evening meal, everything else having been consumed to feed the children. Matías and I walked among the children in the courtyard after supper. Little Pablo and Juan followed us like puppies as we sought to encourage the others.

The clatter of hoofbeats and wheels on cobblestone sounded beyond the gate. Visitors to the lower city after dark were most uncommon. We opened the gate. Moonlight gleamed off the crest Casa y/Vega. A footman opened the carriage door, giving a hand as Condesa Maria Rosa stepped down.

"Padre," she smiled.

"My Lady, to what do we owe such honor?"

"My children. May I come in?"

"Of course. Please. May I present Padre Mathias Goni. Matías, Condesa Maria Rosa de la Vega."

Matías bowed, stepping aside for her to enter the courtyard. The children's noisy prattle fell silent in awe of the beautiful lady. Her rose satin gown splashed moonlit color on the drab dusty palate of curious faces staring at her in amazement. We showed her into the rectory.

"Tell me, My Lady, what means this 'My children,' " I asked.

"This." She drew two fat purses from beneath her cloak. She handed one to me and the other to Matías.

My jaw dropped. "There is a fortune here."

"Not a fortune, an orphanage with food and clothing."

"How did you bring your husband to such a change of heart?"

"I did not. These are the proceeds from the sale of my jewels. Conde Carlos de la Vega does not know."

"Will he not be angry?"

"He will have children. Send for me when you have your orphanage established. I should like to see my children in a better place."

"Of course, My Lady, with all gratitude and my blessing."

"Thank you, Padre."

Reverend Father Rector's mood improved with newfound support for our ministry. We located a building in the lower city not far from Loyola House that would suffice to start and commenced renovations. With our plans to sail for New Spain on the first available ship, we needed someone to operate the orphanage. Reverend Father Rector introduced us to Mother Superior of the Sisters of Our Sorrowful Mother. Mother Superior was quick to see the merit of our mission and was overjoyed to find sisters who would see to the needs of our children. We suggested the home be called Mother Maria Rosa House. Mother Superior approved of the gesture to our benefactor.

With the renovation complete and the sisters and children in residence, we sent word to the condesa, inviting her to visit Mother Maria Rosa House. She replied by return messenger she would be unable to come. Her husband the conde strongly disapproved of her actions in selling her jewels and forbad her to have any further contact with such foolishness. For this I felt remorse. The Lady's act of generosity deserved more than her husband's rancor. I thought I might speak with the conde and convince him of the blessed goodness accomplished by the condesa's generosity. Secure in my resolve, I set off for the upper city.

The liveried servant at the Casa de la Vega gate remembered me with distaste. Disputes such as the one posed by the orphanage could not remain secret in such a household.

"What do you want now, Padre?"

"A word with the conde if I may."

"Are you sure this is what you wish? My master is, shall we say, put out by your dealings with the condesa."

"I understand and I am most regretful for that. The condesa's generosity has done much good. I only wish to explain that to the conde in hope he will harbor no anger toward the good Condesa. Please, tell him that as my request for an audience."

"Very well," he said with a scowl.

I held out little hope. The porter returned soon after wearing a troubled expression.

"My master will see you. This way."

We crossed a broad plaza to an imposing front entry to villa de la Vega. The porter led the way across a tiled reception, past double arcing staircases leading to the upper floors. We continued down a paneled corridor, lit by wall sconces braced in golden candlesticks to a pair of polished double doors, one of which he held open to me. Inside I found a large sunlit room furnished in the most elegantly carved and upholstered manner gathered around a massive stone fireplace. At the far end, Conde Carlos de la Vega sat at an ornate desk haloed in shadow by floor to ceiling windows at his back. Hat in hand I approached, presenting the best possible smile I could muster.

"Excellency, thank you for the privilege of seeing your humble servant."

"Humble servant indeed. Humble servants are not nearly as expensive as you, Padre." He curled a long dark waxed mustache. His coat trimmed in the finest brocade, his britches of the softest wool tucked in boots that gleamed to his knees.

"I didn't mean to be a burden to you,

Excellency. I merely came to see if you might help orphan children. The condesa must have overheard my request. When you were too busy to see me, she inquired after my purpose. I did not ask that she sell her jewels. She did that out of sweet charity in her own heart. She has done much good with her gift. We now have an orphanage, called Mother Maria Rosa House, that cares for some two hundred homeless children. It is my prayer that you see all the good made possible by your wife's generosity and hold no harsh feelings toward her charity."

He folded his hands and pursed his lips. "Two hundred you say."

I nodded. "The need is great, but it is a beginning. A beginning made possible by the saintly offering of your devoted wife. If you would be willing to come and see it, I believe you would find reason to rejoice with her."

He drummed his fingers on the desk. "Where is this orphanage of yours?"

"In the lower city, near Loyola House on the Avenue of Ashes."

He sat in silence, studying me as though a specimen of some foreign insect.

"I will consider it, Padre."

"Gracias, Excellency. I shall take no more of your time." I took my leave.

CHAPTER NINE

Mother Maria Rosa House

Three days later they arrived by carriage, Conde and Condesa Carlos de la Vega. Matías was at the orphanage helping Sister Maria Concepcion. He sent Juan, running to Loyola House to fetch me. We both ran to the orphanage. We found Matías conducting a tour of the facility. Dormitories upstairs, one for the boys, another for the girls, classrooms, a refectory and kitchen.

"We don't have room for a chapel," Matías explained. "In good weather we use the chapel at Loyola House. If the weather is inclement, we say mass in the refectory."

I followed along listening to Matías conduct the tour. The condesa smiled broadly at all she saw, remembering some of the children she'd seen with me in the upper city, their faces clean, their rags replaced in plain, clean clothing. Conde Carlos said nothing. He showed no expression as we returned to reception. He fixed me with one eye.

"Very impressive, Padre," he said. "You said it was a start. It looks as though you have accomplished a great deal for a simple 'start.'"

"This is but a small pool drawn from a river of need."

"Would you expand if you could?"

"We would. The building next door has potential. A second facility would allow one for the boys and one for the girls."

"That still doesn't sound like a river."

"It is a beginning."

He smiled. "See what you can purchase that building for. Figure your needs to furnish it along with a proper chapel and come see me."

I for once found myself speechless. It was left to Matías to express our gratitude for so benevolent a generosity.

The Conde and Condesa Carlos de la Vega departed to tearful smiles.

Loyola House
1679
Under the patronage of Conde de la Vega we purchased the house next to Mother Maria Rosa and the following spring opened San Carlos Home for Boys. It was a joyful

time, made more so by news a new fleet prepared to sail for New Spain in July. Matías and I bid painful farewells to our children, confident we left them in the loving care of our sisters. We departed for Cádiz, renewed in the purpose of our mission, inspired by the charity of Conde and Condesa de la Vega.

Cádiz

We arrived in time to secure passage on a West Indian fleet in convoy of two Spanish galleons. We again availed ourselves of the bishop's hospitality for a brief stay, awaiting our departure. We boarded a merchant vessel on the tenth, a sunny day buffeted by stiff breeze on a sea roiled by chop. I wondered after Matías's sea readiness nearly a year removed from his last voyage, though riding at anchor he seemed to quickly recover his sea legs. Accommodations were spare, but we took joy in anticipation of our voyage to New Spain.

The fleet sailed July eleventh. The twelfth dawned to an ominous sky, darkening rapidly to flashes of lightning and peals of thunder. Headwind blew furiously, lashing the decks in torrents of rain. For a blessing the storm caught us not far off the coast. Battered and buffeted by wind and high seas, our ship floundered, driven toward shore. Matías and I spent the hours of this ordeal in prayer, not knowing the fate of our ship or our mission. We placed all trust in divine mercy and took it for God's will when our ship ran aground before the storm blew itself out.

Brokenhearted, Goni and I were ferried back to Cádiz in a small boat. With no immediate prospects for passage we returned to Seville, once again taking up residence in Loyola House and service to our orphan children.

Mother Maria Rosa House

A year passed to the autumn of 1680. Late one warm afternoon a carriage under the seal of Casa y/Vega clattered to a halt at our gate. It bore the condesa, come to look in on her children. I greeted her in the court-yard.

"Padre, what are you doing here? I thought you would be in New Spain by now."

"So, we hoped."

She listened with sympathy to the tale of our misadventures.

"Your new flock must grow impatient with your long-delayed arrival."

"I'm afraid it is we who grow impatient.

Our flock does not yet know they miss us."

She laughed, a melodious sound I'd come to appreciate in her friendship.

"Perhaps Carlos can help. He is a man of some influence. I shall speak to him of your plight."

"You are most gracious, My Lady."

Word came from the conde during Advent to Christmas. He booked commercial passage for Matías and I aboard a ship sailing for New Spain in January. Yet another gesture of generous charity done in our cause. To the joy of Christmas, we said a mass of thanksgiving for the conde's intention.

Cádiz
January 28, 1681
She rode at anchor, her gun decks evoked visions of Barbary pirates. I nudged Matías.

"San Crystobal," I said lifting my chin to direct his attention.

"Not the fondest of memories."

"You became a seaman aboard her decks."

"No less painful an experience."

"Remember your sea legs. The voyage to New Spain will have us at sea three months or more depending on winds and currents."

Matías lifted his eyes heavenward and crossed himself. "Pirates, shipwrecks, seasickness, what more might we ask of this mission?"

"Come now, my friend, it can't be so bad as all that."

It was only when we spoke with the harbormaster, we learned our passage would reunite us with the *San Crystobal*. We were shown to a longboat and rowed out to the ship. I smiled at the familiar rope ladder bobbing at the gunwale.

"After you, Matías?"

He declined with a gesture.

"Suit yourself." I hiked up the hem of my cassock and grasped the ladder, letting the swell lift me from the longboat. I climbed to the rail where Capitán Santiago assisted me aboard.

"Padre," he smiled. "We meet once again, welcome aboard our humble ship."

"Our good fortune to sail with you, Capitán."

"And Padre Goni?"

I nodded over the side.

He smiled and looked over the rail. "Padre, welcome! Come aboard."

Matías tucked the hem of his cassock into his belt and eyed the rope ladder with apprehension. At last, he grabbed it much as I did and allowed himself to succumb to the swell. Once committed, he found foot purchase and climbed with determination, until the capitán was able to claim him over the rail. Firmly planted on the roll of the deck, I watched his complexion for the least sign of green. His stomach may have roiled but he managed it and soon found his sea legs had not deserted him.

"We sail at dawn," the capitán said. "The mate will show you to your cabin. Join me at my table for supper."

We accepted his gracious invitation and repaired to our cabin.

Over supper Capitán Santiago told us he'd come into port at Cádiz to spend Christmas when a messenger from Madrid presented new orders for a voyage to New Spain. He found out sometime later we would be sailing with him. I thought it likely Conde de la Vega may have prompted a change in the capitán's orders, but I kept my own council on such a thought.

"Have you made this crossing before?"

Matías's question bore a note of uncertainty.

"I've not, Padre. We will explore the Atlantic together."

"Without a coastline to follow . . . ?"

"Have no fear, Padre. We have charts. We have the stars. We have our compass. We have all the time we need for the crossing."

"And the protection of the Almighty to guide us," I added.

"And the Almighty," the capitán agreed.

We awoke next morning to the bustle of crew preparing to weigh anchor and set sail.

February 1681

We sailed steel dark seas under cloud-rumpled gray skies three weeks out. Westerly winds had us tacking a southwesterly course at an agonizingly slow rate of progress by my simple reckoning. Late of our third week, wind shifted north by northwest. Our progress improved for a fairer wind. Capitán Santiago and the lookouts up top kept keen watch to the north and northwest. In two days' time the reason for their vigilance darkened the horizon.

"Weather," the capitán said in response to my question. "We are in for a blow."

"Blow?" I said.

"A storm. Winter on the Atlantic can spawn them."

Matías took the news with some dread. He'd adjusted to life at sea though I doubted he'd ever be a comfortably seasoned sailor. He took to our cabin, his hammock, and the comfort of his rosary. I can't say I blamed him. Nothing could have prepared either of us for what lie ahead, or rather loomed to starboard.

A dark wall built on the horizon, ever larger and darker. The wind picked up and with it the sea. Foreboding gray waves crested white, crashed into troughs. *San Crystobal* surged and sloughed from one swell to the next, running as best she could ahead of a billowing pursuer bent on our aft quarterdeck. I held to the rail, wind whipping my cassock and hair. A gust of rain lashed my cheek. Time to join Goni in prayer.

I made my way down the slippery deck to our cabin. Matías looked perfectly miserable there, seated in a ball on the floor, cabin wall to his back. A single candle affixed to a rough-cut tabletop by a puddle of its own wax. Only his lips and fingers moved over the beads, taking comfort where none could be had by any other endeavor. I joined him.

"Hail Mary, full of grace . . ."

Rain lashed the ship in sheets. Wind howled, battering broadside. Sails trimmed the helmsman fought to hold some semblance of a course, though no course could be made with any pretense at precision. The wind and storm would have its way with us. Should the Good Lord see us safely through, we'd need stars to right our way.

Rocked and rolled roughly about by a tempest no man could withstand, I found my way to another storm on a sea in Galilee. That storm ended well when the Lord walked the waves. I felt something of the drowning Peter, reminding myself he was saved by a Lord who rebuked the sea and becalmed it. With that I found becalm within. The storm would blow its furious force. The Lord would walk her waves. In time we too should be saved.

By the gray light of dawn, we survived. The sea heaved and fell as if panting exhaustion, but without the violence of the darkest hours. The wind, still strong, ceased to howl. I chanced a peek out the cabin door. The rain abated. Stars could be seen overhead to the west beyond the mantle of cloud overhanging the dregs of the storm. The crew let out some sheet. The bow swung starboard amid course correction. Sail on. Sail on to the coming light.

CHAPTER TEN

Cosari
Pimeria Alta

Late spring sun glittered on the surface of a gently flowing aqueduct bringing water from the river, east to fields in the foothills of sierras to the west. Black Thorn and Yellow Feather bent sweat-slicked bare backs to shovel-like wooden tools. They cut furrows in rows for seeding the fertile flood plain. Rain and Sweet Grass followed their husbands, seeding the furrows. Giggling and splashing nearby, Hawk and Fawn played in the stream, glistening copper bodies clothed in natural innocence.

Rain minded the children with a watchful eye as she patted soil over seeds sown by Sweet Grass. Sweet Grass rocked back on her heels.

"You see them."

"Um," Rain nodded.

"Black Thorn and Rain, many summers ago."

"You make it sound so long ago, but yes. We were children together."

"And here you are now. Maybe they will follow your path."

"Who can say?"

"Yellow Feather."

They laughed.

"The children have a say before that," Rain said.

"For now, let them be children."

Yellow Feather paused to wipe sweat from his eyes and his chest.

"Soon the maize will be in."

Black Thorn swept his gaze over the field. "Beans, squash, cotton, and melons, more to do."

"Good planting makes a fine harvest." Yellow Feather grinned. "Here comes the spring harvest." He lifted his chin over Black Thorn's shoulder.

Black Thorn's father, Red Sky, came down a twisting trail out of the hills, bent by a heavy basket strapped to his back.

"What have you there, Father?" Black Thorn's eyes smiled with mischievous jest.

"You know very well," the old man huffed dropping his burden beside the field.

"Agave hearts."

"If you know so much, why ask?"

"Fermented elixir for feasting. We toil for food while my father harvests for pleasure."

"You'll have your harvest of pleasure too when you grow to my age and wisdom. For now, bend your back to feed my belly as I did for you when you were a stripling."

"He never forgets," Black Thorn said.

"May you live long enough to receive return of the favor from your son."

Apacheria
Mogollon Mountains

The boy ran, his breechclout soaked, his naked body slicked with sweat. He sucked a pebble to beat back his thirst. A boy of fourteen summers, coming into his manhood, he ran because Chiricahua warriors run. He ran to be the best Apache warrior. He ran long and hard, pushing his body to the limits of endurance. Endurance and dogged determination became his strength, his medicine. Apache traveled swiftly and silently, seizing the precious gift of surprise over their enemies.

The trail he ran snaked its way unseen through a narrow defile up the side of a mountain. In this run he would be observed by no one save a scorpion, a snake, and a hawk, riding the mountain winds aloft in lazy circles. The prize at the end of this run, a hidden rock cistern with a store of winter rainwater. Here in the high desert water was life. The Apache lived at one with the land. The land opened her secrets to the people. Where to hide, hidden water places and trails to game. Apache lived on the land by cunning and stealth.

The boy reached the end of the trail. He dropped to his knees, cupped his hands, and dipped water from the shaded cistern. He let the water moisten his mouth, swallowing slowly, absorbing life-giving nourishment. When he had his fill, he lay on his back watching the hawk soar among wisps of white cloud. He rested, restoring his body for the long run back to the village.

Water sustains life. All life in arid country. Scent drew the puma to the cistern. Perched on a ledge above the cistern, human scent overpowered water. The big cat crouched, eyes riveted on the boy at the well.

Strong urine scent summoned the boy alert. He held still. Above a tawny tuft gave away the cat's presence. Slowly he grasped the bone handle of his sheath knife. Small defense if needed. Instinct told him to move. As he did, the big cat sprang. Silhouetted against the sky, it pounced, claws bared. One great paw raked cheek and shoulder a glancing slash. The boy buried his knife in the chest cavity behind the left foreleg. The cat screeched ear-splitting agony. The boy jumped away as the great cat thrashed deadly claws and fangs bared to its death throes.

Pain fired the boy's gashed wounds. Blood flowed. At last, the puma lay still. He retrieved his sheath knife. He cut off a paw for its claws before setting off for his return to the village. He would survive his wounds. He would wear the puma claws on a thong around his neck, along with the ragged scars of the attack he survived. Both marked him a warrior, symbolic of victory. A warrior who would be called Ndolkah Sid.

Veracruz
May 3, 1681
The rigors of open-ocean sailing gave way to gentler seas as we threaded our passage among the islands of the Caribbean toward the gulf waters of New Spain. Sun-warmed winds favored our course on blue-green seas dotted with coral reefs. Anxious as we were to reach New Spain these days and nights brought us much peace as we prepared to depart on our mission. After three long months, *San Crystobal* at last dropped

anchor at the port of Veracruz. Capitán Santiago accompanied us ashore.

He helped us locate Antonio, a short stout caravan master of swarthy complexion, bound for Mexico City. The city, former center of the Aztec empire, now served as capital of New Spain. Passage was quickly arranged. Capitán Santiago then bid us Vaya con Dios. Before he departed, he presented me with a most marvelous gift.

"Padre, I wish you safe journey. I know you go with God, but I know too you will put this to good use."

The compass was a miniature version of the one mounted on the wheel deck of *San Crystobal.* The dial floated in a polished wooden box.

"Hold it level and it will guide your travels," he said.

"Thank you, Capitán. I shall treasure this to a safe journey home. God speed your return voyage."

With a wave of his plumed hat, he returned to the docks to provision his voyage home.

The caravan Antonio led was made up of mule-drawn carts loaded with trade goods. A man of few words, Antonio provided Matías and me donkeys to ride. Embarking on our mission in this way put me in mind of our Lord and Savior's triumphal entry into Jerusalem on the Sunday of Palms in Holy Week. Our mission to spread the good news of the Gospel sprang from events undertaken from the back of a borrowed colt, the offspring of an ass. I made it a fortuitous sign our mission destined to succeed.

The journey afforded our first taste of New Spain. From the salt tang of sea air, we plunged into lush coastal forest and climbed mountainous high desert as we made our way inland to the capital. Everywhere we looked we were treated to novel manifestations of creation heretofore unknown to our experience. From brilliantly colored birds to wildly chattering colonies of monkeys swinging and scampering among the canopied limbs of forest trees overhead. These were soon replaced by voracious wild pigs called javelina, serpents, and clouds of biting flies and insects common to the desert places we crossed. The former fascinating and beautiful, the latter reminiscent of the plagues of Egypt. We endured these latter pestilences, offering them up in prayer for the success of our mission. In the fullness of time, we survived passage to the breathtaking magnificence of the destination awaiting us.

CHAPTER ELEVEN

Mexico City

Mexico City sprawled in broad avenues, spacious sun-washed plazas, thronged markets, massive temples, elegant palaces, and densely populated barrios covering an island in the midst of Lake Texcoco. Here ancient Aztec stood beside Spanish conquest. The Cathedrals of Holy Mother Church invaded shadows left by pagan temples, steeped in bloody stains of human sacrifice. Palaces of tribal authority and pagan gods served Spanish civil authority. The Aztec empire now bent at the knee of royal authority.

On arrival, we proceeded to the college of Ignatius, maintained by our Company of Jesus. There we were welcomed by Father Provincial, Bernardo Pardo. He showed us to a well-appointed parlor, where he introduced us to the college and its curriculum. I was surprised to learn the college enrolled some fourteen hundred students. Father

Provincial then inquired of our backgrounds. In my turn, he showed keen interest in my facilities with astronomy and mathematics.

"Interesting, Padre Kino. Have you applied these skills to navigation?"

"I have, your reverence, cartography as well."

He lifted his brows. "I see. You could well find a useful place on our faculty, if we can keep news of you from reaching the viceroy's ears."

"And why is that?"

"The crown has a voracious appetite for exploration and territorial expansion where wealth is found in gold, silver, or pearls. But for the work of the society, a faculty position seems a most appropriate appointment to your skills."

Science once again. In New Spain, not Cathay, yet science nonetheless. What of my call to the salvation of souls? God's plan for me remained shrouded in mystery.

"The porter will show you to your rooms. Vespers are sung at four o'clock. Supper is served in the refectory promptly at six."

With that he dismissed us.

That evening Matías and I found seats at a table in the refectory. Introductions were made. I struck up a conversation with a brown-skinned reverend father to my right. He introduced himself as Baltasar Mansilla.

"Have you a teaching position with the college?" I inquired.

He shook his head around a bite of bread. "I am on my way to Acapulco. From there I sail the Philippine galleon to Manila. I have been appointed procurator to missions there. And you?"

"My colleague and I only arrived this very day. It appears I am to take a faculty position."

"In what field?"

"Astronomy, mathematics, perhaps navigational arts."

"Truly? Not common skills among our company confreres."

"I studied I thought in preparation for scientific admission to China, where I hoped to follow in the glorious footsteps of my beloved patron, San Francisco Xavier. Instead I am sent to New Spain."

"Do you still wish to go to Cathay?"

"I do, though I am accepting God may have another plan for me."

"Perhaps His plan had you sit with me this evening."

"How so?"

"Philippine missionaries have been sent to

85

China. With your scientific credentials, I should think you an excellent candidate. Perhaps Father Provincial will spare you to me."

"Could you do this?"

"If you wish, I can try."

"Then, please, your most reverence, try."

Cathay, dared I hope? As it happened Reverend Father succeeded in having my appointment considered. I put my cause before Our Lady of Guadalupe at her shrine near the city and waited in prayer. Once again, my cause was decided, this time by lot. My place remained in New Spain with another appointed to the Orient. I felt a kinship with Our Lord's vesture for which they also cast lots. I thought the matter of my faculty appointment settled. Then once again, it was not.

It came with a summons to Reverend Father Provincial's office.

"Ah, Eusebio, thank you for coming so promptly."

"Is something amiss?"

"Hmm, good question. Have a seat."

I took a hard seat before his desk in spare surroundings, warmed only by a golden glow of late afternoon sun.

"It seems we have not succeeded in keeping news of your considerable talents from the ears of the viceroy. We are summoned to audience with him on the morrow."

The following day we made a short walk to the royal palace and audience with the archbishop who presently served as interim viceroy. I was pleased to find we were joined by Matías who appeared as puzzled as I by the summons.

Civil and Church authorities existed side by side in New Spain, with civil matters reserved to the viceroy and spiritual matters deferred to Holy Mother Church. For a time, both offices were vested in the archbishop, pending appointment of a replacement to the office of viceroy. We soon learned such harmony of purpose was not often the case and still more often failed to reach mission frontiers. Yet those discoveries lay in the future.

The Most Reverend Archbishop Viceroy greeted us warmly.

He introduced us to Don Isidro Atondo y Antilion, recently appointed Governor of Sinaloa province and Admiral of the Kingdom of California. A vigorous man, youthful for so prestigious an appointment, he cut a fine figure of a military man, tall, strong and lean, dark skinned with coal black mustache, shoulder length curls, and eyes glittering with authority. The don evidenced a dedication of singular purpose to his post. The significance of his presence would soon be made clear.

The archbishop apprised us of the needs we would encounter on the mission frontier. He inquired of our backgrounds and interests for Don Isidro's benefit, Goni's facility for languages and my interests in the sciences. Don Isidro became most intrigued by my background in mathematics, astronomy, and navigation, of which he chose to interrogate me. He observed to the archbishop his expedition to California could surely benefit by the services of a surveyor and cartographer who also served the spiritual needs of the mission. The archbishop had of course anticipated the wisdom of such an appointment, an appointment which could do no harm in currying favor with his royal superiors.

Matías and I were forthwith assigned to the Atondo expedition. Further to this assignment, the archbishop appointed me vicar of California, thereby aligning my spiritual authority with Don Isidro's civil authority. The wisdom of aligning our offices notwithstanding, in so doing lines were drawn, putting secular duties in contention with my ecclesiastical mission, though the significance of these lines would not be observed in the comity of audience with an archbishop viceroy firmly ensconced on both sides of the line.

CHAPTER TWELVE

Ensuing days became a whirlwind of preparation as Matías and I arrived late to Atondo's intended departure. We departed Mexico City days later bound for the Atondo party base camp in Sinaloa. We traveled northwest by way of Guadalajara, which we reached on fifth November. Here we encountered delay over securing ecclesiastical authority to open mission in California, as the territory was embroiled in diocesan dispute between the bishop of Guadalajara and the bishop of Durango. We received the authorities necessary to our purpose in Guadalajara, reckoning California far removed from the disputants and relying on the expediency of forgiveness over permission should the eventual outcome fail to fall in favor of our appointment. We reached Village de Nio on the Sinaloa River in March 1682, where members of the Atondo expedition gathered in preparation for

California exploration.

Two great ships along with a smaller barca awaited launch at the mouth of the Sinaloa River. Each ship commanded a crew of ten with four seamen assigned to the barca. Engineers and craftsmen would accompany the expedition to see to maintenance of the vessels and equipment. These included carpenters, a wheelwright, gunsmith, and a surgeon. Indio laborers too would see to all unskilled physical labor. The expedition would be secured by a company of thirty soldados armed with eight cannon and fifty arquebus. All totaled the expedition numbered one hundred.

Matías and I plunged into preparations for our mission journey. Owing to our late arrival, we found ourselves behind our secular companions. Not wishing to be cause of any delay, we undertook long days of labor, assembling provisions for our journey. We carried with us sacramental vessels used in celebration of the Holy Sacrifice of the Mass and such small accoutrements as may be used to establish a chapel or small church.

Ships of the expedition were launched to maiden voyage in autumn 1682. Supplies were gathered at nearby river ports with final preparations for the expedition returning to Sinaloa in early 1683. There we loaded livestock, horses, cattle, and chickens.

Cosari
Pimeria Alta

Coxi, Cacique of the Cosari Akimel O'odham, (Chief of the Cosari Pima), sat before his olas kih bathed in firelight. Night sounds rested peacefully on the village. Planting progressed. The people were at one with one another and the land. A shadow appeared out of the darkness beyond the circle of firelight. The medicine man Scorpion stood arms folded at his chest. The planes of his sweat-slicked naked body sculpted in moonlight and shadow.

"Speak, Scorpion."

"Sacred peyote ritual has granted Scorpion a vision."

"Come. Sit by the fire."

He squat, a snake skull, hung by a thong about his neck, caught firelight in eye sockets, an ominous sign.

"Tell us this vision."

"I saw Apache village. A young warrior has come of age. He is marked for a great war-chief by the sign of a puma."

"The Apache have many war chiefs."

"This one I see with Pima slaves."

"He is a raider then. How is he called?"

"Ndolkah Sid."

"Scar. Can you make medicine to ward him?"

"Scorpion can try. The puma is strong in him. His warriors will make strong medicine of this."

"How long before his medicine is strong to the hunt?"

"There is time. Scorpion will pray over it."

"Pray well, medicine man. While you pray, my warriors will prepare."

Village de Nio
March 18, 1683

With preparations complete, our small flotilla rode at anchor in sun-splashed, blue harbor waters. The three ships were smaller and lighter than the heavy, oceangoing galleons of my experience, well suited to navigate the Sea of California. The *San Jose* and *La Concepcion* would sail the mission voyage bearing the bulk of supplies and expeditionary forces. The *San Jose* would serve as command ship, which Matías and I boarded in company of Don Isidro. Accommodations were smaller than those we enjoyed aboard the *San Crystobal,* though we were not overly inconvenienced for the brief voyage across the Sea of California.

We set sail on a pleasantly warm winter day with great anticipation to begin our long-awaited mission work. Atondo charted a southwesterly course on a favorable breeze. As we stood at the windswept rail, Matías gave voice to our thoughts.

"Where do we begin, Eusebio?"

I smiled. "At the beginning."

"In the beginning was the Word and the Word was with God."

I laughed. "Our beginning may require a few steps before we reach Holy Scripture. That will require some command of a language we do not yet know."

"My point," Matías said. "Where do we begin?"

"We know little of the Indios we will serve. We know they are primitives. There is much we can teach them of practical matters and more to be shown by example."

"What are you thinking?"

"Temporal need will be shown to us first. Food, clothing, medication, perhaps shelter. Spiritual need we know will be there. This we must show by example to begin. Tap the people's natural curiosity and thirst for God. That will bring them to us with their questions, their language, and their customs. Once we understand them, we must impart the faith in terms understandable to them. Baptisms will follow."

"You make it sound so simple."

"It is simple. It is only in doing difficulty is found."

This last thought proved one we would return to many times in the coming seasons of our service.

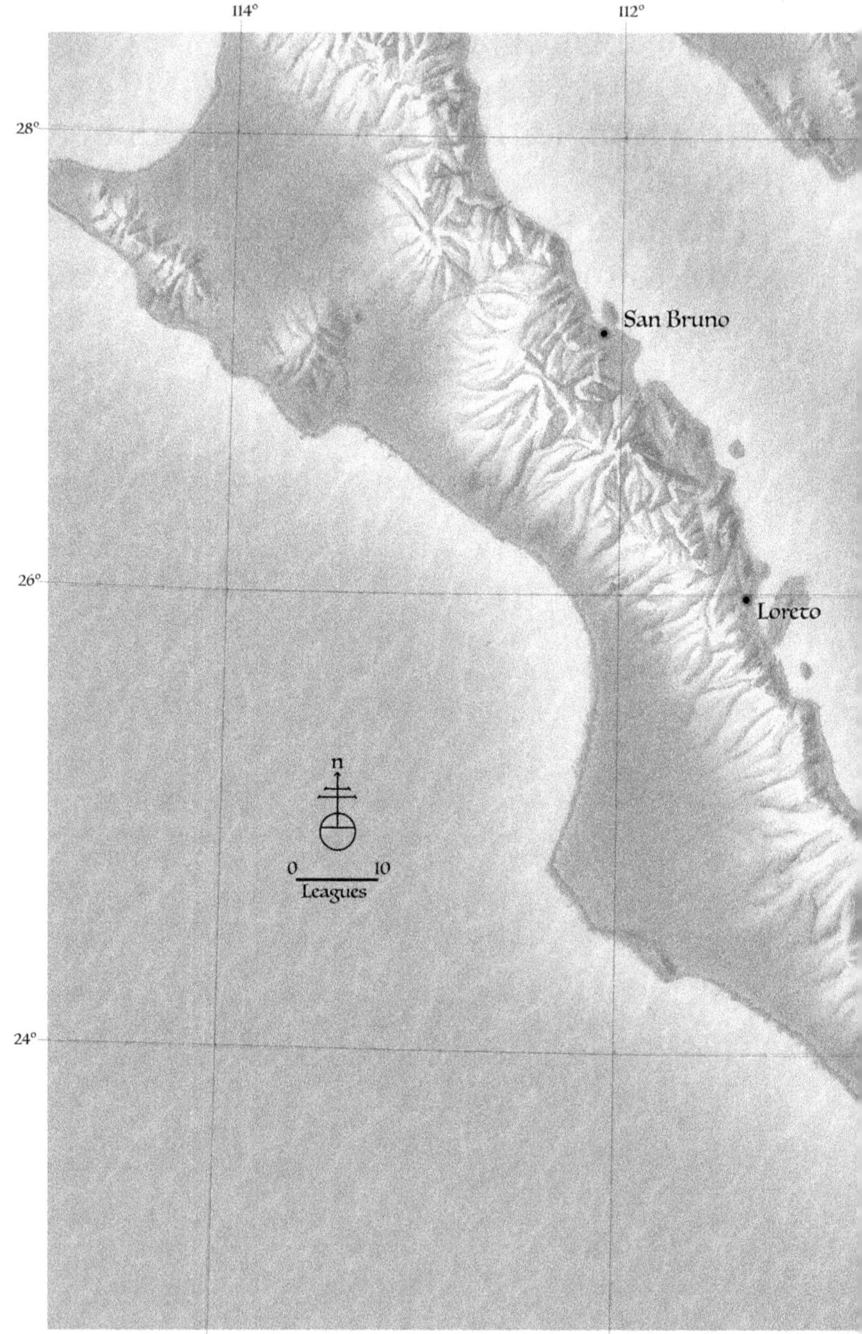
114°
112°
28°
San Bruno
26°
Loreto
n
0
10
Leagues
24°
114°
112°

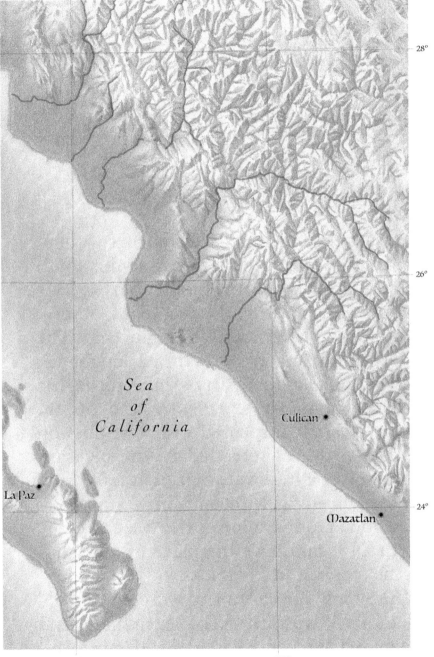

110°

108°

28°

26°

*Sea
of
California*

Culican •

24°

La Paz •

Mazatlan •

110°

108°

CHAPTER THIRTEEN

La Paz
April 1, 1683

We reached the coast of California without incident and dropped anchor at the south end of a bay affording safe harbor. We remained aboard ship the first night, observing the shore on which we might land. The following morning, we boarded longboats, ferrying our landing party ashore through a gentle surf to an expansive sand beach. There we first inspected our new mission field. A grove of trees led us the pleasant discovery of a freshwater spring not far from the beach along with an ample supply of firewood. Goni explored the beach to the north. Not far above the place of our landing he stopped in his tracks.

"Eusebio!" He called and waved. "Come!"

He said it with irresistible excitement and urgency. I lifted my cassock and ran to his side.

"There," he pointed.

Footprints. Bare human footprints. The trail came down the beach to become lost in the surf. We exchanged glances. Here our first encounter with evidence of our new flock. A humble first encounter to be sure, but a beginning of sorts nonetheless. I offered a brief prayer of thanksgiving.

At that the moment was broken by a summons to return to the ship.

The next few days were spent ferrying material and supplies ashore. On Sunday, April 4th, we partook a day of rest with celebration of the most Holy Sacrifice of the Mass. Later that day members of our party caught a great quantity of fish we roasted for our evening meal. Matías and I made the fish a catch, symbolic of the rewards awaiting our work.

The next morning, Don Isidro led a landing party ashore. He called the assembly together and planted a royal standard there on the beach. A volley of arquebus discharged in salute to cheers of long life to King Carlos. Atondo, as Admiral of California, proclaimed the land with all precious metals, pearls, and riches a possession of the crown. He further ordered fair and gentle treatment of any Indio peoples found there, though none were present to hear this most magnanimous pledge. His order salved, for the moment, any misgivings I might have harbored for the future of our, as yet unmet, flock. He cautioned the party against trading or congress with any Indios encountered until peaceful relations could be assured. Precious metals or gems as might be found would be subject to a one-fifth-part tax to the crown.

His proclamations were fully expected, though I wondered at what those whose footprints trod this land before our coming might think should they understand the full measure of its meaning. This we would come to understand soon enough.

With royal possession established, I proclaimed ecclesiastical possession of the land by authority vested in me on behalf of Holy Mother Church. By these claims we asserted sovereignty over lands heretofore in possession of those who preceded us.

With that, we commenced exploring coastal regions in the area of our landing. Goni and I erected a cross near the freshwater spring, claiming the site for Holy Mother Church as a mission. There also Don Isidro proposed to construct a presidio and establish a settlement.

Construction had no more than com-

menced on the skeleton of a crude fortifica-
tion and chapel with shelters for our small
garrison and stores, when we awoke one
morning to angry cries voiced by a band of
Indios. They stood apart from our clearing,
brandishing bows and arrows, their naked
bodies, painted in unknown symbols,
agleam in morning light. By gestures they
made known to us their desire for us to
leave. Atondo puzzled over how to respond.
He ordered his soldados to prime their
weapons. I understood the precaution, still
it caused me alarm.

"Don Atondo, I do not believe they mean
us harm. They only bear weapons in the
event of hostilities much as your men now
prepare. Let us not provoke trouble. With
your permission, perhaps Matías and I
might make known our good intentions by
offering gifts."

"Understand, Padre, if you go out to meet
them, I may not be able to assure your
safety."

"We will not go unprotected." I held up
the crucifix worn at my breast.

And so, we left the shelter of our clearing
beneath the sign of the cross. We held out
gifts of hard bread and small wooden crosses
affixed to thongs that might be worn about
the neck. We managed to approach to within

half the distance separating us, where we were stopped short by a guttural command accompanied by the nocking of arrows. We held up our cross and our gifts, for which we received curious inspection. By sign we were instructed to put down our gifts and go back from whence we had come. I confess we complied with more haste than dignity. With us returned to safe distance, a few came forward to sample the bread and inspect a cross. With signs we encouraged them to put the little crosses around a neck or two. With that all went away, satisfied for the time we meant them no harm.

Matías and I put our shoulders to the building of a chapel, assisted by a young lieutenant, Juan Mateo Manje, detailed to our work by Atondo. A pleasant and respectful young man, Juan Mateo possessed some skill in the art of building. Owing to his proficiency with a machete, we soon had a simple poled structure covered in thatch. We felled a tree of sufficient size. The base of the trunk might serve as an altar.

As we sat by our evening fire after one of those backbreaking days at hard labor, I first noticed the change. Dirt under the nails. A hardening of the flesh and a raising of calluses. The soft hands of an academic priest, beginning to change. It set me to wonder, what more change might be wrought by the journey of this mission?

No sooner had we a place to celebrate the Holy Sacrifice of the Mass, the first of our curious flock arrived. They appeared among the trees and undergrowth where the beach melted to desert scrub. Dark-skinned, naked Indio men armed with bows, arrows, and spears. Instinctively wary, they stood off at a distance observing. We must have looked strange to them with our pale faces, Matías and I clad in flowing black robes, and soldados in polished breastplates and helms, colorful pantaloons, and high boots.

At length, one stepped forward. He was small and wiry brown with straight black hair and dark eyes, wrinkled at the corners as a sign of his years. He approached tentatively. We greeted him with welcoming smiles. He seemed curious about the construct of our little chapel. I folded my hands as in prayer and pointed to the heavens. He followed my fingers, searching the sky for what manner of meaning this might be.

Matías held up one of the small wooden crosses we brought as gifts for our visitor to inspect. He put it on himself with the reverence of a kiss, under the watchful eye of the first sheep come to our flock. He then removed the cross and offered it to our new friend. He took it and examined it closely. By encouraging signs, he was persuaded to put it on. We added three ears of corn to the gift of the cross. These were received with much enthusiasm. We smiled broadly at our success. He nodded and smiled in return. Corn again. I was reminded of little Pablo, the orphan. I remember seeing Jesus in the boy. He spoke to me from the heart of this one also.

"What is your name?" I asked.

His response came a puzzled stare.

"I am Padre Kino." I pointed to myself. "This is Padre Goni. What is your name?" I pointed to him. He took a step back, wary.

"All in God's time, Eusebio," Matías said.

I offered a blessing which proved enough catechism for one day. We dubbed our first lamb Adam, as he backed away to join his brothers.

Adam returned the following day with perhaps a dozen others, including three women, two with infants at the breast. These at least wore skirts woven of reeds. All sought the wooden crosses we were only too pleased to provide. We did so by inviting them to sit in the shade of our little chapel. There we presented them crosses, blessed the children, and showed them how to make the sign of the cross while we prayed the Lord's Prayer. This seemed to please them, and all departed happily.

In the days that followed more came as word spread. Soon our little chapel filled to overflowing. We began our gatherings with the Holy Sacrifice of the Mass. This our flock did not understand, but showed much curiosity over the mystery. The people's questions revealed a crude introduction to their language. Simple words gave us a beginning. We learned these people were called Guaicuros, though how these might relate to other people of California we did not know.

We followed mass with small instructions, beginning with the sign of the cross and simple prayers of the faithful. More words exchanged. Following mass and instruction, Matías and I served a simple meal for the people to partake in. These were greeted with much appreciation.

Small steps. Simple beginnings. Greater appreciation for the enormity of the task before us. Matías and I prayed over it and took our encouragements where we found them.

CHAPTER FOURTEEN

As the days passed, we experienced harsh desert conditions. It seldom rained, making water scarce. The people we observed did not farm. Our own attempts at raising crops sprouted, but quickly withered and died. The people subsisted on small game, some fish, roots, wild plants, cactus, insects, even snakes. This no doubt accounted their appreciation of our every offering of food. Corn seemed unknown to them. We served it as a stew called pozole and as pinole, a cookie ground into flour, sweetened with sugar and fried.

For all the mean circumstances of their existence and abject poverty, the children were delightful. They made a game of everything. One day to their amazement I produced a rubber ball, bouncing it off a flat rock to shrieks of amazement and fear for some thought the ball alive. When they found they could bounce it too, they chased the ball and each other endlessly, consumed in new sport.

Atondo also took occasion to impress our new friends, though for a far more serious demonstration. He set up a hardened leather shield as target for a shooting contest. He invited Adam to take the first shot with his bow. He hit the target with much pride, though the arrow failed to penetrate the shield. Atondo congratulated him on his marksmanship with a cheer, a smile, and all hail from his men. He then selected a musketeer from among his men. The marksman primed his arquebus, taking careful aim he fired. The flash, charge, and smoke visibly startled the Indios. Atondo retrieved Adam's arrow and the target, pierced by the musket ball. He returned the arrow to Adam and made him a gift of the shield, ever to be reminded of Spanish war might.

While we endeavored to befriend our new flock, Don Isidro sent reconnaissance parties out to the north, south, and west to better understand our surroundings. Hills to the west climbed toward a distant mountain range. Some distance inland a small lake could be seen with smoke sign suggesting presence of a village.

Matías and I led our Spanish community

107

in the observances of Holy Week beginning with Palm Sunday. Our nascent Indio flock took much pleasure in observing the procession of palms. Later in the week we commemorated solemn celebration of the Lord's Last Supper and initiation of the Eucharist. Ritual washing of feet sparked great curiosity among our visitors. Good Friday led us in the stations of the cross. Holy Saturday we sang the sacred litanies leading to Easter celebration of the resurrection. This we marked by the ringing bells and a cannon salute at dawn. Fiesta followed though our exhausted guests returned inland to sleep.

As spring turned into summer the prospects for supplying our party off the land dimmed. Hot dry, desert conditions withered any attempt to plant and grow crops faster than our ability to water them. Don Isidro dispatched *Concepcion* to Rio Yaqui for supplies. Following *Concepcion*'s departure, he approached me one evening as Matías and I finished our supper.

"Good evening, Padre."

"Good evening, Don Isidro. How may we be of service?"

"I need your services as a cartographer."

"What is it you wish to map?"

"The coast, north and south of here, and

some leagues inland."

"I see."

"I regret interrupting your mission work, but if for no other reason than defensive purposes we should better understand our situation here."

I nodded. "Matías, can you carry on without me for a time?"

"The Lord will provide until your return."

"Good. It is settled then," Isidro said.

"When do you wish to depart?"

"We make our preparations tomorrow and depart at dawn the following day."

And so, we did, leaving the company in command of Capitán Francisco Zevallos. In military and civil matters, he stood second in command to Don Isidro himself. A swarthy man of arrogant demeanor and authoritarian bearing. While the capitán caused me some apprehension, I kept my own counsel as to this for I had no more to base them on than instinct.

Journal Entry

I noted our La Paz position at twenty-four degrees north latitude. We struck a course south along the coast for several days. I charted our progress, recording all we encountered on the pages of this journal. We made our way easily along white sand beaches with little difficulty in negotiating the occasional rocky outcropping. We traveled in safety, accompanied by a squad of soldados under the command of Lieutenant Manje. Young Manje made an affable traveling companion without the formality of Don Isidro's imperial demeanor.

The days passed sunny and hot with only gentle sea breeze to relieve a brow from the heat. At night we camped on the beach beneath lush palm canopies, dazzled in brilliant starlight from which navigational readings could be taken and added to my cartographic notes. Young Manje found this work interesting, entertaining me with his questions. Don Isidro kept to himself once the evening meal was done. He, like the soldados, took to his sleeping blanket early. Mateo and I stayed up talking quietly into the night until lulled to drowsiness by the gentle lap of surf on the shore.

Some ten days south of La Paz, Don Isidro announced we would turn inland toward what appeared to be a rocky ridgeline some distance from the coast. Trekking inland through rock-strewn high desert, we observed cactus formations and all manner of desert scrub eking out survival in unforgiving arid conditions. It took three arduous days to reach and climb the face to the crest of a ridge. From there we were re-warded by vistas of the coast in the east and further desert expanse to the west.

The following morning Don Isidro set our course north traveling just below the crest of the ridge. The vantage point to our journey allowed us sight lines to the coast with occasional pauses to take in western vistas. By my reckoning we were less than a day's march south of La Paz when we observed smoke sign east of our evening camp. The number of cook fires suggested a large Indio village, likely the one observed by earlier exploration. I suspected these might be Adam's people. I spoke with Don Isidro over our evening meal.

"Might we go down and visit the village?"

"To what purpose, Padre?"

"We are here to minister to the people. This is the first village we have encountered. Given their proximity to La Paz these people may be some of those who have visited our mission."

He thought for a moment as he filled his long-stemmed pipe, lighting it with a straw from the fire. "We are here to map this region," he puffed. "Yours is a spiritual mission. Now that you know where the village is located, you and Padre Goni may visit it on our return."

"Speaking of our return, how much further do you plan this excursion to go?"

"We should pass La Paz on the morrow. Ten days further on we shall turn east to the coast and return to La Paz by the shore. This should give us a mapping of some fifty leagues of coastline with another twenty, inland."

I was disappointed by the delay in extending our spiritual mission, though comfortable in knowing Matías continued our work in my absence.

CHAPTER FIFTEEN

Cosari
Pimeria Alta

Sun burned brightly out of a clear blue sky, warming the hillside. Proud saguaro stood sentinel in clusters here and there. In season, they bore rich red fruit ripe for the taking. Rain, Sweet Grass, and Willow worked as a team. Rain wielded a knife lashed to a long pole, prying bulbs from tall spiny arms. Sweet Grass caught the falling fruit for Willow to place in their baskets. The fruit would be boiled and reduced to a sweetening syrup. Some would be fermented for ritual consumption.

Nearby Hawk and Fawn sat, each with half a ripe fruit. They scraped soft sweet flesh up in fingers they sucked clean, eager for more. They laughed at the red juicy smears on each other's faces. Harvest times like these were good times for children occupied with good fruits.

Four eyes watched the women and children, unseen. A rattlesnake watched from a rock where it sunned itself, unthreatened by those of no further interest. Higher up in the rocks a more sinister predator looked down on the scene.

Ndolkah Sid traveled alone, a wolf, to scout the Cosari Pima. A wolf who bore the sign of the puma. Two women, not much older than himself. A fair prize by themselves for slaves, or even a second or third wife. Children too who might be raised Apache. The boy looked sturdy. He stalked the village unseen for days. He knew them. He knew their strength. The village offered still greater prizes. He could lead his brothers on a raid, promising prizes for all. Such a raid would bring him much honor. Honor in the sign of the puma.

La Paz

We returned to La Paz some twenty-five days later toward the end of April. Much progress had been made in construction of fortifications and housing. I was greeted by an anxious and concerned Matías. He spirited me off to our hut, which served as sacristy to the chapel.

"I am thankful you have returned, Eusibeo."

"You seem troubled, Matías. What is amiss?"

"The soldados. They press the Indio into service, building the fort. There have been incidents where Indio were mistreated."

"Mistreated?"

"Beaten like slaves. I tried to intervene, but my protests were dismissed by Capitán Zevallos as a civil matter. Once the capitán marched out to the village with a squad of soldados to conscript a work crew. We are not building trust with our neighbors. Some still come to the mission, but mostly women and children too young to be conscripted to work crews."

"This is most disturbing. We must bring these matters to Don Isidro's attention."

"I agree."

With that we set off for Don Isidro's hut. We found him in the company of the very Capitán Zevallos of our concern. The capitán proudly reported all the progress made in Atondo's absence. He greeted our approach with a dark scowl, anticipating the nature of our visit.

"What is it, Padre?" Don Isidro said.

"Matías tells me much of the progress we observe on our return was made on the backs of our Indio neighbors, impressed to hard labors."

"The capitán has just made a most excellent report of his progress."

"Did he also report these conscriptions were forced and included mistreatments and beatings?"

"Is this true, Zevallos?"

"Only for those who shirk their duties or perform clumsily or stupidly."

Atondo knit his brow.

"When Father Goni protested," I continued, "he was told these were civil matters."

"There are differences between civil matters and ecclesiastical matters," the don said.

"Beatings? Forced conscription? You said yourself, on the occasion of our landing, the Indio must be treated justly. How does this condone conscription and beatings?"

"So, I did. Capitán, you will restrain your men from further mistreatment."

"Sí, Don Isidro."

Zevallos accented his ascent by a bitter glare directed at me.

One might hope this put an end to abuses. One might hope; but while the situation improved, incidents continued to occur from time to time.

Matías and I determined to venture out to the village observed on our mapping expedition. We hoped we might repair the damage done our little flock by the ill-advised actions of Capitán Zevallos and his men. Don Atondo assigned young Manje to accompany us with a squad of soldados. I told the don we would be most pleased to have Mateo accompany us, but a soldado presence might evoke distrust if not anger among the Indio. Don Isidro graciously deferred to my wishes, and we departed the following day.

We found a trail trod by our visitors leading southwest to the village. The village nestled in a shallow valley served by a seasonal stream still flowing with fresh water. The camp could be identified by wisps of smoke rising in columns from cook fires scattered along the banks of the stream. The people lived without shelter owing to the warmth of the climate and the nomadic nature of foraging for food and for water.

We halted our approach at the edge of the forest in hope of an invitation. A small crowd gathered nearby. We had come to know them from their visits to our mission, but saw them afresh here in their natural setting. The crowd come to meet us grew in number. Red brown bodies tattooed in riotous patterns glistened in the sun. Some adorned themselves with feathers and shells. Black hair hung in gleaming plates around glittering black eyes. Again, I saw Our Lord present in those eyes. He called out to me, pained at the hostility he felt there.

Those who set eyes on us for the first time viewed us with a mixture of curiosity and suspicion. They wore the experiences of those victimized by conscription in a palpable air of distrust. I offered a blessing for the appreciation of those who visited our mission. Adam came forward. We exchanged signs of friendship. He led us into the village. The crowd parted as the sea before Moses and the Israelites, flowing around us as they followed along behind.

We learned these people sustained themselves here in the desert, gathering acorns, wild roots, fruit, some fish, and small game. Soon after we arrived, we were treated to something of a feast and shown to woven mats where we might pass the night. In all of this it soon became apparent we were welcomed by the old ones, women, and children, all of whom sought our small wooden crosses. The men remained aloof, their weapons ready at hand. It was clear they harbored resentment for mistreatments suffered at the hands of Capitán Zevallos and his men. Mateo took particular note. He spoke of it when we retired to our mats.

"Padre, the warriors of this village do not

118

welcome us."

"I have noticed this too, Mateo."

"I will stand watch through the night against the chance of treachery."

Matías crossed himself. "You believe we are in danger?"

"It is possible. We have only one chance to be certain."

We passed an uneasy though uneventful night. In the morning, we applied our best efforts to invite Adam and all to return to the mission. We sought, as far as we were able to communicate, to assure them they would not be abused by the soldados. With these apologies made, we took our leave. On the path back to the coast, Mateo kept a watchful eye on our back trail against the possibility we might be followed by those with hostile intent. God willing, we returned safely to the mission compound.

CHAPTER SIXTEEN

La Paz
July 1683

Our journey to the Guaicuro village resulted in some of our flock returning to the mission. They came accompanied by armed warriors who stood watch from the perimeter scrub. This led to a general sense of unease with Capitán Zevallos holding his men on a state of high alert. About this time, a young cabin boy numbered among our expedition disappeared. Zevallos asserted foul play with the boy either taken captive to slavery or killed by hostile Guaicuro. He confronted Adam with the accusation, a charge our humble Indio did not understand. He did manage to understand the capitán's threatening demeanor and fled.

The following morning a party of warriors appeared out of the hills. Capitán Zevallos deployed his soldados in defensive positions along our fortifications. Regrettably an arrow harmlessly struck a wall. The capitán ordered a cannon fired in response. Three warriors fell. The rest of the party vanished into the hills. Sadly, damage done by this exchange of hostilities ended any pretense of peaceful equanimity.

In the aftermath of this incident, Capitán Zevallos raised concern with Atondo one Sunday morning after the Holy Sacrifice of the Mass.

"A word, Don Isidro?"

"Sí, Capitán."

"Our situation here grows grave. With no crops to sustain us we depend on the mainland to supply us by sea. *Concepcion* has yet to return to replenish our stores. Who can say what may have befallen her? We have no more than a few weeks' provisions remaining. With supplies so depleted our situation grows desperate. The Indio warriors remain restless and prone to hostility."

To this I felt compelled to speak for our flock. "The Indio mean us no harm. It is only the wrongs done them that cause them to be wary of you and your men, Capitán."

"This is a civil matter, Padre. We are isolated in this remote outpost. Should the Indio attack in force we lack the powder and shot to hold out long against any prolonged or determined siege."

Don Isidro stroked his beard. "Capitán Zevallos raises valid concerns, Padre."

"We are only just beginning to make inroads with our mission of conversion. Give us a little time and I am sure relations with our Indio brothers and sisters can be restored."

"Little time is what we have, Padre," Zevallos said. "Our supplies see to that."

"The Indio gather. There is food to be had here. We have only to seek it."

"My men cannot subsist on wild roots, insects, and snakes. Who would protect us should we engage in a foraging enterprise?"

"The capitán presents a sound estimate of our situation, Padre," Don Isidro said. "The *San Jose* can take us to Rio Yaqui to resupply. From there we can seek a more hospitable location further up the coast. There too we further our cartographic mission."

And so it passed, on July 14th we weighed anchor and set sail on a return voyage to Sinaloa. Matías and I were saddened at abandoning our Guaicuro flock to their old ways for a time. We provisioned a second expedition in port at Sinaloa, setting sail two months later for a return to California.

■ ■ ■ ■

San Bruno
October 6, 1683

We explored coastal waters north of La Paz, investigating several sites to evaluate suitability for locating a mission and presidio. We found the first few wanting in fresh water or building material. At last, we made safe harbor at the mouth of a river fifty leagues north of La Paz; we proclaimed the site San Bruno.

The river we learned was among those flowing seasonally. Suitability of the site would depend on finding a reliable source of fresh water. From the beach we followed the riverbed inland through a narrow arroyo. At a distance of but a league we found a deserted village with good water. Below the village a gentle plain rose above the riverbed to a valley, offering ample pasturage, a promising site for a new mission and presidio we christened San Isidro.

As we made our inspection, we were greeted by curious and friendly Indios who seemed much more accepting of intruders than the La Paz Guaicuro. Once again Matías and I began the painstaking task of making outreach to the Indio, beginning with the curious.

We had no more than completed a hut to go along with a thatched roof chapel, when Don Isidro again requested my assistance as cartographer. He proposed to explore the immediate vicinity around San Bruno to better understand our circumstances at our selected location. We set out on a day's ride of six leagues south and a second day's ride north.

South of San Bruno we encountered an Indio clan known as Edues. Tall, gentle people, they were led by Cacique Dionisio, the Sun. We were met by a second friendly clan to the north. These Didius were governed by Cacique Leopaldo. To complicate the work of evangelization, the two clans spoke different languages. To hasten our progress Matías and I agreed, he would study the Edu while I the Didius.

This division of duties aided our progress, though progress came grudgingly slow. From the doubtful and humorous responses we received from those with whom we spoke, we concluded our comprehension, pronunciation, and grammar to be crude at best. We made use of signs to supplement broken communications and by them, extend our learning of the language. These methods sufficed for daily interactions, but left Matías and I to pray over how we might instruct our flock in the mysteries of faith. We waited for some manifestation of the Holy Spirit to give us a gift of tongues, such as bestowed upon the apostles at Pentecost, that all might hear, each in his own tongue. Such a miracle would have much aided our cause, but miracles are reserved to those who receive miracles. We, it seemed, were reserved to learn by the twist of the tongue, tone of the ear, and small revelations of understanding.

By the end of October, we set about building a more substantial chapel and shelters, during the month of November. Our new friends and neighbors proved most willing to assist us without coercion. It made cordial occasion to share meaningful work and the refreshment of a meal. As in La Paz the people were drawn to the chapel, the sacrifice of the mass, and the statues and paintings displayed there.

In late November Atondo ordered the *San Jose* to return to Rio Yaqui for supplies and reinforcements. He sent dispatches to the viceroy with the capitán, describing our progress in charting California and plans for continuing the work. With knowledge of the coasts already established, Atondo proposed another exploration, this time setting a course inland. Here I once again encountered conflict between my ecclesiastical mission and the demands of duties to the crown. The conflict weighed on my conscience. I felt my duty to Holy Mother Church, yet at the same time the scientist in me, the student of navigational arts and cartography, reveled in these explorations.

Journal Entry

We rode west from San Isidro on horseback with a mule train carrying supplies. We were accompanied by a squad of soldados again under the command of Lieutenant Manje and Edu and Didius guides. We climbed a spiny ridgeline and continued west three leagues through dry, arid high desert. We discovered a seasonal cistern of fresh water at the foot of a mountain and camped there.

The following morning, we could find no trail west passable by horses and mules. We left the animals with Don Isidro and a detachment of soldados to guard them. Mateo and I with our guides undertook an arduous climb up the mountain. Our effort was rewarded at the summit by beautiful vistas of a broad valley. We observed a small lake in the distance and determined to explore it the following day.

We reached the shores of the lake the next

afternoon. We saw signs of an Indio village, deserted by those who inhabited it. We camped there for the night. Under a blanket of stars, beside the soft lap of the lake, we took our evening meal at our fire.

"How much further do you plan to go, Padre?"

"We should return to San Isidro soon. We are not provisioned to go further."

"One wonders how much further it might be to the great sea."

"It is a curiosity in need of exploration. Exploration if indeed California is an island."

"Is it not, Padre?"

"That is accepted belief."

"You have reason to doubt it?"

"It has yet to be confirmed."

"Then it is up to us to prove it."

"Or disprove it."

He arched a brow. "You sound as though that is the outcome you prefer. Why so?"

"We have already experienced the difficulty of supplying California by sea. Should the valley of San Isidro prove as difficult to cultivate as we found at La Paz, our work here will be subject to the same risks we encountered there. A land road to California, should one exist, could prove a blessing to our work."

"I see. Do you think it possible?"

"Until we prove it or disprove it, it is as possible as not possible."

Mateo knit his brow in the firelight. "As to that, Padre, I shall take your word on it."

CHAPTER SEVENTEEN

San Bruno

Matías greeted our return with good news. Our Indio cooperated willingly in building our mission and fortifications. He reported Capitán Zevallos to have performed honorably with no incidents of maltreatment in our absence.

We also returned once again to the prospect of dwindling stores and the onset of winter. Atondo dispatched *Concepcion* to Rio Yaqui for supplies. This time, favorable winds attended both crossing and return, completing her mission in a matter of days.

I was pleased to resume my spiritual duties, having been so long away on civil matters. Goni and I were able to tend our small but growing flock. We began by caring for the people's temporal needs for food and medical treatments. These we dispensed in prayer as gifts of the crucified Christ. Our medical skills were most graciously appreciated, finding favor with those we treated and their families. Word spread and soon we were visited daily by a steady and growing stream of those in need of healing. First the body, then the soul.

Always we sought diligently to improve our facility with the Indio tongues. Sounds wore hard on our ears in this struggle. To make matters worse, dialects varied from one village to the next, rendering progress slow and painful. What the Indio lacked in writing, he made up for in pictures. Drawings depicted clan history and significant events. These we could use by pointing and halting communication to extend vocabulary and comprehension. Slowly but steadily the Lord's work progressed.

In early December we set out to explore the coast to the north, in search of a passage through the mountains horses and mules might manage. Such a passage would permit exploration inland in hopes of finding a route to the sea. Thirty leagues north of San Bruno we found a promising passage. A large Didius village occupied the mouth of the pass. In response to our inquiries, they seemed to affirm we might find passage to the sea.

We made our way inland a few leagues.

We were encouraged in finding fresh water and good graze for our stock. We continued climbing the following day suffering harsh desert conditions surrounded by glorious vistas. At day's end, we again confronted a mountain pass too difficult to traverse by horse and mule. We camped at the base of the pass. The next day we climbed the pass on foot. From the summit, we observed rugged, mountainous desert as far as the eye could see. We camped at the summit, making the decision to seek a more favorable passage. We returned to San Isidro in time to celebrate the feast of Christmas.

San Bruno
March 1684
We returned from our exploration to the realization our supply ship was long overdue. Food supplies ran low, rendering our situation difficult once again. Relief came with word of sails sighted against a bright blue sky. The news put an end to the day's labors. Everyone hurried down to the shore to greet *San Jose,* returning from her supply mission. Blessed by a fair wind, she swiftly swept to her anchorage. Boats were lowered. The capitán came ashore while offloading supplies commenced.

The capitán reported to Don Isidro, handing him a leather pouch bearing the official seal of the viceroy. The contents of which would soon become known to me. Also coming ashore with the capitán, we were pleased to greet Father Visitor Juan Bautista Copart, come to inspect the progress of our mission.

That evening, I was summoned to sup with Atondo, thus leaving Matías to care for Father Visitor. I made my way across the presidio compound by light of the moon. The sounds of merriment hummed from the barracks area where twenty new soldados made acquaintance with those already stationed on post. The supply shipment replenished our wine casks, thus ensuring the new arrivals a convivial welcome. My rap at the door to the don's hut drew a muffled,

"Come."

I found him seated at a candlelit rough table in the midst of his spare quarters.

"Good evening, Don Isidro."

"Good evening, Padre. Please have a seat. Would you care for a glass of sherry?"

"It seems an occasion of celebration; but as you know, I do not partake of strong spirits apart from sacramental wine."

"Tea then?"

"Por favor."

Don Isidro poured. The table was set with roast venison, root vegetables, and fresh bread. The don lifted his glass.

"Salud."

"Salud." We took our sips.

"I presume you wonder why I sent for you this evening."

I nodded.

"The viceroy is pleased with the charts and maps you prepared on our early explorations. He sends orders for further inland exploration of the mountains."

"What of our plan to follow the coast north by sea?"

"I'm afraid that must await another time. We need to provision an inland exploration along with procuring horses and mules. I am sending the *San Jose* back to the Yaqui River in a few weeks. I would like you to go along and oversee the provisioning."

"But my spiritual work is here. Must I depart from it again on matters for the crown?"

"Regrettable, Padre, but you are my cartographer. It may be a matter for the crown, but you do serve in that capacity. How is the venison?"

"Most excellent." It seemed the subject closed.

■ ■ ■ ■

So it was, in the company of Father Visitor the *San Jose* set sail for Rio Yaqui. Atondo apprised me of his plan for the exploration, estimating the livestock and provisions we should require. I undertook the voyage with a heart torn in two directions. We were only just beginning to bring forth the fruits of our labors in the vineyard of souls and now I am once again called away to the crown's work. It came with the knowledge that beyond provisioning the work to follow promised a long and difficult exploration. An exploration to chart the unknown. An exploration of discovery and there I felt the lingering tug of my scientific training at cross-purposes with the call of my vocation.

Had I known this to be the nature of my work, I might have joined the army rather than pose the illusion of my service to the Company of Jesus. I said as much to Father Visitor in a quiet moment during our voyage. He assured me my talents were being put to the Lord's purpose as he saw it. The explorations and mappings would pave the way for other missionaries to follow. I hadn't thought of it that way; and yes, I could see the possibility he foresaw. I felt better for it, though I still felt removed from my call to follow the footsteps of our most sainted Francisco Xavier here in California of New Spain.

Matanchel
April 29, 1684
On our arrival in Matanchel at the mouth of the river, Father Visitor directed me to the mission at Torin under the pastoral care of Padre Cervantes. I was given lodging and assistance with the gathering of supplies. Much of my time was devoted to choosing horses and mules for the expedition, some eighty in number. Sturdy well-formed animals were needed to withstand the rigors of mountain and high desert trails. Further to that, quiet docile dispositions were much preferred to face the uncertainties of the trail. I have some facility with horses and mules. Handling them comes naturally to me, though I have no notion as to why. I take it for a gift, a gift that was to serve me well in missions yet to come.

Properly inspected, mules nearly select themselves. They are sturdy by breed trait. Find the willing and you have a fine beast. They are not by nature stubborn as some believe. Unlike a horse whose vision is peripheral, mules see the way forward. As a result, they have a more acute perception of potential danger the handler must skillfully manage. The mule's reputation for stubbornness is born of mismanagement by unskilled handlers.

Horses require greater scrutiny. The Spanish are renowned for breeding fine horses. We found many of strong confirmation in Iberian bloodlines. Spirit is prized in them for demonstrations of power and beauty. Such spirit is less appreciated climbing narrow mountain trails or crossing wilds where the unexpected may be flushed out from behind the next boulder or nearby bush. Well-mannered is more to be prized under such conditions. I took my time, inspecting each animal as to confirmation and disposition. Patience and diligence proved equal to the task. I was rewarded with a fine remuda of sturdy docile stock.

While I saw to the livestock, the capitán looked after foodstuffs and trade goods for transport. At the last I took a chance on an idea Atondo and I had not discussed. I procured five young steers, reckoning them a source of fresh meat to accompany us on the trail.

Loading took considerable time and care. Given the number of animals, additional voyages would be needed. Fodder to feed those transported on our return voyage had to be added to the stores we carried to supply our exploration. *San Jose* rode low in the water by the time we set sail. It minded me of what Noah must have faced.

CHAPTER EIGHTEEN

San Bruno
June 25, 1684

San Jose dropped anchor in the San Bruno harbor on a breezy warm afternoon. Golden sun warmed blue green cove waters. The crew immediately commenced unloading cargo. I was put ashore in a longboat, borne on a gentle surf. Lieutenant Manje greeted me on the beach with horses for the short ride to San Isidro.

"Padre, welcome home." He warmed it with a smile. "I trust you had a pleasant voyage and a successful mission."

"Juan, my son, thank you. I believe we are blessed to have accomplished our purpose."

"Don Isidro sent me to meet you. He wishes to receive your report as soon as possible."

"Allow me to drop my belongings at the mission and I shall accompany you to see him."

"Very well, Padre."

We swung into saddles and set off at a canter. We rode the dry riverbed, reaching San Isidro within the hour.

Matías too greeted my return with news we had much to discuss. I left my traveling kit in our hut and departed with Manje to make my report to Atondo. We found Don Isidro seated at a rough-hewn table in the shade of a cottonwood in the yard before his hut. He poured over dispatches from the viceroy delivered by the *San Jose.* He stood in greeting, sea breeze ruffling shoulder-length gleaming black curls.

"Padre, welcome. Were we favored with a successful journey?"

"I believe so."

"Come then, sit. Tell me all of it." He gestured to a seat at the table. "That will be all, Lieutenant."

Manje came to a crisp salute and departed. I produced a parchment on which I recorded the materials and stock procured for our mission and the expenses associated with each. Atondo read, tracing the page with a finger.

"What is this? Five steers?"

I smiled. "A small improvisation on my part. Fresh meat to accompany us on our journey."

Comprehension dawned in the don's smile. "Clever, Padre. Very clever. Had you not found station in the Company of Jesus you most certainly could have had a successful military career."

"The don is too kind to think so, though I am drawn to my spiritual calling and most anxious to resume my pastoral duties."

"I understand. Forgive me for imposing secular demands on your considerable abilities. It is only that you have talents the crown is much in need of in this service. I shall restrain myself wherever possible. Now as to these stores."

"With so much stock and supply we were unable to carry it all on our return. The rest is in the care of the garrison at Torin."

"Just as well then. We have constructed corrals for the stock, but more will be needed when the rest arrive."

"With your permission, I should like to select a horse for my personal mount."

"Of course. *San Jose* must return to the mouth of the Yaqui a time or two more to complete our preparations. With your concurrence, I propose to send Father Goni to accompany the next voyage."

"Sí, Governor General." I said it with a private sigh of relief, having apprised him of my desire to see to the duties of our spiritual mission.

"Will you dine with me this evening, Padre?"

"If it please your Excellency, I have been long away from our mission. I am sure there is much Matías has to tell me and important he do so if his departure is imminent."

"As you wish. Another time of greater convenience then."

With that I left the don to his dispatches and made the short walk to our mission.

I found Matías seated in chapel on a log in the company of a bright eyed, handsome Indio youth.

"And who might this be?" I inquired.

"Our converted son, Abel," Goni said with a smile.

The boy crossed himself at the sound of his name.

"So, you have been at work in the vineyard in my absence."

"With a few souls to show for it. Little more than a beginning, but beginning, nonetheless. Did your report please Don Isidro?"

"We were able to procure the stock and stores for our exploration. Not all of it could be transported by our return. The *San Jose* will return to Torin as soon as the unloading is complete. The governor wishes you to accompany the next voyage."

"Is that necessary? I am needed here."

"We are both needed here. Appeal the call if you do not wish to go. Perhaps you can persuade Don Isidro where I could not."

"I shall try."

"Now tell me of this beginning of yours and how Abel comes to follow Adam."

"I thought you'd approve the name."

I smiled. "Better Abel than Cain."

A cloud passed Goni's eye. "Yes, well there may be that too. One more thing you should know. We've had no rain."

"I noticed the riverbed dry on our ride from the beach."

"Crops wither in the fields."

"Perhaps it is but a drought that shall pass."

"We can pray. As things stand, it does not bode well."

CHAPTER NINETEEN

The *San Jose* crew completed unloading by the following afternoon. I made my way to the corrals eager to select my personal mount. There I found Lieutenant Manje inspecting the stock beneath a thin veil of dun dust rising from the milling herd.

"Buenas tardes, Padre."

"Buenas tardes, Juan."

"How may I be of service?"

"Don Isidro has granted me the favor of selecting a personal mount."

"Do you see a horse to your liking?"

"I do. I picked him out in Torin when we acquired our first consignment of stock. I made certain he was included in this first shipment."

"Ah, then I presume to know the horse you prefer."

"You do, do you, my son. Then pray tell me my selection."

Manje lifted the point of his goatee to a

blooded black Andalusian stallion with powerful bowed neck, thick chest, and long flowing mane and tail. The horse tossed his head with a snort as if alert to our interest.

"The black."

I smiled. "So obvious is it, my son?"

"Without question. Fortunate for you to come calling for him before the don himself has had opportunity to make his selection."

"The don will be well mounted by choices yet to arrive."

"Have you given thought to a name for so magnificent an animal?"

"I have. He shall be called Damascus."

"Damascus? He is to be named for a city? But why?"

"Paul, Apostle to the Gentiles, found conversion on the road to Damascus. Damascus will bear me on the road to conversion of many."

A few days later Matías boarded the *San Jose* and set sail for Torin. In the days that followed I took time to acquaint myself with Damascus, seeing to his feeding and grooming. Gently we introduced him to bridle and saddle, which, with patience, he willingly accepted. Day by day we worked his gaits at the end of a line, preparing him for our introduction as horse and rider. Abel observed all of this with much curiosity. Like a sponge he soaked up the nuances of horsemanship.

On a bright breezy morning near the time I planned to test him under saddle, we stood at the center of the corral. Abel, as was his custom, watched from the rails. I motioned him to come in. He did so, eagerly at first, more cautiously as he came near the horse's sleek muscled power. I encouraged him to stroke his shoulder, which he did with a tentative smile. Next, I showed him how to pet the horse's nose. Soft warm velvet. The boy recoiled at first touch, but grew more confident with Damascus's gentle acceptance. I drew an apple out of my cassock. Abel's eyes brightened at the prospect of the treat. He accepted it and made to take a bite. I stopped him with a gesture. I spread his hand palm up with the apple placed in the flat of the center. I gestured for him to offer it to the horse. He eyed me with a mixture of disappointment, fear, and excitement. He offered the apple. Damascus lipped it from his hand with an appreciative nuzzle. The beginnings of a bond were born. I drew a second apple from my cassock and handed it to the boy, bringing a light to his eye and an appreciative smile to his lips.

In the days and weeks that followed Damascus learned to accept me as a rider and to respond to pressures and touches governing his movements. Abel would watch us work in the corral or follow along behind when we ventured out to the beach or into the hills. One day as we rode out of the corral, I reined Damascus up beside him. Dark eyes alight, smiling the face of an angel, I reached down. He took my hand in both of his. I swung him up behind me. He grabbed hold of my habit as we picked up a trot down the riverbed to the beach.

We wheeled north in the surf. Sea breeze filled Damascus's nostrils, tossing his mane in gauzy furls. He picked up a proud prance in the foamy lap of the waves. Abel laughed feeling the power of the horse beneath him; salt sea splashes and wind ruffled his hair as we rode along the beach for perhaps half a league. There we paused to rest the horse beside a tidal pool. Abel slipped down and happily ran off to splash in the blue green waters.

As I watched him, it occurred we may have taken another step. The lad could ride. Next, he would lead me to his village where others would see the beauty and mysteries to be found in approaching the faith.

My halting attempts at Abel's Didius tongue

gave rise to equal measures of confusion and humor. The boy for his part rather quickly made for himself a rudimentary facility in Spanish. By combination of the two languages and sign we soon communicated with some proficiency. At that point I broached the subject of a visit to his village. It elicited an apprehensive reaction I did not expect. Something of the home he'd left to spend his days at the mission troubled him. When I proposed we ride there on Damascus, his chest swelled with a look of pride sufficient to overcome whatever misgivings he harbored.

We set out a few days later, climbing into the hills to the northwest. We traveled by the markings of a trail Abel guided us on, though for my part I should never have recognized the signs for a path to anywhere. At a distance of less than a league, I noticed smoke sign from cook fires in the distance. As we drew near, I felt Abel grow tense on his perch behind me.

The village formed a crescent along a shelf in the hillside below the mouth of what appeared a large cave. I observed two styles of dwelling. Low huts formed of adobe like clay toward the back of the village were used for warmth during the cooler rainy season. Similarly constructed brush shelters were inhabited in warm weather. The village was located not far from the beach, close enough to hear the lapping of the surf. Naked men could be seen fishing with nets and spears in the shallows below. Women clad in skirts roamed the hillsides and brush, gathering roots, nuts, berries, insects, and the occasional snake. Children played among the lodges and in the women's wake while older men and women tended cook fires and bean pots.

Our entry into the village was greeted with much curiosity for Damascus presented an imposing and unfamiliar presence. As the villagers gathered, Abel anxiously scanned the crowd as if searching for someone. The person must not have been present for he soon relaxed and enjoyed his celebrity mounted on the back of this strange and powerful beast.

We dismounted at the lodge of Abel's mother. I was given a guest lodge and with Abel's help picketed Damascus with fodder and water. When I inquired about his father, he told me his father was dead. Abel showed me around the village, introducing me to family and friends. As afternoon sun drifted over the hills to the west, the fishermen returned to the village with their day's catch. The women selected their choices and set about preparing the evening meal. Abel stayed close to me, once again seemingly uneasy.

The cause of his alarm soon became apparent. A boy, larger than Abel and powerfully muscled. He looked to be a year or two older than Abel. Intense dark eyes took in Abel and then turned to me. I smiled. The boy's eyes did not return the gesture. He turned away and stalked off with the men.

"Who is that?" I inquired.

"My brother."

Cain, Goni's words came back to me. The boy Cain did not join us when we took our evening meal at Abel's mother's lodge. Later when I retired to the lodge provided for me, Abel begged he might stay with me. I took advantage of the opportunity to ask.

"What is the trouble between you and your brother?" He seemed reluctant to answer at first.

"He blames me for our father's death."

"Why?"

"I was there."

"What happened?"

He sat stone-faced, turning over a painful memory.

"My father was a great warrior. Respected in our clan and well known to our enemies.

He took me with him one day to learn to hunt. We were far from the village when we were seen by a Yuma war party. They recognized my father and attacked. My father told me to run. I did."

"And for this your brother blames you for your father's death."

He could only nod, a tear glistened, visible in low lodge light.

"Black Bird says I am a coward. He says I disgrace my family and for this I should die."

"You were but a boy. You did what your father told you to do. This does not make you a coward. This does not disgrace your family."

"You say so, Padre. Black Bird does not."

This did not bode well. I rested little that night with a wary eye. Our ministry here could not include young Abel unless we made a change of heart in his brother. I must have dozed in the small hours before dawn, for I awoke to pale first light. The boy's sleeping mat lay empty.

Alarmed I scrambled out of the lodge. I cast my gaze about squinting in the dim light. There. A shadow. A glint. A blade. *Cain.*

"No!" I ran toward the picket.

Damascus wheeled out of the shadows.

Nostrils flared eyes wide to the whites with Abel astride. He towered over Black Bird. The boy dropped his knife and ran.

"Now see who runs," Abel crowed.

We returned to the mission that day. Ministry to Abel's clan would await Matías's return.

CHAPTER TWENTY

Cosari
Pimeria Alta

The boy Hawk, now eight summers, trotted behind his father Black Thorn as he jogged the twisting trail into the hills above the village. Always they ran now. Hawk knew the summer beginning his warrior training would come. It was not here yet, but it would come soon. In running he prepared. His bow, more toy than weapon, prepared him too. Serious bow and shield awaited warrior training. This day his father meant to teach him to use a sling. For now, the sling suited the games and purposes of boyhood.

The trail spilled out on a plateau, bordered on one side by a shear rock wall. Black Thorn signaled a halt. He unfastened a leather pouch from his waist thong and laid it on the ground. With a charred stick he drew a circle on the rock wall.

"Kawad." He spoke the word for shield. Hawk nodded.

Black Thorn measured a distance of ten long paces from the target. He opened the leather pouch and removed the sling. He poured out the remaining contents, a pile of hardened mud balls. He cradled a mud ball in the sling, swung it around his head, releasing the ball to shatter in the center of the target. He held out the sling to Hawk.

Hawk cradled a mud ball in the sling. Black Thorn sat on the ground behind him. He swung the sling and released too soon. The mud ball missed, low and far right of the target.

"Once more," Black Thorn said.

Hawk repeated the procedure, releasing the ball too late. This time striking the wall high and left of the target.

"Again."

Mud ball after mud ball, the target remained untouched save his father's first sling. Hawk felt foolish and then ashamed he could not please his father and hit the target. Black Thorn took his hand and guided him to the proper release point.

"Now try here."

This helped. The misses came closer. Sill he missed. Three balls remained. Hawk fought back disappointment. A warrior would not cry. He took a ball, fixed his eyes on the target, and swung. The ball shattered on the wall, inside the circle this time. Hawk whooped in triumph.

Black Thorn ruffled his hair and picked up the last two balls and put them back in the leather pouch. He placed the sling in the pouch and handed it to Hawk.

Hawk understood. He fastened it to his waist thong in the manner his father carried it on the trail. They set off at a jog down the trail for home.

Returning to the village they came to an olas kih where Fawn sat watching her mother weave a basket. Hawk looked to his father who nodded. Black Thorn continued to the family lodge. Hawk stopped to visit his friend. He made a show of his new pouch, removing his sling for the girl to examine. Fawn saw him with bright eyes. He felt a swell of pride. The sling was more than a child's toy. It symbolized a new beginning. The beginning of more serious training. Training to progress toward warrior skills. The skills of a man.

San Isidro
Matías returned to the mission with the *San Jose*'s second supply voyage. When I de-

154

scribed for him the situation with Abel's brother he nodded understanding, having surmised something of the sort. Visitors continued to come to the mission from Abel's village. His brother was not among them, though we remained watchful for the boy's safety. We made all welcome with food, instruction in the faith and baptism for infants and those suffering illness. Catechesis progressed for souls seeking salvation. Our days passed amiably and fruitfully in conversions of our growing little flock.

Once again, the *San Jose* set sail for Torin and another cargo of stock and stores. Preparations for Don Isidro's inland expedition proceeded apace. Matías and I determined to make our own exploration of a new mission while I was available to assist and not occupied by secular duties. We planned a second mission to serve clans further inland. We determined to undertake explorations to that end with Abel to accompany us, serving as guide and interpreter. In this he would assist in establishing our mission, safe from his brother's vengeful ways.

With Don Isidro's blessing, Matías selected a sturdy mule from the herd to carry him on our exploration. We packed supplies for the journey and set off, Abel and I mounted on Damascus with Matías trailing behind.

We rode west, limiting our search to a day's ride for purposes of keeping the missions in close contact for reasons of security. We ranged north and south on our trail, seeking a location served by fresh water. On our swing to the north, we came upon spring-fed wells in a pleasant wooded area. We made camp and christened the site the Wells of San Isidro, reckoning the don would be pleased. In a few days' time we constructed a rudimentary shelter and made a good start on a small chapel.

Our efforts were soon rewarded by the arrival of curious Didius from nearby villages, Abel's among them. With their help, the mission soon commenced to serve. Our days were long and rewarding in the fruits of our labors.

We took our evening meals under a canopy of stars, warmed by a small fire. Matías took stock of our progress.

"We have the makings of a mission here, Eusebio."

"We do."

"I think it is time for you to return to San Isidro to continue our work there."

"It is needful."

"It is. I have made a list of supplies and

materials we shall need here. Take Abel and the mule with you. He can return with the supplies."

Abel brightened at the prospect of taking on such an important part in our work.

San Bruno
October 1684

They came out of the hills to the north and west, gathering in great numbers across the valley from our mission and presidio. They came painted, bodies covered in exotic designs and festooned in feathers and shells. They took up a dance to a steady drumbeat, rolling distant thunder across the valley floor. Atondo ordered our soldados alert. I turned to Abel.

"What does this mean, my son?"

"They dance to the god of gathering. The harvest has been scarce this season. Winter comes. The people are fearful of a season of starving."

It was true of course. Our own stores were depleted, dependent on ships reaching us from the mainland. I informed Atondo as to the meaning of the dances.

"Are you sure, Padre? My scouts tell me Dionisio and the Edu have joined in league with Leopaldo's Didius against us."

"How would your scouts learn such a

thing? The boy is Didius. He knows the ritual of gathering. The people mean us no harm. They are only fearful for the hunger of a harsh winter."

"I can't be so sure. They may blame us for the drought and the shortage of food."

Tensions remained on edge until the dances ended and the people returned to the hills.

CHAPTER TWENTY-ONE

December 14, 1684

Preparations for our inland exploration completed in early December. Atondo would lead a party of twenty-nine soldados under the command of Lieutenant Manje. My charge would record notes on navigation, survey measurements and rendering cartographic features of the terrain we traversed. Thirty-seven horses provided mounts with thirty mules to carry supplies in addition to our commissary cattle on the hoof. Reliable Indian guides were recruited to see us on our way and assist in relations with any Californians we might encounter.

With so much effort having gone into preparations for the expedition and the viceroy's keen interest in the enterprise, Atondo was determined to complete the mission, though without unanimity under his command. California suffered severe drought. Supplies off the land were scarce and fresh water seasonally in short supply, these combined to increase the risks of our undertaking. These risks were not lost on veteran soldados who were heard grumbling to their superiors. Their concerns notwithstanding, we set off on a bright sunny day touched by cool sea breeze.

Journal Entry

We traveled north along the beach to a place scouts reported passage over the mountains possible. Turning west we traversed high desert valleys and plains, climbing gently into steep mountain passes. Though difficult the mountain trail proved passable. Rock-strewn climbs and descents strained the stock. Many went lame or required reshoeing. In four days' march, we descended an arroyo to the Santo Tomas riverbed.

There our guides informed us we were being followed. Atondo ordered the soldados alert. He instructed a few of our scouts to determine who followed us, in what strength, and to what purpose. They made off to the north as the rest of the party undertook an arduous climb of six leagues, to the crest of a divide. The scouts rejoined us early that evening.

They sheepishly reported a small party of Didius led by Cacique Leopaldo.

"To what purpose?" Atondo demanded.

The scout leader, uncomfortable in my presence, mumbled. "He is accompanied by five very beautiful young maidens."

The don pursed his lips in surprise.

The whispered word spread like grass fire through the ranks.

Mateo chewed a lip as though embarrassed for me.

"I am a priest, Mateo. Temptations of the flesh are not unknown to me. I have been known to hear confessions, you know." My assurances notwithstanding the situation remained uncomfortable as we began a three-day descent to the river gorge winding southwest below.

The presence of Leopaldo and his maidens nearby became a discipline problem for Atondo and Manje, especially when it came to maintaining night watch. Sentinels slipped away from their posts, or worse, distracted themselves while on duty noisily enough to disturb the hearing of those awaiting their turn at duty.

"What is to be done, Padre?" Don Isidro asked in awkward frustration. "Am I to keep watch on the watch?"

"Let me see what I might do."

I would like to say I imparted the light of moral virtue to the cacique and his companions. I would like to say that, though in truth I bribed them with gifts to return to their village and leave us to our purpose. Higher purpose in this case need be served by expediency.

December 24, 1684
River passage now arrested our full attention. The gorge narrowed. We were forced to wade rock-strewn rushing waters. Footing became uncertain for men and animals alike. More than a few slipped and fell. We learned to stay alert to those preceding and following us in file. In an instant a fallen person might find himself at the mercy of rushing water. A companion might become the difference between life and death. By patient and deliberate passage, we managed to find our way through to a high desert plateau, arriving in time for Christmas.

We paused for a day of rest and to celebrate the feast of Christmas with the Holy Sacrifice of the Mass, giving nourishment to our spirits and thanksgiving for the safety of our river passage. We slaughtered the first of our cattle for a celebratory feast. Fresh meat for the body, and a day of rest buoyed the men's spirits. Continuing onward we reached the shores of the great sea December twenty-ninth. We journeyed two weeks over a distance I reckoned by celestial sightings at no more than thirty leagues. The difficulty of the terrain rendered the effective distance two to three times that reading.

On reaching the coast, we slaughtered the second of our cattle. We roasted great portions on spits producing another fine meal. The refreshment taken from fresh meat proved the wisdom of including cattle in the stores for our expedition, receiving many accolades from appreciative comrades. For my part, I saw husbandry as a possibility to diversify food sources available to our Indio children. Little could be accomplished with agriculture. Attempts at cultivation suffered the poor soil conditions of arid desert. Hunting and gathering too offered meager yield. I noted ranching and husbandry as potential for future consideration.

At our campfire that night, enjoying the satisfaction of our meal, we discussed further exploration.

"Curious," Don Isidro said.

"Curious?"

"Little more than thirty leagues from coast to coast. Do you make California an island?"

"That is the accepted perception, though we do not know what lies further north."

"That then is our mission, Padre. We must explore northward along the seacoast."

I thought our conversation had come to an end as he packed his pipe bowl with fresh tobacco. "You know, Padre, it seems I made a costly mistake."

"Mistake, Don Isidro? I do not understand."

"I did not think of it at the time, but clearly I should have had pick of the horse herd before allowing you your choice. How does it feel to be mounted on the finest horse in all of New Spain?"

I smiled. "He is magnificent, though you are by no means shamed by your charger."

"Yes, well my gray is well bred with many fine qualities, but if I am any judge of horseflesh, and I am, he stands in the shadow of your Damascus. That too I find interesting. Damascus, odd name for a horse."

"Not odd, Excellency, symbolic."

"Symbolic of what?" He drew his pipe to light.

"Not cartography explorations I'm afraid; but you may recall from Acts of the Apostles, our most blessed Saint Paul the Apostle encountered his conversion on the road to Damascus. Damascus will carry me on the road to many conversions."

"Ah, I see. Very well then. Should your mission here prove any measure of your patron's, Holy Mother Church will be most pleased by your work."

"The holy apostle Paul, great as he may be, is not my patron. I took San Francisco Xavier for my patron many years ago. Paul and I, I am afraid to say, have a much different relationship."

"How is that?" A fragrant cloud mellowed his words.

"I struggled with my studies of Paul in seminary."

"I'm surprised. You are an intelligent man. Paul a missionary such as yourself. A prolific writer of letters, I give him that. What is to misunderstand?"

"His letters."

Don Isisdro shrugged. "He preached. You preach. I don't see the problem."

"The problem is mine. Greek and Hebrew mingle in Paul's teaching. His theological messages are, may I say, circumspect. I am a man of science and mathematics, given to more straightforward thinking."

"And for this Paul cannot be your patron?"

"Not for that, San Francisco has already taken that place."

"Then there is only one thing remaining

to be done."

"What is that, Excellency?"

"Paul the great apostle must be patron to your horse."

We departed the next day, following the seashore north. A week's trek produced no sign of island formation before we encountered high rocky cliffs blocking further passage by shore. We made camp to contemplate a way forward. It was here, I discovered a curiosity, destined years later to shed unexpected light on a path to mission in California.

I walked the beach late of an afternoon, reading the prayers of daily Holy Office. I came to a large flat rock worn smooth by centuries of surfs and high tides. There I sat to finish my prayers in the golden glow of sunbeams, settling over ocean waves stretching to the horizon as far as the eye could see. As I closed my breviary, my eye caught a beautiful shade of blue washed free of its covering sand. I brushed it off and was rewarded by discovery of a beautiful blue shell. As I examined it, I looked around and saw others. I gathered several, never having seen any such as these.

The blue hue made these shells distinctively striking. I wondered at what manner of creature might have clothed itself in so colorful a manner. I puzzled over why I should find shells such as these only here. We traveled near fifteen leagues along the coast to reach this cove, nowhere in that journey had we come across any shells the like of these. I secured a few more specimen in my pack. Time would prove the discovery auspicious.

That evening Don Isidro summoned me to his fire once more.

"What think you now, Padre, an island or land bridge to the mainland?"

"California may yet be proven an island, but this exploration leads us only to further exploration."

"True. It also leads further and further from San Isidro. The proper way to continue northward exploration may be best under sail."

I nodded. "It would seem a faster and less arduous route to confirm an island formation."

We turned south the following morning, following the coast to the high desert crossing, returning to San Isidro by the route over which we had come. We suffered the onset of winter rainy season with its chill, but counted it a small inconvenience for the comfort of journeying home.

CHAPTER TWENTY-TWO

San Isidro
January 1685

We returned from our western exploration early in the new year. Drought conditions persisted through a dry winter. With *Concepcion* docked at the mouth of the Yaqui, San Isidro depended on the little *San Jose* for its supply needs. Rations and drinking water became scarce and restricted. Atondo mounted explorations along the coast, seeking a site more hospitable to our circumstances. These efforts produced no fruitful result. I grew fearful for the future of our work here. Matías saw it the same way. We prayed. If only it would rain.

The *San Jose* sailed a successful supply mission in March, but these supplies too quickly began to dwindle. Drought continued, rendering any form of agriculture impossible to sustain us. To make matters worse, water sources became tainted with salt. Men became ill. Symptoms told us scurvy spread pestilence among us. Men became restless. Fearing for the future of our mission, I mounted Damascus and rode into the desert to pray.

Desert

Why is it, hot dry desolation invites us to pray? How often does scripture tell us Jesus went out to the desert to pray? The desert afflicts us with harsh conditions. Conditions we cannot control. Conditions to remind us, all is in God's hands. And so, I prayed. I prayed for our mission. I prayed we might be given to see it through. Surely God must see his purpose at work in our mission. Surely, he must see.

The desert blooms in spring rains. Wildflowers blossom. New growth bursts forth. Rain stores are replenished. I waited. I prayed. The desert remained an unyielding taskmaster. Hot and dry it could not be bent to my will. It had to be His will. It would be. Not yet. *Thy will be done.*

May 1685

Don Isidro called together Capitán Zevallos and me. I went to the gathering with a sense of dread. Don Isidro enumerated our predicament.

"I am afraid we have reached a moment of truth. Consider what we face. Little grows in these drought-stricken desert conditions. What water we have is prone to foul. Mining and pearl gathering fail to reveal prospects for meaningful commercial return. Disease decimates the ranks of the men. The viceroy has come to the end of his patience and treasury at the cost of this enterprise compared to the paucity of conversions. What say you then to all of this?"

Zevallos spoke first. "San Bruno, as La Paz before it, San Isidro cannot sustain itself. We have no choice but to return the sick to Yaqui for medical attention and abandon this salt desert."

"But what of the Indio come to our mission? What is to become of them?"

"There are not enough of them, Padre," Don Isidro said. "Certainly not enough to outweigh the conclusion Capitán Zevallos draws for us."

"Our work here has only begun to bear fruit. Surely with the assistance of the Indio we can preserve our presence here at San Bruno."

I made the argument hopeful of a favorable hearing, though I could see Atondo wavering over concerns for his men.

"Padre, I am sorry; but I must weigh the safety of all in this matter. Our situation here is too fragile to trust to uncertainty. We must make preparations to return to Torin."

"I will need a few days to withdraw Father Goni from the Wells of San Isidro."

"Regrettable as that may be, I must ask you to see to it."

"Sí, Don Isidro."

The Wells of San Isidro

I departed for San Isidro the following morning. Abel listened as I broke the news to Matías.

"Abandon all our work?" Matías shook his head incredulous. "We could stay. Our Indio flock will help see to our needs."

"These undertakings by royal decree are taken jointly by ecclesiastical and royal authority. Our superiors would not permit such a course of action. I'm afraid we have no choice."

"What of me?" Abel said.

"What of our son indeed." Matías affirmed.

They raised the specter of abandoning the boy to the vengeful designs of his brother. I saw the need though it was not for me to decide."

"Would you prefer to come with us, my son?"

He nodded.

"I shall put the request to Don Isidro."

San Bruno

We returned to San Bruno the following day, Matías astride his mule, Abel perched behind me on Damascus. I made our request for the boy to accompany us to Don Isidro. He seemed reluctant at first; but when I explained the threat to his safety posed by the brother, we called Cain, he gave it some measure of preserving our work in the mission. We weighed anchor with the tide and sailed for Matanchel at the mouth of the Rio Yaqui, with Abel in our custody.

Matanchel

Father Cervantes welcomed us to his mission at Torin. Matías, the boy Abel, and I lent our backs and hands to the work of his mission in the weeks we were there, though these pleasant days of service were not destined to last long. Atondo received orders from the viceroy to conduct a pearl harvesting expedition along the coast of California. He invited Matías to accompany him. With our duties at the mission in Torin temporary, there seemed no reason he should not go. On the eighth of May with a rising tide and a fair wind, the *San Jose* set sail for San Ignacio, Sinaloa, where they would provision for the voyage.

Soon thereafter Capitán Guzman of the *Concepcion* proposed yet another voyage north in search of a site suitable for a military outpost and mission. Supplies were assembled at the mission and packed to the port for loading on the *Concepcion.* Accompanied by Abel, we sailed north along the sea to the coast of Seri. We landed at Salsipuedes in June and spent three days as guests of the Indio there. We were welcomed with great hospitality and good wishes to establish a mission there with offers of assistance, food, and materials.

While the appeals of the people tugged at my heart, Capitán Guzman insisted we continue our explorations. His insistence caused me to reflect on the progress of our mission. It occurred to me the secular dictates of the crown and the spiritual mission of harvesting souls struck at cross-purposes. Explorations were of necessity temporary and migratory. Mission building needed time to develop community, earn the trust of our flock, and instill the faith in their waiting hearts. Something must be done to free our sacred mission from the pressures of constant search for treasure and trade. I prayed over these ponderings in search of guidance as to how to affect them.

By the time we returned to Matanchel on seventeen September, I had a plan as to how I might appeal for change to the fortunes of our mission. Leaving Abel in the care of Father Cervantes at Torin, Damascus and I set out for Guadalajara. Over the days of my journey, I refined my arguments in favor of freeing our ecclesiastical mission from the transitory quests of the crown. In truth the key to the argument must come in harmonizing the desired outcome with furtherance of royal interests. In evenings on the trail, I recorded my thoughts of the day in a journal so that by the time I arrived in Guadalajara I was prepared to draft the report I planned to present to Father Provincial there.

Guadalajara
October 1685
The Company of Jesus maintained a house in the central city. There our confreres were welcome while awaiting assignment to a mission or, as I, taking a respite from one. Father Rector assigned me a room for my stay. In the days that followed, I divided my time between the chapel and composition

of the report I would present Father Provincial.

Journal entries from my days on the trail provided the buttress of my argument for a permanent mission presence in California. I began with the needs of the flock, the souls there in search of salvation's true faith. So great was the need it could not possibly be satisfied by itinerant comings and goings of the sort we experienced in the party of explorations.

Settled missions are required to assist the people in their temporal as well as spiritual needs. To this end, I recommended establishing a mission at Loreto, some leagues south of San Bruno. Here fresh water favored agriculture. I described the clan-centered nature of the people's society. They subsisted on hunting small game, fishing, and gathering wild stores of fruit, roots, and insects. I put forward the opportunity to introduce animal husbandry to their temporal benefit. I drew on my experience of the cattle driven on our inland exploration to the western sea. There we observed grasslands and water sufficient to sustain the maintenance of herds. In addition to cattle, I postulated sheep might be suited to more mountainous climbs. The California mission could be further supported by a sister settlement on the mainland with service between the two performed by small swift barca.

The spiritual and temporal needs of the people made a powerful ecclesiastical argument for permanent missions, but more would be needed to satisfy the purposes of secular authority by whom the proposal must also be approved. In this I felt the Holy Spirit's inspiration at work and trusted the promise of colonization would secure secular purpose compatible with permanent mission. New Spain, I wrote, must not only be explored, it must be settled. Colonial settlements and missions, taken together, provide stepping-stones to further exploration while consolidating the crown's territorial claims.

With my proposal so structured, I had only to add the customary flowers of salutation and introduction and the flourishes of deferential signature, *Your most humble and faithful servant, Eusebio Kino, S.J.*

I delivered my report to Reverend Father Provincial Ambrosio Oddon along with a request for audience with the bishop. Father Provincial accepted my report, giving it prompt and due consideration. He passed it on to the bishop with my request for audience. The bishop's auxiliary accepted my report and request with the assurance his reverence would give it proper consideration. I retired to our rectory to await a response or a summons.

Response came in a week's time in the form of a note from Father Auxiliary. He informed me the bishop would put my recommendations forward to the archbishop and viceroy in Mexico. More than this I could not have hoped for at the time. With some sense of accomplishment Damascus and I prepared our return journey to Matanchel to await further instruction.

On the eve of our departure, an emissary from the viceroy arrived with an official dispatch addressed to Atondo. I was obliged to carry it with me. My plans for a leisurely return became preempted by the urgency accompanying the missive.

CHAPTER TWENTY-THREE

Matanchel
November 1685

On my return I made straight to the residence housing Don Isidro before returning to the mission. I showed the aide in reception the viceroy's seal on the dispatch pouch I carried and asked to see Atondo. Forthwith I was shown into Don Isidro's office.

"Padre, welcome. I trust you had a successful visit with the bishop."

"I presented my proposal. We shall see if it might meet with success. I received this before embarking on my return."

I handed him the pouch. He broke the seal and retrieved the vellum within. He strode to the window and read by golden light of late afternoon. He arched a brow, tapping the sheet to the point of his beard.

"We have a mission," he said.

"We?"

"I'm afraid I must once again impose on

178

your navigational arts, Padre. His Majesty's Manila galleon is in route to California. The viceroy has received reports English pirates operate in waters off the coast. With the closing of the California presidio, I am instructed to intercept her and divert her from danger to safe harbor in Acapulco."

Pirates again. I remembered our brush with the Barbary pirates. Somehow the English seemed less threatening; but pirates were pirates, nonetheless. I doubted we should enjoy an encounter with the English any more than Moors. None of this would alter the viceroy's order or the impress on my navigational services.

The next two days passed in the blink of an eye. Vested with the authority of the viceroy, Atondo passed over a galleon at his disposal in port to commandeer a sleek merchant barca at anchor there. The ship was quickly provisioned and outfitted with a battery of culverin, powder, and shot. We boarded, accompanied by a company of soldados under the command of Lieutenant Manje. I plotted a course south by southwest calculated, as best I could reckon it, to intercept the Manila galleon along a course plotted to reach California from the Philippines, that being the estimate on which prospects a successful enterprise would rest.

Given the forces of wind, weather, and sea, the possibility of actually intercepting His Majesty's ship more precisely rested in the hands of the Lord.

We weighed anchor the following morning with the tide, setting sail on a fair wind, flying the king's colors at the viceroy's rank. This would signal our authority to the Manila galleon, a necessary recognition. It would also provide fair warning to any pirate who might judge us a fat merchant prize. Lookouts searched the seas for any sign of His Majesty's ship or pirate threat.

The barca proved swift transport when compared to the plodding pace of a wide beam, deep draft galleon. We took comfort she could acquit herself effectively should we be forced to engage a fast, maneuverable vessel of the sort employed in piracy. And while the recognition gave some comfort, I still had no fondness for the prospect of facing another sea battle with pirates.

Two weeks at sea brought sighting of a sail on the southwestern horizon. Atondo ordered a course correction to intercept her. Manje deployed his troops to the gunwale port and starboard. The culverin aboard, four in number, sat their caissons amidships, manned to respond to targets on either side of the ship.

Sail slowly swelled against the bright blue horizon as we closed, though we remained unable to discern her colors. Atondo studied her intently through his glass. We waited, tense uncertainty for knowledge to come.

"She's ours," Isidro said at last.

I loosed a breath I hadn't realized I held.

"Heave to, hailing distance." The first mate echoed the capitán's order.

We showed our colors and signaled our intent to approach. Atondo prepared to extend our warning to the galleon. I set myself to charting a course for Acapulco.

Matanchel

We saw the Manila galleon safely to port and returned north along the coast without incident. On our arrival, we were greeted by yet another dispatch from the viceroy. It seemed my report to the bishop must have come to some effect. Atondo and I were invited to conference with the viceroy and archbishop in Mexico City, where we would consider the way forward to a California mission. At this development I took some sense of progress toward finding my purpose in New Spain.

I found Matías returned from his exploration and reunited with Abel. Over supper I explained my report to the bishop and hopes for a settlement approach to California missions.

"And so Reverend Bishop presented my report to the archbishop and viceroy. It now appears both are willing to consider it. The viceroy has invited Atondo and me to meet with him and the archbishop in Mexico City."

"Another long and perilous journey, Eusebio."

"If it leads us to mission in California, Matías, it is God's work."

"So is saving souls, work we have managed precious little of in our time here thus far."

"I understand your frustration. I share it. That is why I undertook my report to the bishop. It is my hope our meeting with the viceroy and our ecclesiastical superior will remedy the situation."

"I will pray for the success of your plan. Abel and I will do what we can here while you are away."

"And I will pray for the success of your endeavors. I have another thought."

"What is that?"

"Perhaps Abel might accompany me to Mexico City. He would provide his excellency the archbishop and the viceroy with evidence of the fruitful harvest awaiting us in a mission to California."

"He would indeed, and on his return, he can tell his people of the majesty and generosity of Holy Mother Church that sends us to them."

"Excellent! We are agreed then?"

"We are. We have only one detail to work out. I shall need the mule while you are away."

"Of course. I shall speak of it with Don Isidro. I am sure he will find a mount for the boy."

With that we undertook preparations for our departure.

Don Isidro saw the merit in my plan to have Abel accompany us to Mexico City. We selected a sweet dappled mare for his mount. He named her Azucar for his favorite flavor, sugar. We departed for Mexico City accompanied by a military escort under command of Lieutenant Manje and a packtrain of mules laden with supplies.

Mexico City traversed a journey of nearly three hundred leagues. We set our course south along the coast for a fortnight, affording comfortable travel for the first hundred leagues. We reached a gentle pass we took southeast and began our assent along the west face of the Sierra Madre. Mountainous terrain slowed our progress. A four-day march of some thirty leagues led us to the shores of a beautiful mountain lake where we camped and rested ourselves and our animals for the final leg of our journey.

Our campsite on the lakeshore invited Abel to memories of his days spent fishing at home. He took to the water the first day of our respite. Fresh fish properly prepared in his native custom made a welcome departure from a diet deficient in meat in favor of peppers, frijoles, and tortillas. We invited Atondo to share an evening meal at our campfire. We finished a sumptuous repast and suitably embarrassed young Abel with effusive praise. Don Isidro filled his pipe as the moon came up over the mountains. Night sounds of insects and the gentle lap of the lakeshore settled as a blanket of peace over our camp.

"It seems your report to the bishop has found favor with the viceroy as well as your superiors, Padre." He puffed a cloud of sweet smoke.

I nodded. "We have learned much in our time here in New Spain, but sadly progress in our ecclesiastical mission has not kept pace with our explorations. Settlement is needed to further the joint causes of Christianity and empire. I simply made humble effort to note these points."

"You are too modest, Padre. You put forward a well-founded case spoken clearly to your ecclesiastic superiors and governing representatives of the crown. The path you recommend is a sound one. My only reservation is that it leads to California."

"California is a fertile field both in souls and territorial riches. Surely you have seen so for yourself."

"I have and both the material and spiritual treasures are as you say. I have also seen the naval and military challenges of supplying and maintaining expeditionary outposts there, let alone sustaining permanent settlements."

I heard concerns of the sort likely to obstruct my plan. "Surely there must be means and methods to overcome obstacles such as these with so much at stake."

"Undoubtedly there are, but one must also ask at what cost."

"Will you speak in opposition to my proposal?"

"No, Padre. Your plan is a well-founded way forward. I will support it, but understand I am duty bound to voice my reservations concerning California. If our Superiors deem the prize worthy the cost, you and I will find a way to do the work."

"Thank you, Don Isidro. Your support will be most welcome at council."

Atondo tapped out his pipe and yawned. "Thank you, Padre, for a wonderful meal. Your idea to bring the boy is brilliant in more ways than I knew. On that note, I shall bid you good even."

I watched the don depart in shadow, beyond the circle of firelight. I hadn't fully accounted the naval and military considerations he mentioned out of an overabundance of zeal for California's harvest of souls. It gave pause to my certainty of purpose. As with most uncertainties, this one was best left entrusted to the care of divine purpose.

CHAPTER TWENTY-FOUR

Journal Entry

We resumed our journey in a few days' time. The difficulty of our climb increased over the span of the next week and a distance of some fifty leagues, though for all the twists and turns our way wended, who could determine distance with any precision. Damascus handled the rigors of the trail with ease. I made a point to follow Abel to assess how well Azucar managed the strain. She proved a sturdy well-behaved lady with pluck.

The mountainous terrain bred rugged high desert vegetation and wildlife to be reckoned with. Snakes, scorpions, and birds of prey abounded. Mosquitoes and biting flies followed us in swarms, testing us with misery and suffering in sympathy with the plagues Moses visited on Pharaoh's Egypt. Our military escort ever on watch for banditos or hostile Indio took on an added element of danger. Mountain lions and jaguar were known to prowl the high country, hunting marked territories. The jaguar is held in godlike reverence and awe by the Indio. The heights of stout trees and rock outcroppings all became sources of sudden danger. Lieutenant Manje and his men kept their arquebus primed.

A day's climb below the high desert plateau we would follow to Mexico City, we camped on a broad ledge that afforded a generous supply of firewood with a freshwater stream tumbling out of the rocky heights above. We gathered wood for our evening cook fires in canopied gloom at early onset of evening. All at once the forest fell silent. Gone were birdsong, even the persistent buzzing of insects. Horses and mules picked up their ears and flared nostrils to the breeze. I followed Damascus's alert nose into rock reaches above our campsite. Something out there set off alarm. I glanced across our campground. Manje had noticed it too. Hastily he deployed his men in a defensive perimeter, weapons at the ready.

We watched and waited. A wild-eyed pronghorn antelope bolted out of the trees up the trail above camp. The giant cat leapt in a blur. Even in faint light and shadow, massive claws and fangs flared. The jaguar let out a primal screech fit to turn a man's blood cold.

"Fire!"

Manje's men loosed a volley of powder flash and smoke. The big cat's shriek choked off in its throat, thrashing the throes of violent death. Silence descended like the fall of a curtain. Juan waited while his men reloaded, then signaled them forward. They moved cautiously up the trail. Curious, I followed.

The jaguar lay next to the pronghorn. The antelope's broken neck bore marks of the big cat's powerful jaws. The dead cat felled by appearance of at least three balls from where I stood. I marveled at the size of the head, the length of the fangs, and vicious curled claws protruding from its massive paws. I shuddered to think what such a beast might have done early Christians martyred in brutal barbarism.

The soldados dragged the jaguar to the side of the trail. Two men carried the antelope back to camp where it was dressed and roasted. That night we feasted on the big cat's prey and were grateful to the jaguar for providing it.

The following day we reached high desert plateau at Chupicuaro, setting a southeasterly course for Mexico City. With more favorable terrain to traverse, we crossed the final fifty leagues in five days.

Mexico City

We paused on a sun-soaked bluff overlooking Lake Texcoco and the city seeming to float away from her western shore. The city stood in all its ancient grandeur ready to engulf our senses as we entered. Here again one could see remnants of pagan Aztec culture, adorned by the spires and steeples of Holy Mother Church. Our journey ended. What awaited? I wondered.

We straggled out of the hills and followed the cobbled causeway leading to the city gates. We followed a broad thoroughfare to the central plaza. There stood the former Temple of Quetzalcoatl, now known as Palacio Real, palace of the sun, housing the viceroy's residence and the seat of royal authority in New Spain. Here Abel and I detached from Atondo's party, continuing on to the nearby cathedral and the archbishop's residence.

Archbishop Ferdinand Roberto received us warmly in his handsomely appointed offices. A portly man of imposing figure, his Excellency possessed the gentle nature of a father figure. Abel, whose living experience ended with mud huts and primitive dwellings we constructed in mission, stood in awe of the opulence and trappings of the dwelling place for what he regarded as a red-robed chief of priests. Wide-eyed he beheld me kneel to kiss the archbishop's ring.

"Welcome, Padre Kino. I have been most anxious to meet you since reading your excellent report on prospects for our missions."

"I am humbled, Excellency."

He smiled at Abel. "And who do we have here?"

"Our son, Abel is a convert of the Didius people of California. He has chosen to follow Father Goni and me in our work. He is one among the many souls awaiting conversion."

"Splendid, then he too is welcome. Please have a seat."

He motioned us to a red-velvet covered settee. I took a seat and patted the cushion for Abel to sit. He did so on the edge, ramrod straight in discomfort. The archbishop and I shared a smile.

"I understand the viceroy has recalled Governor Atondo to join us in discussing your proposal."

"We traveled together with Don Isidro. He reports to the viceroy as we speak."

"Good. Then we shall not be delayed in

our deliberations. How was your journey?"

"Largely uneventful save an encounter with a jaguar."

"A jaguar, oh my. Was anyone hurt?"

"Thankfully none of our party. The jaguar did provide an antelope for our nourishment before the soldados of our escort shot him."

"Such risks are endemic to travel in New Spain. It goes with our mission it seems."

"May I ask, Excellency, have you had occasion to discuss the recommendations of my report with the viceroy?"

"We did, not long after we received it."

"How did he view it?"

"He sees merit for ecclesiastical and territorial gain. I must say your coupling of settlement with mission was a brilliant stroke."

"Thank you, Excellency. Perhaps then he will find our mission to California worth the cost."

"Cost?"

"Don Isidro has reservations about the difficulty of sustaining permanent settlement in California by sea. Settlements too must be garrisoned against hostile Indio."

"I see. It appears we have more to discuss than I imagined. Now I'm sure you must be weary from your journey. Let us show you

to your rooms and make yourselves comfortable before we take our supper."

"If it please your Excellency, the Company
of Jesus maintains a house, Casa Profesa,
near the university. My brothers would
welcome us there."

"As you wish then," he said with a nod. "I
shall send for you there when we are to meet
with the viceroy."

CHAPTER TWENTY-FIVE

Tepeyac Hill

In the few days it took to arrange audience with the archbishop and viceroy, I took advantage of the opportunity to make a small pilgrimage. On a bright sunny morning, having obtained directions from the stable boy, I rode Damascus out of the city into the hills overlooking Lake Texcoco. I followed a well-worn footpath set down by thousands of pilgrims who trod this path for more than one hundred and fifty years since the events that occurred at this site.

Tepeyac Hill I found little more than a dusty knoll in the province of the poor beyond the grandeur of Mexico City itself. I drew rein and dismounted at the foot of the hill, leaving Damascus to crop dry grass. It was here a young peasant boy, Juan Diego, heard someone call his name in his own Nahuatl tongue. A young Indian maiden addressed him. She instructed him to ask the bishop to construct a church here on the site of an ancient pagan shrine. I imagined the scene as I climbed the hill. I felt the disbelief of a young peasant boy called to deliver so improbable a request to one in auspicious authority. Another unlikely instrument chosen to heavenly purpose. Not surprisingly the bishop ignored the boy's plea.

Returning to the site, the maiden informed Juan that she was the most Blessed Virgin Mary, Mother of God. The revelation did little to impress the bishop with the truth of the boy's claim. At his next encounter with the lady, Juan poured out his sorrow at being unable to fulfill her request. He certainly must have felt the inadequacy so often expressed in scripture by prophets and those chosen to do work, important to the Lord. Looking back over my time in New Spain, I felt kinship to young Juan in that. For all we had done, we accomplished little to advance our mission purpose.

As is often the case in matters such as these, Our Lady wasn't finished with young Juan. She showed him roses, growing out of season at her feet. She instructed him to gather them and fill his cloak with a bouquet to take to the bishop once again with her request. The boy did as he was bid. When he presented himself to the bishop, he opened his rough-spun cloak to a beautiful portrait of the Holy Mother herself. At this last the bishop was moved.

As I approached the chapel erected as her shrine I could not but reflect on the fruits of a humble messenger's quest. Heavy, carved wooden doors opened to the chapel, dimly lit by stained-glass windows. I entered the stillness, letting sight return in the gloom. There before me, beautifully framed, the cloak, the portrait. I approached in awe. I bent to read an inscription, affixed beneath the image.

"My dearest son, I am the eternal Virgin Mary, Mother of the true God, Author of Life, Creator of all and Lord of the Heavens and of the Earth."
Apparition of Our Lady to Juan Diego

I took to my knees in the presence of her heavenly portrait. I lifted my eyes to the apparition as she might have spoken. Of all the Blessed Virgin depictions in my experience, painted or sculpted, none ever spoke to me such as this. All those others, self-styled as one of the artist's kind, were the work of human hands. This one was the work of the Virgin herself. Her Indian likeness made a powerful connection to the mission for which I had come.

I fixed on her face. Her features prefigured a flock I had yet to meet. I saw in Our Lady of Guadalupe a bridge to faith for a new flock. She had the power to make her Indio brothers and sisters one with her Son and the Gospel Good News. Her appearance and presence to the people here, foreordained the success of my mission. Our Lady would show the way to California. I was sure of it. At that, she may have smiled.

Palacio Real

Viceroy Christiano y Amaro occupied a palace fit for a pagan god, which it was prior to the coming of the conquistadors. Of course, graven images were now replaced with the standard of the king and appropriately elegant symbols of Holy Mother Church. We were shown to a large well-appointed room, suitable for a throne room, which it was before repurposing to meetings of state. Our little party took seats at one end of a long table, leaving the seat at the head to await the viceroy's arrival.

Atondo preceded us. We exchanged greetings and he reacquainted himself with the archbishop. The tatter of bootheels on stone tile announced the viceroy. A tall, swarthy

197

Castilian, Amaro cut a dashing, aristocratic military bearing in crisp purple doublet, cream-colored pantaloons, and luxuriously tanned riding boots. Bright black eyes with impeccably trimmed goatee bespoke an air of authority. He smiled as he extended his hand to me.

"Padre, Christiano Amaro."

"Eusebio Kino, Excellency."

"A pleasure to meet the author of such a farsighted proposal. Please, have a seat."

We took our seats, the viceroy at the head of the table, the archbishop at his right, Atondo on his left. I took my place beside the archbishop.

"Welcome," the viceroy intoned. "Especially you who have journeyed so far from our frontier. We appreciate your dedication to extending the crown's holdings in New Spain. We are here to discuss the excellent report of recommendations penned by Padre Kino. The archbishop and I have both reviewed it and see merit in the arguments put forward. Have you any introductory comments, Archbishop, before we turn the floor to Padre Kino?"

"I can only add our prayer the Holy Spirit guide our deliberations here this day and onward."

"Amen, Eminence. Padre Kino the meeting is yours."

I reaffirmed the arguments put forward in my report. Salvation's true faith cannot possibly be instilled by itinerant excursions such as our explorations. Permanent missions are needed to provide for our flock's temporal needs, while preparing them to receive spiritual guidance and instruction.

Amaro spoke up. "In regard to the temporal needs you speak of, explain your thinking on animal husbandry."

"The Indio live in small clan-centered villages. They subsist by hunting small game or fishing for those who dwell near the coast. They also gather fruits of the vicinity such as root vegetables, wild berries, cactus, even insects and snakes. Grasslands are plentiful in many of these locals. Water for more fulsome agriculture is scarce. Conditions are dry, much of the land desert. The Indio could easily be taught the raising and keeping of cattle. Sheep too should thrive in mountainous regions. Both would serve to ease the demands of daily living."

"Very clever, Padre. Please, continue."

Continue I did, acknowledging the benefits of exploration to further the crown's interests in New Spain. I went on to argue New Spain must not only be explored, it must be settled. Colonization would advance the king's interest in a manner compatible with permanent mission. Colonial settlements and missions together would provide stepping-stones to further exploration while consolidating the crown's territorial claims. Colonies will succeed in furthering mining interests and harvesting natural wealth such as pearls. In this combination of settlement and mission we reach out to secure the resources, riches, and harvest of souls awaiting colonization and redemption in California. I placed the scroll of one of my maps on the table.

"With your Excellency's permission, may I speak to conditions of a California mission?"

"Of course, Padre."

I spread the map showing the coast of Sinaloa, Sea of California, and the eastern coast of California. The viceroy and archbishop rose to bend over the map.

"Our mission efforts in California first located here at La Paz. When that proved too difficult, we moved to San Bruno, here a league inland from the coast. As you know concerns for fresh water and arable land along with difficulties of resupply from the mainland led us to abandon both. Here I recommend changes to advance a new California mission. We should locate our

mission and colonial presence south of San
Bruno, here at Loreto. Water is more plentiful there, improving prospects for locally
grown crops. We should supplement local
produce by a smaller mainland supply
operation. This would be based out of an
agricultural settlement on the Sinaloa coast,
with a fleet of small barca serving supply
operations.

"Our presence in California should prove
sustainable at Loreto for both mission,
colony and a small garrison. Sustained presence will advance territorial settlement
along with the spread of our faith. Have you
any questions?"

The viceroy nodded. "You make powerful,
logical arguments, Padre." He turned to the
archbishop. "Do you agree, Eminence?"

"Most assuredly."

"Don Isidro?"

The don met my gaze before answering.

"I agree with the means and methods of
Padre Kino's plan. I question directing our
efforts to settle California. California is a
worthy prize in riches and souls as Padre
has correctly stated."

"Then what gives you pause?"

"The Loreto site Padre proposes is somewhat more favorable than our experience at
San Bruno and La Paz before it. Still mis-

sions and settlements in California must be sustained by sea. Conditions are harsh and dry, arid deserts and mountainous inland of the seacoasts. We experienced great difficulty, sustaining our attempts at settlement there by sea. While Loreto offers some advantages, anchorage there lacks the shelter of harbor, increasing susceptibility of supply operations to the effects of open sea.

"Missions and settlements in California must also be garrisoned for protection. It spreads our military thin, drawing forces away from the security of mainland New Spain. I know I am putting forward arguments, hostile to lands over which I serve as governor, but as a military man I am duty bound to put these cautions forward. There is a cost to colonize California, cost that can be managed more efficiently here on the mainland."

The viceroy stroked his beard in thought. "Eminence?"

"Both arguments have merit."

Amaro nodded. "Indeed, they do. On one hand we have agreement on the wisdom of uniting colonization with mission. On the other we have reservations on the suitability of California to colonization. The question remaining is where and how best to embrace Padre's proposal. If it please, Eminence, I should like to give the matter further thought."

"Prayerful thought, my son. I concur. We await your direction."

CHAPTER TWENTY-SIX

Cathedral Rectory

Two days later I was summoned to meet with the archbishop. He informed me he received a message from the viceroy requesting audience that afternoon. His eminence responded with an invitation for the viceroy to join us for lunch. A private room off the refectory was set aside for our use. The viceroy was shown there on his arrival.

"Eminence, thank you for agreeing to see me on such short notice. Your gracious invitation to luncheon is most generous."

"Welcome, my son. Please be seated."

The archbishop offered his blessing, signaling lunch service to begin. The viceroy wasted no time on society.

"Padre, I have consulted with my military advisors who have listened to Don Isidro's concerns. I'm afraid I must conclude that while your plan is most certainly worthy, California is not at this time."

I was disappointed at hearing this though not surprised. I was taken aback by Amaro's next statements.

"Atondo has told me much of your skill in mathematics, navigational arts, cosmography, and cartographic talents. These are valuable abilities in New Spain. I wonder if his eminence the archbishop might indulge us the use of your services. You could remain here in Mexico City and be of invaluable service to both church and state."

I looked to the archbishop without saying more than my eyes could speak. He nodded some recognition.

"Now it is I, my son, who must take time to consider your request. Any assignment Padre Kino might receive must come from his superiors in the Company of Jesus. I am in position to but recommend and request."

"Sí, Eminence. I understand. I hope you will find it in our mutual interest to put such a recommendation forward. I see a rare opportunity to employ a most valuable talent to the benefit of all New Spain."

Lunch ended. The viceroy took his leave. The archbishop turned to me.

"I sense you are reluctant to embrace the viceroy's offer."

"I will do whatever finds favor with the

needs of Holy Mother Church, Eminence. There was a time I should have greeted the viceroy's offer with great enthusiasm. Even now, I confess I find his offer flattering and the prospect of exploration exciting, but I have also seen the face of Our Lord Jesus in those awaiting the good news of salvation."

I held up my hands, calloused and knotted by the strain of hard labor. "Once these hands were those of an academic, a scientist. Now they have become something more. I set out on the journey to priesthood in the footsteps of my sainted patron, Francisco Xavier. That journey led me to New Spain. I hear a call to work in mission fields, building salvation for souls. If it please, if it possible, I would return to the missions. If it is not to be California, let it be some other needful place. I have learned language and methods to teach the sweet comforts of catechism. Others can see to scientific pursuits. I know the plan for mission and settlement. I would see it bear fruit."

"Bear fruit or bear cows?" He said it with a twinkle in his eye.

"As you say, Eminence, both." I smiled.

Mexico City
November 1686
The archbishop summoned me to audience

a fortnight later. I was shown into his private study where I found him seated at his desk. Soft golden light suffused the room in red-velvet glow.

"Ah, Padre, please have a seat."

He dispensed the formality of kissing his ring with a hand wave. I took the offered chair set before his desk.

"Thank you for coming. I thought you would want to learn of your new assignment as soon as I was able to resolve the viceroy's offer."

"And you were able to do that, Eminence?"

He smiled with a nod. "I discussed the matter with your Reverend Father Oddon. He had some reservation with regard to opposing the viceroy's wishes. Privately I suspect he may have harbored ambitions of a faculty position for you at the university. I managed to convince him I could deal with the viceroy and with that he agreed I should try. Scarlet, as it happens, carries some weight in church matters.

"I next spoke to the viceroy. I can't say he was happy about it, but I pled the need of our ecclesiastical mission so long indulged by your work in Atondo's explorations. Reluctantly he relented."

"Thank you, Eminence. Now how may I

be of service to our holy mission?"

"I took the liberty of consulting with your provincial on that matter as well. We discussed your plan to advance mission and settlement and are now both agreed. He will confirm the details of your assignment with you."

"But where am I to serve?"

"Pimeria Alta."

"Pimeria Alta? I'm afraid I don't understand."

"Pimeria Alta is home to the Pima people. Come." He rose and led me to a side table. He spread a crude map of northwestern New Spain. "Forgive a man of my rudimentary knowledge, presuming to explain a map to a cartographer," he chuckled. "Pimeria Alta is bounded by the Altar River here in Sonora, north to the Hila Rio Grande, west to the Rio Colorado in the north, and south to the Sea of California."

"It is a large mission, though it stops short of my hopes for California."

"Patience, my son. California is not to be just now. Pimeria Alta is a fertile field for souls. It leads to the shores of your California dream. One day, the Lord willing, you may yet reach it."

"When am I to depart?"

"A month's time should be soon enough.

Until then, perhaps you might offer assistance to the viceroy to soften his loss of your services. Then even as Our Lord and Savior sent his apostles to spread the Good News, so we send you now to your new flock."

"Gracias, Eminence."

Guadalajara

Accompanied by Abel, I departed Mexico City sixteen December and arrived in Guadalajara two days before Christmas. We took lodging in a house our Company of Jesus maintained in the city. I was full of questions concerning our mission destination. I interrogated any one of my brothers who might have knowledge of the people to whom we would minister. Little help was available to me beyond tales of the Pima people Abel heard in the lodges of his people. He believed them to be farmers and gatherers. Peaceful by nature but able to defend themselves when threatened by hostile Yaquis to the west or Apache from the north and east.

On Christmas Eve there arrived for us a most pleasant surprise. Atondo, hearing of our new mission, dispatched Lieutenant Manje and a squad of soldados to see us safely to our destination. I invited Juan to celebrate Christmas with us. This we observed with mass at midnight and later a mass at dawn. We shared a fine Christmas dinner with our Jesuit brothers, whereafter Juan and I took seats by the parlor fire.

"Juan, my son, what can you tell me of this Pimeria Alta to which I am assigned?"

"I have some knowledge, Padre, though I confess not much. I will happily share with you what I know, but first, how do you feel about this appointment? I well know your heart was set on California."

I shrugged. "California, it seems, is not meant to be, at least not yet. Once upon a time, I saw my mission follow the footsteps of blessed San Francisco Xavier to Cathay. That vision was not meant to be. Our Lord's plan took me halfway around the world in the opposite direction. California to Pimeria Alta is but a minor detour northwest. A flock, perhaps in greater need than I know, awaits me there."

"And your ambition is at peace with this?"

"Of course, my son. I am after all but an instrument. I go where I am sent. As Luke says in chapter ten, verse five 'Into whatever house you will have entered, first say, peace to this house.' Perhaps one day the house will be California. It is not for me to say.

Now what can you tell me of the house at hand?"

"Pimeria Alta is home to tribal clans comprising the Akimel O'odham, by their tongue, Upper Pima nation by ours. Clans gather in villages along river valleys where irrigation can be brought to their fields. Northwest along the lower Hila and Rio Colorado certain tribes of Cocomaricopa and Yuma also reside, though the Yuma speak a language different from the Pima. The Pima are generally a peaceful people, though they can acquit themselves satisfactorily in battle when called to defend against Apache raids or other hostiles."

"Are they receptive to our coming?"

"They are, so long as we treat them fairly."

"You say, 'so long.' Are there problems?"

"There have been. Primarily forced labor abuses. Though these practices have recently been outlawed by the crown. King Philip has issued a Royal cédula prohibiting forced labor of the recently converted. The provincial governor has received it, though in New Spain such things make their way to outposts on the frontier slowly."

"I see. Then I must see the governor before we depart. We shall carry a copy of the king's proclamation with us to prepare

ourselves to serve as advocates for our people."

We stayed in Guadalajara long enough to
provision our journey and obtain a copy of
the king's proclamation. We procured three
mules to serve as pack animals and departed
with our escort at dawn the year of our Lord
one-thousand six-hundred and eighty-
seven.

CHAPTER TWENTY-SEVEN

Oposura
February 25, 1687

We followed the Yaqui River north, arriving at the office of the provincial superior for Sonora in late February. There, Father Provincial introduced us to Francis Pintor, a convert of the Lower Pima. More than a convert, Francis served as a catechist. Father Provincial assigned him to our catechetical mission in Pimeria Alta in addition to serving as interpreter. Further to our journey, Father Joseph Aguilar, pastor to his flock at Cucurpe, would accompany us on his return to his mission. Cucurpe, we learned, would be the closest mission to those we would establish in Pimeria Alta.

With these happy additions to our party, we continued our way west, passing through the mining camp at San Juan with its guardian garrison some two leagues west of Oposura. Ten leagues further west we reached

Huepec on the Sonora River. Continuing west, we reached the San Miguel River, turning north. Ten leagues on we arrived at Father Aguilar's mission, Cucurpe, nestled in a river valley in foothills to the Agua Prieta Mountains.

Over the course of these pleasant days and evenings on the trail, Francis and Father Aguilar were most agreeable to answer my endless questions. I was able to learn more of the Pima people, their culture, and the challenges of ministering to them. I was further delighted when Father offered to accompany me five leagues further north along the San Miguel River to Cosari, the southernmost village of the parishes I would serve.

Cosari
Pimeria Alta

The boy Hawk, now ten summers, sat in shadow beyond the circle of firelight. Only his eyes spoke his presence in the darkened olas kih. His grandfather, Red Sky, lay on his blanket beside a small lodge fire. Black Thorn sat beside his father, saddened and concerned for the journey Red Sky was about to undertake. The medicine man, Scorpion, chanted softly, his naked body painted vermillion and black. His arms followed fire smoke to the night sky. His chant prayed, beseeching Prophet of the Earth to dispel evil sorcery and restore Red Sky to good health.

"If then, oh Great One, this cannot be, spare our father Red Sky from the clutches of the Malevolent One and bear him safely beyond to the land of the rising sun. See his ancestors welcome him there even as we pray."

Somewhere in the darkness an owl hooted.

"He comes," Scorpion said.

Red Sky heard his death call, and silently slipped away.

Scorpion lowered his arms. "He has gone to the land hereafter. We speak of it no more."

In bright morning light Hawk helped his father gather wood to build a pyre. There they laid father and grandfather wrapped in his blanket, armed with his bow and rations of pinole to protect and sustain him on his journey. The family gathered to pray while the flames did their work.

Cosari
Pimeria Alta

We departed Cucurpe on the ides of March, following the river north into Pimeria Alta. At a distance of no more than five leagues

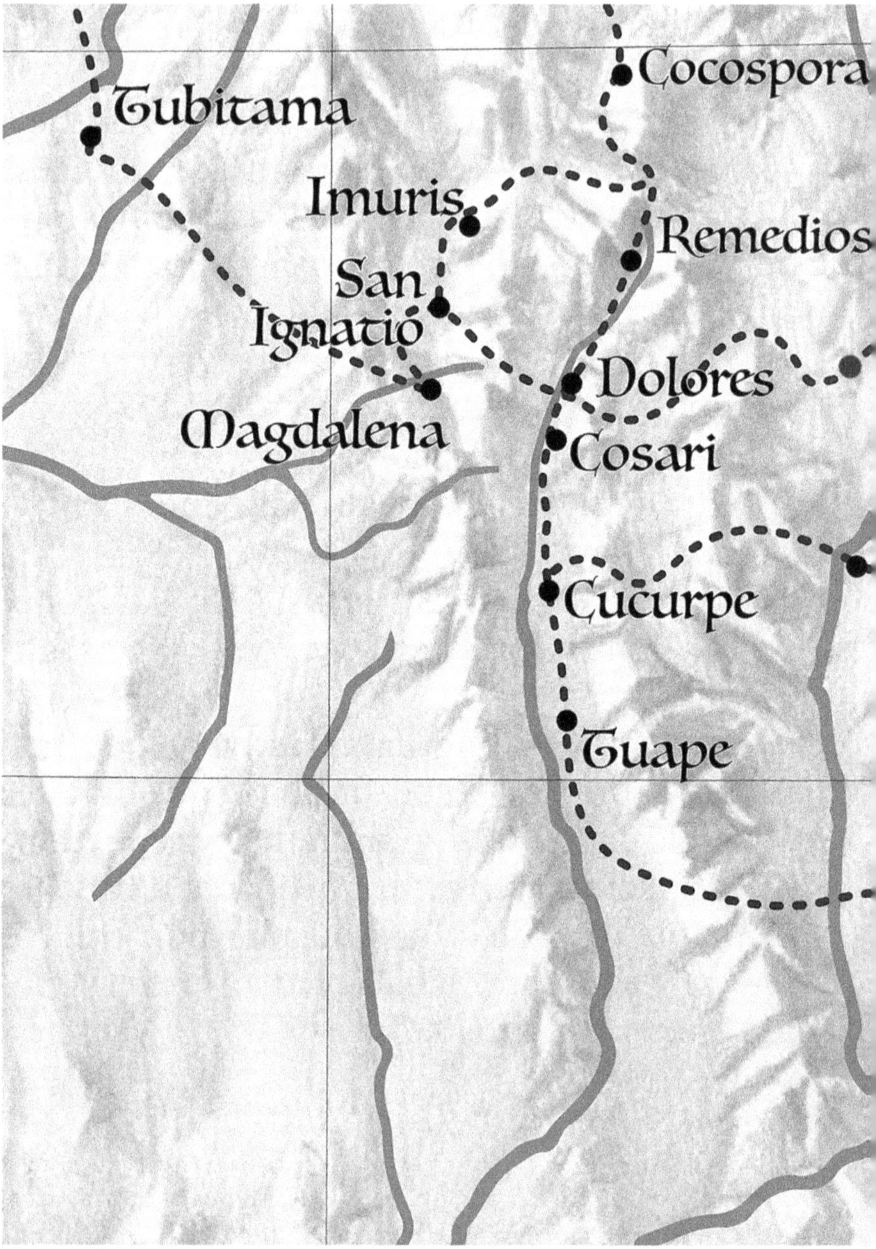
Cocospora
Tubitama
Imuris
Remedios
San
Ignatio
Dolores
Magdalena
Cosari
Cucurpe
Tuape

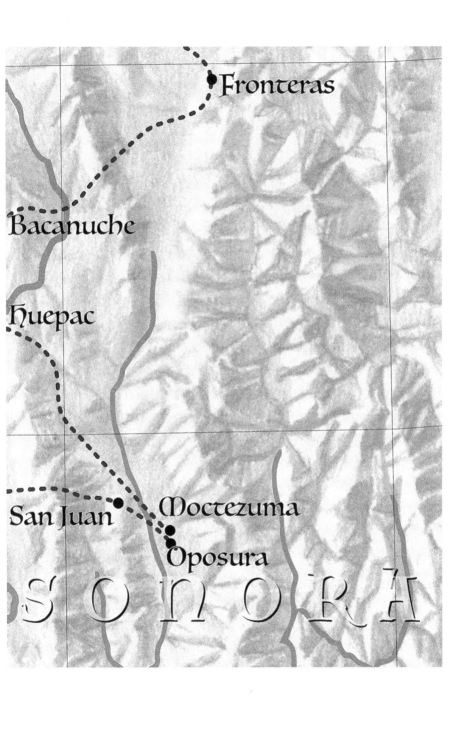

we came upon the village of Cosari, the first of four villages in the parish of my ministry. Set in a lush river valley, at the mouth of a mountain canyon, the village was surrounded by verdant fields planted in maize and melons. The fields were served by an ingenious network of canals, diverting river water to irrigate the crops. I sat astride Damascus, letting the land speak to me. *Milk and honey, truly a promised land, a land from which a river of faith would flow, claiming innocent souls in the name of Christ Jesus.* I said a small prayer of thanksgiving as we nudged our horses forward.

We entered the village and were at once subject of intense curiosity. People gathered to greet us. Shy at first, they warmed to our smiles and gestures of goodwill. We dismounted. The children were first to give in to the wonder of the black-robed strangers and armored soldados astride great beasts. They clustered about us, dark skinned, dark eyes turned up to us. The bravest among them ventured to touch our clothing, clothing being unknown to these people beyond a simple breechclout or skirt. When we proved harmless and friendly, they turned their attention to our horses and mules.

As the children warmed to us so did their elders. The women began to chatter among themselves with a giggle here and a pointing there at some observation found amusing. The mature women bore facial tattoos; younger girls did not. We would learn tattoos marked those who were married. The men maintained somewhat more reserve though they too spoke among themselves in quiet tones.

I sensed a feeling of home from the moment my feet touched the ground. I exchanged a glance with Abel. He nodded response to an unspoken question. At that, a wiry lean man of proud bearing detached himself from the crowd to approach us.

"I am Coxi, Cosari Pima Cacique. I bid you welcome. Why are you come?"

Francis stepped forward to translate.

"I am Padre Kino from the Company of Jesus come to bring the Pima people joyful Good News of Our Lord and Savior Jesus Christ and the blessings He will bestow on his Pima people."

Coxi listened carefully as Francis gave him my words. In turn he spoke to his people. The words were greeted with smiles and nods of agreement.

"We wish to establish a mission here to live and work beside you. Will you allow us to serve you?"

Francis repeated my petition. Coxi again

spoke to his people, obtaining more nods of agreement.

After so many years of journeying we'd at last reached home.

> "Peace to this house. And if a son of peace is there, your peace will rest upon him."
>
> (Luke 10:5b)

Peace indeed came to rest.

We made camp on the riverbank at the mouth of the canyon. Next morning, we rose to offer mass for our new community. A few villagers came to witness this new curiosity. One of the women brought us tasty maize tortillas flavored with cinnamon to break our fast. She was accompanied by a boy of about ten.

"Thank you, my child. What is your name?"

Francis made my words understandable.

"I am called Rain, wife of Black Thorn. This is Hawk."

I tousled the boy's hair. "Welcome. Come anytime."

They went off to be about their daily business. Lieutenant Manje watched them go.

"Padre, our assignment is complete. Our orders were to see you safely to your destination and then return to Matanchel. I will give my men a few days' rest before we depart. May I be of any further service until then?"

"Ah, Juan, you have done so much already. I shall miss you, my son. Do this for me. Carry a message to Don Isidro. The presence of the river at the site of this mission suggests to me it is a strategically attractive location for a settlement. A presidio with a small garrison would promise a good start. Perhaps Atondo will consider it. One never knows, he might place you in command to continue our explorations together."

He smiled. "Always a man with a plan, Padre. I shall carry your message to Don Isidro."

"Not a plan, Juan, only a suggestion. God alone plans. Oh, and one more thing."

"Sí, Padre."

"When Atondo sends you back to me, ask him to send cattle, horses, and mules with you. Rancherias will flourish here also."

"Of course, Padre. I shall carry your suggestion to the don just in case ranching is also part of God's plan."

I smiled. "I have on good authority, it is."

CHAPTER TWENTY-EIGHT

Journal Entry

The following morning Father Joseph and I, accompanied by Francis and Abel, departed on a circuit to visit the villages, making up the missions I would serve. The villages, four in number, stretched north and west from Cosari forming, if I may draw on my studies of Euclid, a loose parallelogram. The first day we rode west through mountainous terrain to the village of San Ignacio, set among shaded cottonwood groves on the banks of the Magdalena River. We were greeted warmly, spending a pleasant evening with our new family there with the promise of bringing them a mission of their own soon.

The next morning, we rode upriver, three leagues north to the village of Imuris, perched on a bluff overlooking the river. There we celebrated mass, baptizing three infants. We shared a meal and passed the evening gaining friendship through the efforts of Francis, who I must say was fast becoming indispensable to the eventual success of our mission.

The following day we turned east through the Huachuca Mountains to the village of Los Remedios, a distance of some six leagues. Here the pattern of our visits repeated. That night as I rested my head on my saddle the enormity of the task and need in the whole of the mission weighed heavy on my heart. So much to do. Where to begin? My thoughts churned in uncertainty. I turned to prayer for guidance. Peace descended in simplicity. *Begin in the beginning. Cosari, the land of promise. Realize the promise and more will follow.*

We turned south in the morning, returning to Cosari that afternoon, a journey of no more than four leagues. Still my thoughts on the trail gained greater sense of purpose in the words of Saint Luke.

"The harvest is great; but the workers are few. Therefore, ask the Lord of the harvest to send workers into his harvest." (10:2)

I said as much to Father Joseph before he returned to Cucurpe. He nodded knowingly and encouraged me to make my plea to for assistance to Father Provincial. Wisely, he further encouraged me to patience, for indeed the laborers are few. Fortified in wisdom, I wrote my first letter of request.

Cosari

In the days that followed we searched for places we might locate our church. One day Francis and I were invited to Coxi's olas kih to partake of his evening meal. He was much interested in our plans for the mission we spoke of. I explained we would build a chapel, a home the Lord Jesus shares with His people. We would build a rectory for my residence. He sat thoughtful for a time as we ate.

"Where will you build this mission?" he asked through Francis.

"We are searching for a suitable location."

He thought more. "Tomorrow come, I show you."

The next morning, Coxi presented himself at our camp accompanied by the warrior Black Thorn and another made known to us as Yellow Feather.

"Come. We go."

I followed along accompanied by Francis and Abel. With Francis having assumed the role of interpreter, I sensed my son Abel somewhat at a loss for his purpose in our work. I prayed a purposeful employment for him might soon present itself.

Coxi took a narrow path, climbing the arroyo wall above the village to a plateau, overlooking the river. The plateau jut out from the arroyo wall, affording scenic vistas on three sides with only the single avenue of approach. A mountain stream trickled out of the heights above affording a source of precious fresh water.

"It is beautiful," I said. Francis nodded.

"Safe Yaqui, Apache come," Coxi said.

Abel gulped on the translation. "Apache, Yaqui very bad."

I hadn't thought about safety. Surely, we had nothing to fear from our Pima flock. With Juan and the soldados departing the region, realization dawned, we could not be so sure of keeping hostiles away.

"Coxi is very wise."

He drew himself up at the praise.

"We shall build our mission here."

I wondered at what name we might give it. Presently I heard in the silence of my heart.

A dedication to Our Lady, perhaps Mother of Sorrows.

"Nuestra Sonora de los Dolores," I said.

Francis and Abel nodded agreement.

■ ■ ■ ■

Mission Dolores

In the days that followed, with the help of Coxi and his clansmen, we began construction of our chapel. With Francis's help we undertook a second task to learn the Pima language. This we judged the first step in imparting messages of conversion. In the days and weeks that followed, our chapel and a small adobe hut to serve as rectory took shape. The Pima were much intrigued by our use of mud bricks to form the walls of our dwelling. Their own olas kih were simple thatched coverings woven over a bent wooden frame, susceptible to the ravages of wind and weather.

While our building proceeded at an orderly pace, the vagaries of language proficiency proved far less certain. Still, we managed to gain the use of some words, and by observation, question, and hand signs increased our knowledge of Pima language, customs, and religious beliefs. They acknowledged a supreme being, translated, Prophet of Earth, along with a malevolent deity translated Evil One. The Evil One they saw for a sorcerer responsible for misfortune, sickness, and death. The owl symbolized the spirit of death.

Their rituals and ceremonies were presided over by a shaman, called Scorpion, who also served as medicine man. As we went about our prayers and offerings of the sacrifice of the mass, Scorpion regarded us with a measure of curiosity and suspicion. The seeds of discord were sown when Fawn, the daughter of Yellow Feather and Sweet Grass, fell ill.

The child suffered fever and stomach pain. Yellow Feather summoned Scorpion who performed his smoke offerings and incantations. When the child's condition failed to improve, Sweet Grass came to me for assistance. We took our small medicine chest along with the oils of anointing and followed Sweet Grass to her olas kih. There Yellow Feather observed, uncertain with suspicion. Scorpion greeted our arrival with disdain.

I examined the child and ordered cool water and clothes to bathe her fever. I administered a powder dissolved in a water to soothe her stomach discomfort. I anointed her with holy oil and offered prayers as we cooled her with compresses. Deep into the night our ministrations were rewarded. The fever broke and she slept peacefully. I sent Francis to his sleeping mat, while I stayed with the child until morning. At dawn Francis returned. Choosing my words carefully I assured Sweet Grass and Yellow Feather the sickness left their daughter by the hand of the Prophet of Earth's Son. The Evil One no longer troubled her. I returned to Dolores for a few hours' rest in hope we may have given our faith connection to their concept of deity. Our Father, by any name, remains Father.

Later that afternoon Sweet Grass came to the mission. I paused my work on a bench that would serve us at our rough-hewn supper table. Speech was halting on my part, but we made do.

"Is your daughter well?"

She nodded and gave me a basket of ripe melon and tortillas by way of her gratitude.

"Good. What more may I do for you?"

"Sweet Grass would know more of this Son of the Prophet of Earth. Pima do not know him."

So, it begins. I offered a prayer of thanksgiving.

"The Son came to earth to teach people the ways of the Prophet. He suffered and died that all might live. To know the Son is to know the Prophet. Knowing the Son comes through the waters of baptism."

She listened thoughtfully before returning to the village.

That evening I prayed in thanksgiving. I wondered what might become of this. I felt it a beginning. *Begin at the beginning.* A beginning best left in keeping of the Holy Spirit.

CHAPTER TWENTY-NINE

Two days later Sweet Grass returned, accompanied by Coxi and little Fawn. I greeted her with a smile and a hug for the little girl.

"Welcome. What can I do for you this day?"

"Sweet Grass wishes this water to know the Prophet's Son. Can Fawn also know this water?"

"Most certainly."

I summoned Francis. "Ask the cacique what we may do for him."

Francis posed the question. "He wishes only to watch."

"Come then."

We led them to the foot of the altar, amid the construction that would become our chapel. Francis fetched a bowl and pitcher filled with water. I motioned Sweet Grass to bend over the bowl Francis held. He explained I would pour water over her head, saying the words of baptism. I poured.

"Ego Baptisto te . . . In Nomine Patris . . . et Filii . . . et Spiritu Sancti."

Sweet Grass next held Fawn for her baptism. We commemorated the Christenings with small wooden crosses for each to wear about her neck.

At last. Two souls. A beginning indeed.

In the days and weeks that followed Yellow Feather too received the sacrament and his cross. Others came in a trickle: Old Willow, Rain, the boy Hawk, then Black Thorn.

By April with the people's help, we completed construction of a chapel and a small adobe to serve as rectory. Construction continued, expanding the chapel toward the dream of a larger church, but first all the people turned to the work of spring planting. Abel, Francis, and I joined in their labors.

The people farmed the river bottom plains, where spring floods deposited layers of rich soil. Land existed for the common good and was free to those who worked it. A family might work a plot or partner with another family in cultivating a crop such as maize, useful in trade for other produce.

In spring planting, men cut the fields in furrows, using a sharpened flat wooden tool.

Women followed sowing seeds and covering plantings with soil tamped down by bare feet. Other women carried ollas filled with water drawn from the network of irrigation canals to water the plantings. Fields were allotted to various crops. Dietary staples corn and beans commanded the largest tracts. Squash and melon completed the crop. Backbreaking long days sowed the seeds of prosperity. Spring rains gave sprout to the promise of a bountiful harvest.

Irrigation canals, as many as fifteen cubits wide, served all the tilled fields. We observed the extension of one to serve a new field for cultivation. Men dug the trenches using crude wooden implements, a larger version of the flat sharpened tools used in planting. Women carried the excavated earth away in baskets with the soil used to sweeten the field served by the canal.

Planting done, we returned to building our church, though not alone. Curiosity and laughter became our constant companions. These were the children. Abel became big brother to the entire village. I seemed an endless source of mystery and magic. I confess to using curiosities to advance the cause of conversion and religious formation. My compass pointed to the Prophet of

Earth so I might never lose my way to him. The sundial we placed in the mission plaza appointed hours that called us to prayer. And perhaps the most stunning fete of all, starting fire by the Spirit of the Prophet with a glass.

The day I caught a sleeping hummingbird provided a spiritual moment of gratitude and joy. Hummingbirds go about their days feeding at a feverish pace. In turn, they sleep deeply. I came upon one at the end of a long day's labor. I held the tiny creature captive in the palms of my hands. As it happened young Fawn and the boy Hawk had yet to depart for their family cook fires. Fawn's cure, attributed to the Prophet of Earth's Son, began our quest for conversion. I bent down to show the children the bird. I opened my hands slowly. The hummingbird lay there, gone from sleep to playing dead against the peril I posed. Fawn's eyes softened in sorrow, believing the tiny bird gone to her ancestors. With that the hummingbird roused and flew away.

Her eyes shot wide. "Ibimu huegite!"

Hawk, equally wide-eyed, squealed his exclamation.

And there I had it. Pima words to reveal the mystery of Resurrection. I repeated them to myself in a prayer of thanksgiving, lest I lose their sound and meaning.

Fawn watched the bird with bright eyes and sweet smile. She and Hawk scampered off to spread word of the dead bird that lives. This we would soon show for the work of Our Lord Jesus Christ, whose *ibimu huegite* brings salvation to those who follow Him.

Damascus too had a part in the children's fascination with our work, especially for the boys. One day riding into the village, young Hawk ran to meet us. I reached down, took him by the arm, and pulled him up to sit behind me. Off we went to squeals of delight. This was to be another beginning. Ever after, anytime we rode into the village, boys would run beseeching a ride. We accommodated as many as we could. It called to mind the story of the Pied Piper, though absent the nefarious purpose of the children's disappearance.

Even at day's end the children came to us. Their laughter and games brightened the mission. We entertained and instructed them with stories from the Holy Bible. Stories and instruction, they could take with them to their families. We taught them to pray along with the rudiments of Spanish language. These too went with them to their homes.

Then at the end of July on the feast of our sainted founder Ignatius Loyola, Coxi came to the waters of baptism with his children. Many in the village came after him. Soon the cross of Our Lord could be seen marking the growing numbers of our flock.

Over the course of the summer, we witnessed a most interesting variety of gatherings. Potato-like wild roots were gathered for the bean pot families kept over coals. In summer, women picked sweet red saguaro fruit. They boiled the fruit, reducing it to syrup. This they put up in jars to be used as a sweetener or fermented for ceremonial use in praying for rain. Bean pods of the mesquite tree were gathered, dried in the sun, and ground to powder with mortar and pestle. Women baked the powder into cakes, stored for the winter. Caterpillars were gathered in season. The heads were cut off and the insides squeezed out in preparation for boiling. Boiled caterpillars were braided in chains and stored for the winter along with dry roasted locusts. These meager sources of meat affirmed my belief cattle and sheep would be of value in building a better life for the people.

So passed the summer growing season. As

the harvest approached, we were roused from our labors one afternoon by the bawling of cattle. They came up the trail southwest from Cucurpe under a dun dust cloud rising to announce the return of Lieutenant Juan Mateo Manje with a garrison company of soldados. We hastened down to Cosari to greet him. We found him surrounded by villagers.

"Juan, my son, welcome."

"Padre. You are well?"

"Very well. You brought cattle, horses, and mules too, I see."

"I did and more. Come I show you."

The small herd consisted of a dozen cows. Juan directed me to one small calf.

"This little fellow was born on the trail. He will give you a fine herd of many more."

"A bull calf, father to our future. We shall call his name Abraham."

"Abraham seems well suited," Juan chuckled.

"I see descendants, as many as the stars."

"Padre, you have the vision."

"On good authority." I smiled.

"There is more," Juan said. He led us to a mule-drawn cart covered over in canvas. He pulled back the cover to reveal a beautiful crucifix, a bright brass bell, and a stunning framed fresco plaque, depicting Our Lady of Guadalupe.

"The bell is a gift from Don Isidro. The crucifix is sent with the blessing of the bishop. My men took up a collection for purchase of the fresco. You will also find mosaics to stations of the cross safely wrapped in the cart."

I gave our bell its first ring.

The assembled people could scarcely contain their joy and amazement at the beauty of the sound and all the riches come to their village to honor of the Prophet of Earth's Most Holy Son.

Juan and his men set to work constructing the crude beginnings of a presidio west of the village. It would serve to shelter them through the coming winter. I began, with Abel's assistance, the work of educating our flock in animal husbandry. We carved a cistern out of the riverbank for water and fenced a small rancheria for the cattle, horses, and mules. In this work Abel and Azucar found new purpose. I smiled at the thought, he would become our vaquero. With the livestock secured, we prepared for the harvest.

Beans were picked by the women over the course of the growing season. Each family warmed a bean pot over coals as a staple of the people's daily diet. Gathering too continued into the harvest with melon and squash. The fruit were cut into strips and dried in the sun for winter stores.

The time of harvest arrived. Maize comprised the bulk of the work. Women harvested maize. Ears were husked and dried or roasted over a bed of coals and hot stones. Kernels were cut off the cob and ground into fine powder using a stone metate. The flour, called pinole, was used to make tortillas sometimes flavored with spices such as red chiles, coca, agave, cinnamon, and vanilla.

With the harvest in, I approached Coxi with the suggestion to plant the new field in winter wheat.

"Winter wheat? What is this winter wheat?"

I showed him seeds. "These produce a golden grain from which to make bread."

"We can do this in the season of starving?"

"We can. I will show you."

We sowed the new field in winter wheat. Green sprouts would turn to golden waves in the months where fruits of the desert and game grew scarce.

Following the sowing of our new crop, I

approached Coxi with the idea of holding a fiesta at the mission to give thanks for bountiful crops and the blessings of Our Lord God, the Prophet of Earth. This would be done with a great feast and dancing. Coxi welcomed any suggestion of celebration and so it was planned for the following Sunday.

We began with the Holy Sacrifice of the Mass and all good intention. Everyone would come to the fiesta, even those not yet come to the mission in search of baptism. In this we might gain the curiosity of those we had yet to reach.

Fiesta included games of chance for the men, races and ball games for the young. All enjoyed a harvest feast followed by dancing into the night.

CHAPTER THIRTY

Cosari
January 1688

We celebrated Christmas and the dawn of a new year with great joy and thanksgiving. We accomplished much in the short time since arriving at Cosari. Mission Dolores slowly but surely took root among the people, planting the seeds of faith. Those flocking to the Word of the Lord grew in number as we continued construction, expanding the church. For all these achievements, much remained to be done, extending our outreach across Pimeria Alta. I wrote of our successes in appeals to my superiors for additional laborers to the harvest of souls in this Pimeria.

With no help yet arrived, I made it my practice to ride the circuit of my villages two weeks in four. I spent a day or two in each village, celebrating mass, giving instruction, performing baptisms, and assisting however I might in the temporal work of my flock. Always my visits were warmly received with joy and generous hospitality. It was most notable when the mood at Remedios became somewhat less welcoming. I was able to put no cause to it for myself. It was only when a kinsman paid a visit to Cacique Coxi at Dolores that some light shed on the cause. He came to me with a troubling report.

"Rumor of abuses in our mission were heard in Remedios," he said.

Francis translated, though my language skills had improved to where I understood much of it.

"They say the Pima here are forced to labor in the mission fields and herds, leaving little time to work for care of the people. Pressed into these labors, rumors say the royal cédula is a lie. Those who resist are punished, some have even been hanged. Too many cattle strain the water supply. Holy oils kill. It is further said people are leaving Cosari, moving further downriver to be away from the tyranny of the black robe."

The allegations of course were unfounded. Still, I was shocked and saddened at whatever misunderstanding might have led to these falsehoods.

"What did you tell your kinsman?"

241

"I told him to see for himself. None of these stories are true."

I was grateful for his help. I prayed it might put matters to rest.

We also began to see the fruits of our efforts to establish a rancheria for husbanding our growing cattle herd. Abel found his place at the mission, tending the herd mounted on Azucar. Boys and young men admired his work. He began teaching them to ride horses and mules. Abel grasped the value of our yearling, Abraham. Assisted by his fledgling vaqueros, he took special care looking after the young bull. Soon we would see the fruits of his work feed the people.

Further to our feeding the people our fields flowered in golden waves of winter wheat.

As harvest time neared, I found Coxi gazing at our wheat field. Golden grain tossed in waves on the breeze. It was a bountiful sight.

"Is it not beautiful," I said.

"What becomes of it?"

Ever the pragmatic. I plucked a stalk and showed him the head.

"This is grain. We will cut the stalks and separate the grain. We grind it like maize to make flour from which to bake bread. Bread you will see is the staff of life."

"It is so small."

"Small yes, but plentiful. And tasty also."

"When do we gather this wheat?"

"Soon. I will show you."

I guided the men in harvesting wheat, cutting and raking by hand. We showed them how to arrange the raked wheat bundles in a ring around a central post. We tethered a horse or mule to the post and drove it around the circle separating wheat from chaff with the animal's hooves. Chaff could then be taken away, leaving the wheat to be gathered. The Pima were much appreciative of a food crop gathered in the season of starving with animals doing most of the work. Pleased as I was, I knew somewhat more might be brought to spring planting by construction of a plow.

February cheered us by the arrival of Reverend Father Augustin de Campos to bolster our Pimeria Alta mission. We made our plan. I would continue the work at Mission Dolores, while Father Augustin extended the reach of our church to the west and north. Further to our prospects the warrior, Black Thorn, offered to serve as our guide. He could also make testimony to the good things attended to establishing a mission to serve the people. On a month's preparation we set out on our journey.

A day's ride west we arrived at San Ignacio. There we were welcomed as always by the people who had long awaited the wonders the black robes would bring to them. We established a second mission there, Padre Campos's first.

We journeyed three leagues to Imuris and again were joyfully received by the arrival of Padre Augustin. We stayed long enough for Padre Augustin to establish the rudiments of mission San Joseph de los Himires. With foundations in place for Padre Campos's mission and ministry, we took our leave, returning to Dolores by way of Remedios.

Here we were once more greeted with some reservation. Father Augustin noticed it just as I had. I explained the unfounded rumors we had heard. Black Thorn having heard our concern spoke with any who would listen, praising the prosperity in Cosari and promising flocks and herds would be given them also. We founded a mission village, calling it Nuestra Sonora de los Remedios. Responsibility for these souls would be added to my ministry from Dolores. Damascus and I would ride this circuit assisting in all the mission work. From these mission outposts the call went out to partake of the black robes' gifts and accept the message of eternal salvation.

Mission Dolores

With our village mission circuit in place I divided my time between Mission Dolores and Mission Nuestra Sonora de los Remedios, allowing time for me to ride the circuit visiting the good works of Padre Campos once a month. All progressed according to God's purpose everywhere except Nuestra Sonora de los Remedios.

Nuestra Sonora de los Remedios

The people resisted the call to conversion. Some remained frightened by my black robes. This was new to my experience and curious. It had to be the rumors. What made them so persistent? Why did all evidence to the contrary fail to overcome these false fears? We prayed for assistance whatever the cause.

A few days passed with no change in the people's demeanor despite my best efforts to encourage equanimity. Unable to understand the nature of their grievance, I confronted the headman with concern for the cause of their distrust.

"We are told the Fathers have ordered people hanged."

"This is not true," I said. "Who told you this?"

"Comandante," he replied.

"What else has this comandante told you?"

"The Fathers require so much planting of the people, there is no time for the people to plant for themselves. So many cattle are pastured at the mission villages, the watering holes dry up. Further they kill the people with holy oils and falsely claim to do all this in the name of the king."

These were the same complaints previously heard. Complaints previously addressed. What made them so persistent? From reference attributing the falsehoods to the military I knew miscommunication existed between civil and ecclesiastical authority. The question was why? Why would comandante of the presidio at Bacanuche put forward false statements concerning the works of our missions? Why?

I assured the headman these claims were untrue and invited him to visit Mission Dolores to see for himself how the people there prospered by taking the faith. I further assured him we would take up these misunderstandings with the comandante and all would be well.

■ ■ ■ ■

Bacanuche
May 10, 1688

We journeyed twenty leagues east to the mining town where Lieutenant Antonio Solis commanded the garrison. The lieutenant received us with gracious good offices and offered his services, which we were pleased to accept. We apprised him of the matter of the calumnies against the fathers among the people of Remedios. The lieutenant pled ignorance of these falsehoods, but when I showed him the royal cédula authority given our mission and assured him of our holy intentions, he promised full support of his office. We further learned Lieutenant Solis served under the command of now Coronel Francisco Zevallos in Guadalajara, a man in my experience with a history of poor relations with the Indio. I suspected the lieutenant curried favor with his superior's sympathies. I hoped he might forego such practices to honor a royal decree. For whatever reason, circumstances in Remedios improved and progress commenced in matters of temporal well-being and spiritual conversion. I thought the matter put to an end.

■ ■ ■ ■

Mission Dolores

Even as work continued, building our church, we guided others of our growing flock to new enterprise. We built shops to house a blacksmith and carpenters. These we gave instruction in learning new crafts. We designed plans for a water mill on the riverbank to water the stock and manage the grinding of grain into flour. We planted orchards to produce fruit for food and trade.

We engaged Coxi to assist us in all these endeavors. With his encouragement, men of the clan willingly came to our aid. These we put to work in mission construction, tending gardens and orchards or working as stockmen. Vaqueros tended the herds while drovers organized packtrains to trade in Bacanuche and Sonora. In all this we sought to harmonize the tribal clan with advances in civilization and evangelization.

In all this I truly felt father to the Pima. I loved the people and they in turn loved me. Everywhere we went children followed us, laughing and playing. We were invited to tribal councils. We celebrated baptisms, spring planting, and harvest with fiestas. The Pima showed us a childlike innocence and a desire to please.

With Mission Dolores prospering and with Francis and Abel capable of managing affairs in my absence, Damascus and I took to riding the circuit to our outlying missions. I visited Nuestra Sonora de los Remedios, San Joseph de los Himires in Imuris, and San Ignacio. Much of what we accomplished at Mission Dolores slowly began to take shape in our newly established missions. I took time to visit with Father Augustin at San Ignacio or San Joseph, wherever I found him. He welcomed the companionship of a confrere and the opportunity to share experiences in our ministries.

Yet amid all the success of our mission, dark unrest lurked on the fringes of our flock.

CHAPTER THIRTY-ONE

Mission Dolores

It broke out as a plague. Black vomit claimed a heavy toll on the old and the young. We ministered to the sick as best we could. We isolated the afflicted in hope of avoiding spreading contagion. It did no good. Outbreaks continued among the otherwise healthy.

I fought it as a disease. Coxi suspected treachery. He called what remained of healthy tribal elders to council. He invited me to join him. There he posed the question.

"What evil spirit has afflicted this sickness on the people?"

No one seemed able to answer. At that the medicine man, Scorpion stood.

"I have not seen this evil spirit before. I will make a vision quest for guidance and return to council when I am granted an answer."

With that, he gathered his medicine bag and left the village, climbing into the hills. I asked Coxi the manner of such a vision quest.

"Scorpion will seek the voice of god in peyote. His vision will be clear. In his words we shall hear the truth."

"How can you be certain?"

"I will know the truth of his words in my heart."

Two days passed. At sundown, the second day, Scorpion returned to the village, his naked body painted blue. He presented himself in the place of council and waited for Coxi and the elders to assemble. When all were assembled, Scorpion spoke.

"The voice of god has given Scorpion vision. The source of this Black Death is the black robe. The sick vomit black teachings."

Coxi nodded at the medicine man's words.

"What is to be done for the people?"

Scorpion lifted his eyes as though in a trance. "Fill our ollas with the blue waters of spring and eat no more of the black robe teachings."

"The evil one stands before us," Coxi said.

Scorpion raised his arms in prayer. "Send the evil one away."

"Scorpion says blue spring water will wash the sickness away. Bring me the olla from

251

the olas kih of one suffering the disease," Coxi ordered.

The water jar was quickly brought from a nearby lodge.

"Now let us see the truth of Scorpion's vision." He drew a gourd dipper from the jar and offered it to the medicine man. "Here, drink."

Scorpion stared at the gourd in disbelief.

"Drink."

The medicine man brushed the water aside. "This is not the blue spring water of my vision."

"It is not. It is water you tainted to bring on the black sickness. You have done this, medicine man, out of envy. Now we shall send you across the horizon to your ancestors."

The council elders fell on him with clubs.

I learned of this too late to intervene in the name of mercy. It left me grateful for Coxi's wisdom. The plague of black vomit washed away in clean water. Divine providence spared our mission.

Mission Dolores
1690
With the treachery of the medicine man dispelled, Holy Mother Church's flock grew

in faith, grace, and joy. Our rancheria herds too grew. Abraham proved a father worthy to the name. Many calves dropped that spring, including two young bulls. These we took to fathering their own herds in rancheria pastures at San Ignacio and Nuestra Sonora de los Remedios. Our Abraham may not father descendants "as numerous as the stars" as promised Abraham of Old Testament Israel, but surely he and his sons would enrich the herds of our people. Abel and his vaqueros tended our herds, as well as adding vaqueros to their number from the villages of our sister missions. Cattle provided meat to feed the people in addition to those taken to market in trade.

Our mission orchards and gardens brought forth produce in abundance: grapes, peaches, figs, pomegranate, pear, and apricots. These along with harvests of maize and wheat beyond our needs became trade goods driven to market by our packtrains. Trade goods were exchanged for tools and material to build our churches as well as other necessities.

Progress followed a similar pattern at the other three missions established on our circuit. The mission San Joseph de los Himires at Imuris logged timber from nearby mountain forests to supply construction needs. Each mission built its church, beginning with a chapel dedicated to San Francisco Xavier. His blessings on our missions followed, building a faithful flock while sowing the seeds of prosperity.

With so much to commend our work, we were dismayed to learn whispers of rumored abuses at Los Remedios, and the treachery of the medicine man Scorpion, found their way to the offices of Father Provincial, Reverend Ambrosio Oddon. These rumors coupled with reports of Indio conscriptions to forced labor in the mines and the levying of taxes on crops to support their Spanish overlords disturbed Father Provincial. Acting out of an abundance of caution and concern, he appointed Father Juan Maria de Salvatierra, Father Visitor to Sonora and Sinaloa where he was charged to investigate reports of abuse and carry out inspections of progress at our rectorate in Pimeria Alta.

Cosari

On a bright spring morning, Black Thorn summoned the boy Hawk, now thirteen summers. He came with his kawad shield and sling to stand before his father. Black Thorn held out his hand.

"Give me the sling."

Hawk did as he was told, puzzled. Black

Thorn set the sling aside and reached through the flap of the family olas kih. He drew out a new bow with a quiver of arrows. Hawk's eyes brightened at the prospect his warrior training would be taken to this next battle skill. Black Thorn handed him the bow and quiver.

"Come. We shoot."

They set off through the village toward a trail into the hills. As they passed, Fawn set aside the basket she was weaving to watch. Her childhood friend grew to manhood. Soon he would take a wife. It made her impatient with her body. She harbored her feelings in hope he would wait.

Black Thorn set the pace at a jog. Hawk followed. They climbed into the hills. Black Thorn led his son to the place he had chosen. A fallen dead tree rotted soft for a target. Black Thorn drew a square of deerskin from his belt and lashed it to the tree trunk. He paced off the distance of a short shot. In one fluid motion he drew an arrow from his quiver, nocked it, pulled his bow, and released the arrow into the deerskin center. He turned to the boy and smiled.

"You try."

Hawk selected an arrow, excited fingers fumbled to nock it. He drew the bow, the arrow tip wavering at the tension. He let the arrow fly. It sailed over the log. He turned to his father, crestfallen at his failure. Black Thorn nodded knowingly, patted his shoulder, and knelt on one knee beside him.

"Again."

Hawk drew an arrow and nocked it. Black Thorn straightened the boy's bow arm sighting arrow tip and target. He lifted the boy's elbow, holding the bowstring, parallel to the ground.

"Now draw and shoot."

The arrow glanced off the top of the log, narrowly missing the target.

"Better. Again."

Hawk repeated the movements, this time without his father's assistance. His shot struck the log just below the target.

"Once more."

This time the arrow flew true, striking the square. Hawk gave a joyous whoop and grinned at his father.

"Again."

The boy shot all the arrows in his quiver, retrieved them, and shot again. His arms began to tire with the strain of the bow. Black Thorn then paced off a shot of longer range.

"Try here."

The shot struck the ground below the target. Confused, Hawk turned to his father.

"The arrow falls. Aim above the target."
He demonstrated and struck the target.

"How much above the target do I aim?"

"There is much to learn of this skill, my son, even before winds blow and targets move. Enough for today. Come, we return to the village."

CHAPTER THIRTY-TWO

Dolores
December 24, 1690

Father Visitor arrived Christmas Eve in time to celebrate the vigil and the birth of Our Lord. The day after Christmas we sought audience with Coxi that he might answer Father Visitor's questions, concerning the matter of Scorpion's treachery.

Coxi welcomed us to his olas kih, affording our visitor the experience of Pima hospitality. We were most agreeably treated to dried caterpillar and tortillas dipped in a fiery pepper sauce. I confess I took private humor in Father Visitor's hesitant acceptance of the caterpillar delicacy.

Coxi described the outbreak of black vomit disease and Scorpion's vision quest laying blame for the evil spirit at the feet of the black robes. He explained his suspicions were aroused at the charge the illness was a rejection of Holy Mother Church teaching.

He suspected the medicine man acted out of jealousy, when clean water was suggested for the cure. He confronted Scorpion with his treachery, ordering the medicine man to drink from the olla of one who had recently died. In this the treachery was exposed.

Coxi's explanation satisfied Father Visitor without further question.

While Padre Juan Maria's charge was to investigate reports of abusive practices in this Pimeria, I was not in the least threatened by his presence. I knew no such abuses should be found among the missions under my care. In fact, I welcomed the company of a brother in the Company of Jesus and one whose authority might serve to bring aid to our work. I found him thoughtful, intelligent, curious, and solicitous for our success in the mission fields. We formed a bond of friendship as we spoke in the early evenings following his arrival.

"Have you any first impressions of your visit, Juan?"

He inclined his head in thought. "You have accomplished much in your short time here at Dolores, Eusebio. If we find more of the same at the remaining missions, I suspect my time here will be brief."

"I pray we shall not disappoint you. Much

remains to be done at our newer missions, but all are started on the path you see here in Cosari. Our greatest limitation is two priests and four missions. As Luke writes in chapter ten, 'The harvest is bountiful, the laborers few.' "

"It is the cross of the missionary."

"We have only touched a tiny part of the souls awaiting the Good News of Our Lord in Pimeria Alta. One day, God willing, we may yet touch the rich prize that awaits beyond the Sea of California."

"I understand your affection for California. I read your report to the archbishop in preparation for my visit here. You make a strong argument for the work to be done there."

"Thank you, Juan. Strong perhaps, but not strong enough to be persuasive."

"There are challenges of concern to secular authorities."

"There are always challenges. Challenges to be overcome by the intercession of our most holy patron San Francisco Xavier."

"Have patience, Eusebio. All will be accomplished in due course and proper season."

■ ■ ■ ■

Nuestra Sonora de los Remedios
January 1691

Early in the New Year Father Visitor and I journeyed north to investigate rumored abuses at our Remedios mission. There we observed an increase in the flock of the faithful and budding prosperity in ranching brought to the temporal well-being of our charges. The headman assured Father Visitor the reports of abuse were told to them by outsiders, and while the people were fearful for a time, no such abuses ever materialized.

A heifer was slaughtered and roasted for a feast served in honor of our visitor. We enjoyed fresh meat along with dried melon, vegetables, and tortillas all prepared from the fruits of the harvest.

"Ah, Eusebio, to return to Luke ten, verse eight, I believe, *'eat what they set before you,'* and we did, with pleasure."

"Are you saying you prefer the fruits of our rancheria to caterpillars?"

He laughed.

"Now that you mention it, I do."

■ ■ ■ ■

Mission San Ignacio

Our next inspection proved much the same as the first. During our visit we assisted Father Augustin in baptizing infants and welcoming others to the faith. We celebrated the Holy Sacrifice of the Mass followed by a fiesta in honor of our distinguished Father Visitor. I doubt our faithful comprehended the importance of the guest of honor to the future of our work here in the mission; but among a happy people, disposed to good cheer, fiesta always proved reason enough to celebrate.

Having completed the circuit of our missions, I fully expected we would return to Dolores. Following mass, the morning after our fiesta, Father Visitor and I broke our fast.

"It is time to return to Dolores," I said.

Juan turned his gaze west. "As long as we have come this far, Eusebio, would you indulge me further exploration?"

"Exploration? Why that is my second name. You have only to ask his Excellency Governor Atondo."

He smiled. "I do not mean exploration for

the purpose of making maps. Rather I would better understand the fertile fields for souls to the west. Will you assist me?"

West, to me, promised the ultimate prize, California. The ambition to evangelize there burned strong in my heart. "I have not traveled west of this Pimeria; but if it is your wish to do so, Juan, I am most eager to help."

"Good. It is settled then. Let us provision to see the Lord's work extended to new lands."

The following day we departed. We rode northwest in the company of Pima guides provided by Father Augustin, reaching Tubutama, a large village on the Altar River, at a distance of some twelve leagues. Arriving like the wise men on January sixth, the Feast of the Epiphany, we were greeted by welcoming Pima people. While we refreshed ourselves, we were pleased to receive ambassadors of the Soba people who inhabit far western reaches of Pimeria Alta. They expressed desire for mission to Padre Salvatierra, promising their assistance in further exploration to Rio Colorado and the Sea of California. At mention of California, I felt a stirring in my breast, the promise of prize within reach.

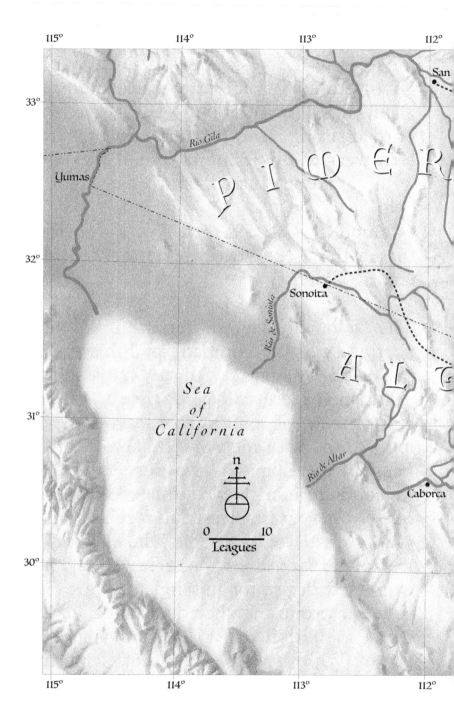

San

Rio Gila

Yumas

P I M E R

Sonoita

Rio de Sonoita

Sea
of
California

H L G

Rio de Altar

n

0   10
Leagues

Caborca

115°   114°   113°   112°

33°

32°

31°

30°

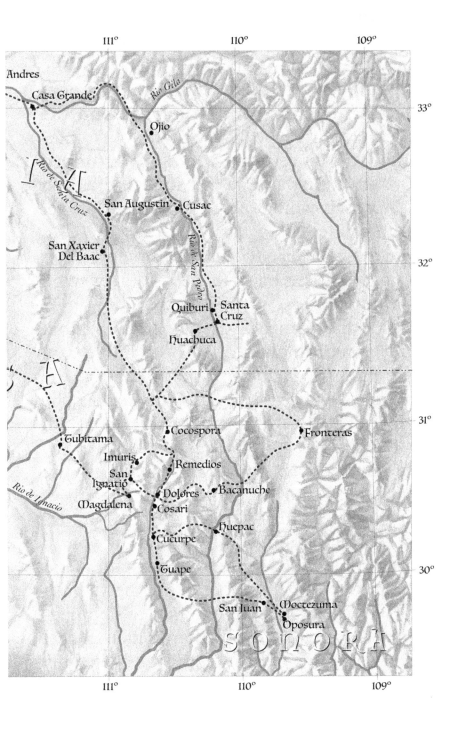

On the advice of our Pima hosts, we continued up the Altar to the village of Tumacacori. Here our exploration of the frontier came to a halt for this expedition. The approach of spring planting and the duties of our respective assignments summoned us to return. At this we stopped short of visiting a large Sobaipuris village at Baac, which would await our arrival for yet another time.

On the trail of our return, I asked Father Visitor what he had learned. He reflected for a time.

"I see the future, Eusebio. I see all that you have accomplished with the model you have made of your missions. I see too the wisdom of your rancherias. They better the temporal lives of the people while the faith nourishes them spiritually. I see also the way you have woven the Good News of the Gospel alongside the beliefs and customs of the people. It makes for a strong foundation. A foundation those who follow you to these people must come to understand. God willing, I shall be numbered among them. I see California on the horizon. I see stepping-stones between here and that golden goal. I cannot say how many stepping-stones, only that there are many. Laborers will be needed. All this I can attest to Reverend

Father Provincial. How does that comport with what you see?"

"I too see the horizon and stepping-stones. I am humbled by your vision of my small part in the work here. I only hope I shall be granted leave to take part in the claiming of California."

"A part for you in California is not for me to say. I can say I understand the zeal in your heart, a zeal I shall surely make known to Father Provincial. Further to the goal of mission in California, you may begin preparations for construction of a small barca to support supply should appropriate ecclesiastical and civil authorities be acquired."

"My thanks, Juan. I can ask no more."

CHAPTER THIRTY-THREE

Dolores
October 1691

Word of our visit to Tumacacori spread throughout northeastern Pimeria. It was amid the music, dancing, and feasting of our harvest fiesta later that year, Sobaipuris ambassadors arrived from the northern village at Baac. They came bearing crudely fashioned wooden crosses to plead that I visit their village. Moved by their piety and sincerity, of course I agreed, promising to visit in summer once spring planting was done. At this they joined in celebration of our bountiful harvest, satisfied by prospects for establishing their own mission rancheria.

I reckoned the overture by these Sobaipuris important for reasons beyond extending the Good News to yet another mission. These northeastern Pima occupied lands on the front line of defense against hostile Apache. A mission rancheria with a presidio garrison would present powerful deterrent to marauding Apache raiders.

Baac
June 1692

We traveled good road eighty leagues north through Remedios and Cocospora to the valley of the Santa Maria River and the Sobaipuris village of Baac. Francis and I traveled in the company of Lieutenant Manje, Cacique Coxi, with Black Thorn and Yellow Feather serving as scouts. Drovers managed a packtrain of some fifty mules. Abel and five of his vaqueros trailed a small herd with sixty head of cattle and a yearling bull along with twenty-five horses and mules. These would stock a new rancheria and provide a remuda to manage the herd.

We were welcomed to a village of some eight hundred souls by Cacique Cola de Pato, Duck Tail. He showed us to three arbors constructed in anticipation of our visit. One they prepared to serve as a chapel for the celebration of mass, a second for our sleeping quarters, and a third to serve as kitchen for the preparation of meals. Whereupon we christened our new mission San Xavier del Baac.

Many were curious to see who these

strangers were and from what land we had come to them. We showed them a map of the world, a marvel to them, and their place in it. We showed them the route the Spaniards traveled by sea to Veracruz and onward to Mexico City, Guadalajara, Sinaloa, and Sonora to Mission Dolores in the land of the Pima.

We spoke to them the Word of God and the articles of faith leading to admission to God's family by acceptance of baptism into the Holy Mother Church. They listened with interest to the story of a Son to the Prophet of Earth and that of his mother, Our Lady of Guadalupe who showed herself to an Indio boy. They asked prayerful questions to which we responded. In the end, many professed their faith and embraced the teachings of Holy Mother Church in baptism.

We observed among the Sobaipuris an industrious people eager for the blessings of faith. They inhabited fertile fields and tranquil valleys. We administered instruction and baptism to all who came to us.

Quiburi

We made our return to Dolores by way of the village at Quiburi, on the San Pedro River twenty-five leagues southeast of San

Xavier del Baac. The San Pedro flows north emptying into the Hila Rio Grande. We made this visit for the purpose of meeting Cacique Coro, a strong leader and warrior by reputation; his village stood at the eastern border of Pimeria Alta, facing the dreaded Apache threat. If we were to form a defensive alliance among Pima, his support must be won. I hoped Coxi's presence would make clear the sincerity and wisdom of our proposal.

Coro did not disappoint. A fine featured, wiry man he hid a joyful, jolly disposition beneath a mask of reserve. With Coxi's help we soon won his trust and interest in the rancheria we established at Baac. He was quick to comprehend the Apache threat attendant to such wealth, revealing the tempered strength of the warrior he became when faced with hostility. I spoke of a league, uniting eastern and western Pimeria in common defense. He became skeptical at mention of Soba's Pima clans, there having been generations of clan warfare and animosity between them. I begged his indulgence to consider the promise of rancheria wealth and the strength provided by the presence of Spanish soldados garrisoned there. Strength he understood. Spanish presence gave him pause. He too must have heard stories of abuse. I assured him that under the protection of the black robes and the royal cédula decreed by the authority of His Majesty King Philip V of Spain, all would be well. Coxi confirmed all this happened as I described in his experience at Cosari. In the end, we won his nod. He would wait to see the truth of our words.

It was a beginning on which we took our leave returning to Dolores. Much work remained to be done in northeastern Pimeria, but in truth we made a promising start.

CHAPTER THIRTY-FOUR

Apacheria
1693

The wolf, Caballo Rojo, presented himself before the wickiup of Ndolkah Sid.

"Sobaipuris welcome black robes to their village. Black robes bring horses and mules. These we can raid without suffering the black robes' religious sickness."

Ndolkah Sid listened to the words of his wolf and nodded. The Sobaipuris village is far from the nearest Spanish presidio. Soldados could not come in time. When they do come, it will not be to the Apache.

San Xavier del Baac

The Sobaipuris' herd offered the Apache an easy prize in the hands of a peaceful people. Ndolkah Sid and his raiding party watched from the hills above the village as families gathered around their cook fires at the end of the day. Darkness fell. The people drifted off to their lodges and sleeping mats. The village fell silent.

Moon rose bright and full. Ndolkah Sid and his band crept toward the corral, ground shadow, flowing around the sleeping village. One by one the raiders slipped through the corral rails and fit a lead tether to a horse or mule. Ndolkah Sid waited at the corral gate holding the lead to a sturdy bay. When his raiders mounted, he opened the gate, swung up on his mount, and led the raiding party out.

He set a southwesterly course at a lope, ghostly silhouettes frosted in moonlight. They made no attempt to cover their tracks, leading anyone following away from Apacheria and into southern Pimeria Alta. With the moon high overhead, the trail cut a stream. Ndolkah Sid rode further south in the streambed until he found a rock-strewn east bank suitable to his purpose. He led them out of the stream, continuing on a southwesterly course, leaving a clear trail to disappear on rocky high ground. Here he doubled back northeasterly to the stream, leaving no trail. Once in the stream the band turned north to Apacheria.

Mission Dolores
We received an urgent message from Father

de Campos of Mission San Ignacio. Reverend Father was most distressed to report troops under the command of Lieutenant Solis out of the presidio at Bacanuche had come to the mission to arrest those responsible for stealing horses and mules from the village rancheria at San Xavier del Baac. The people of San Ignacio knew nothing of the Sobaipuris' loss. Lieutenant Solis insisted the trail left by the thieves led to Pimeria Alta. I sent for Lieutenant Manje who came at once. I handed him the message from Father Augustin.

"This does not sound like the work of Christian Indio," he said.

"That is as we see it also."

"Solis is another who can be a zealot to his duty, especially where he curries favor with his superior."

Coronel Zevallos again. I recalled our encounter with Capitán Zevallos over the abuse of our flock at La Paz. "What can we do, Mateo?"

Manje shrugged. "Perhaps Solis can be made to see reason. Come, let us go to San Ignacio."

We set out at once leaving Francis to look after Dolores. Abel rode with us should we find ourselves in need of his language skills. We reached San Ignacio the following morning. Father Augustin greeted us with much relief. He took us to the hut occupied by Lieutenant Solis.

"Padre Kino, Lieutenant Manje, to what do I owe this visit?"

Mateo took up our response. "Padre de Campos and these people say they are innocent of this charge. Why is it you believe they are responsible for the Sobaipuris' loss?"

"The trail the Sobaipuris showed me led us here."

"Led you here to this village?"

"Near here. Clearly in this direction."

"So the trail did not reach this village?"

"No."

"Can you show us where you lost it?"

"Sí, but why?"

"Is it possible the thieves made a false trail to deflect blame from themselves?"

"Anything is possible. Though the thieves used a stream to throw off any pursuit. It was only by great diligence we found the place where they left the stream to continue their escape here."

"A stream you say."

"Sí."

"Please Lieutenant, show us this place."

Solis had his horse saddled and with much grumbling led us out on a northeasterly course. It was late afternoon by the time we reached the stream used by the thieves. We followed the stream bank to the place where the raiders rode out to continue their trail toward San Ignacio. The trail from the stream did not go far before it became lost in rough stony ground.

Abel peeled away to the north walking Azucar slowly, searching the hard, stony scrabble. At a distance of no more than a single stadia he drew rein and stepped down.

"Padre!" He waved.

We rode to his summons and stepped down from our mounts.

"There," he pointed to dried horse or mule sign. "Here the thieves doubled back to the stream."

"Why would they do this?" Zevallos asked.

"Old trick," Abel said.

"Can you tell which way they went?" Manje said.

Abel shrugged before lifting his chin back upstream to the northeast.

Zevallos scowled. "Back to the Sobaipuris?"

Abel shook his head. "Apacheria."

"Apache?" I queried.

Manje nodded. "A false trail to cast accusation on the Pima. Now Lieutenant, will you follow the stream to a north trail leaving for Apacheria?"

"Better to follow smoke in the wind."

In this we averted punishment of our flock. For this all were most grateful. We were treated to a fiesta in celebration as Solis and his men returned to Bacanuche.

CHAPTER THIRTY-FIVE

Mission Dolores
April 26, 1693

Francis and I stood at the back of the church making inspection of arrangements for dedication. Sun-softened golden light spilled from oilskin covered windows, turning the church a sepia glow. The altar reached a high arch, ornately carved to our design in polished wood sections meticulously assembled to beautiful effect. Carved tabernacle doors gleamed in relief of loaf and cup. Candles braced the tabernacle. Altar cloths draped their proper places. The fresco of Our Lady of Guadalupe hung in its place beside the altar. Frescos depicting stations of the cross lined the walls on both sides of the nave. High above carved oaken doors at our back our bell hung in its steeple, its clarion tones there to call all to worship.

"Six years," I said, taking it all in.

279

"Hard to believe it is finished at last."

"A day at a time, soul by soul, we achieve our mission."

"Much remains to be done, Padre."

"Sí, but the laborer is entitled to celebrate the Lord's blessing on our work."

"Then we are truly blessed."

Padre Augustin arrived that afternoon with a delegation from San Ignacio. Others trickled in from San Joseph and Nuestra Sonora. The Sobaipuris Cacique Coro led a small delegation from Quiburi, followed closely by Cola de Pato with his children of San Xavier del Baac. Relations with the San Ignacio Pima restored by reports Apache were culprit in raiding their herds.

Last to arrive were a curious delegation from the western regions of Pimeria Alta. Ancient tribal and clan hostilities existed between the Pima in the east and those in the west. These new arrivals led by their Cacique El Soba evidenced the first softening of the feud in anyone's recollection. Here we were given further indication of our mission work. Coxi, accompanied by Black Thorn and Yellow Feather, welcomed the visitors to Cosari, expressing pleasure they had come to celebrate dedication of our church. Coro remained cool to the presence of the new arrivals, though he offered no sign of hostility. Padre Augustin and I saw in El Sabo and his people a new opportunity for peace in Pimeria Alta and conversion in the west.

We dedicated our church the next morning, Padre Augustin and I concelebrating Holy Sacrifice of the Mass. The church filled with our flocks and visitors who could not help but note the delight our faithful found in their beautiful new church. Many had never seen so glorious an edifice.

The day continued with a fiesta. Our people made merry with music, dancing, and a feast. Padre Augustin and I watched with much satisfaction. My attention turned on two of the young ones. Hawk now grown to a young man of sixteen and his childhood companion Fawn, now a maiden of fifteen. Soon she would dance her womanhood. I watched as they shared a meal side by side in the circle of their families. Time was coming for a wedding. Time to give thought to how we might weave ancient custom and the Holy Sacrament of Matrimony together in a manner respectful of both. I posed the question to Francis who well understood the customs we must honor. With his help, when the occasion arose, we were ready.

■ ■ ■ ■

Mission Dolores

Autumn arrived on a cool breeze; following a successful harvest, we celebrated a joyous fiesta. During fiesta Augustin and I found a moment to discuss mission in western Pimeria.

"Much has been accomplished here in the east, Eusebio," he said, admiring our church, our flock, and the numbers of our herds.

"We have accomplished much, yet so much more remains to be done. Somewhat more begins with mission in the west."

"I have been thinking as much myself, though I scarcely know where to begin."

"In that we must assist from the abundance we enjoy in the east. The Soba people await us. Cacique El Soba said so on his visit to dedication of our church. He is a man of good heart. I think he is open to a treaty of peace with Pima clans here in the east."

"A treaty of peace we might seal with the promise of mission and rancheria."

"The Pima people have been divided by generations of animosity and feuding. We discussed the need for the Pima to unite with the Spanish in opposition to Apache hostilities."

"How are the Apache a problem for western Pimeria?"

"We must make a connection for the Soba. Peace within Pimeria allows Cacique Coro and Cacique Coxi to meet the Apache threat without need to guard against treachery from within their own Pimeria. Your coming will further the cause of peace with the faith you bring and the wealth that comes with it."

"Wealth? I come with no more than vows such as yours. One of which you may recall is poverty."

"Poverty I am well acquainted with. The wealth we will take to Caborca comes on four hooves. Cattle, horses, and mules bring wealth to our Indio flock. Peace comes easiest to prosperity."

As soon as we were properly provisioned, we departed for the village at Caborca. Abel accompanied us with vaqueros to trail one hundred head of cattle, one of Abraham's sons, fifty horses, and twenty-four mules. The journey would take us west at a distance of fifteen leagues.

Caborca

The village stood on the south bank of the

Altar River, which empties into the Sea of California. Its geographic significance to our California ambitions struck me at once as propitious. El Soba greeted us with warm welcome extending his hospitality to Padre Augustin as a long-lost brother. Abel went to work with young Soba, anxious and willing to learn vaquero work tending their new herd.

El Soba was pleased to show us primitive preparations for establishing a mission we christened La Concepcion del Caborca. Steeped in goodwill, I broached the subject of peace among the Pima people.

"Pima people should not pose a threat among themselves. Coxi and Coro face the Apache in the east. They are the threat Pima must oppose. It is their gesture of goodwill that brings the prosperity of a mission rancheria to the Soba."

He listened, sober in thought.

"Pima must unite with the Spanish for common defense. Peace is the path to prosperity and mission. Can the Soba join us in this?"

"El Soba sees wisdom in these words. Let us choose this path."

I smiled. "Excellent."

Thus assured, Augustin could begin mission work, we rested a few days, baptizing those who wished to embrace the faith and celebrating the Holy Sacrifice of the Mass.

Dolores
February 7, 1694
We took steps to complete our peace mission with alacrity. We summoned Cacique Coro to join us, along with Coxi and Lieutenant Manje. We rode west to El Tupo on the Altar River, following rich fertile river valley southwest to Caborca. There we were greeted by El Soba and Augustin. Progress on mission was notable, but this journey was to bring lasting peace to the Pima people of Pimeria Alta.

Pledges of peace and gifts of goodwill were exchanged among the cacique. Padre Augustin and I solemnized the occasion and pledges, concelebrating Holy Sacrifice of the Mass. Thus blessed, a fiesta was held in honor of the visiting headmen.

While our party rested, celebrating new friendships, Mateo and I undertook a small, yet important exploration. We rode west, crossing difficult desert, to reach Mount Nazareno. There we negotiated a climb on foot to a vantage from which observed eastern shore on the Sea of California and from there to the horizon, California itself. I estimated the crossing at a distance of no more than fifteen leagues. California. The goal. Within reach. Buoyed by discovery we returned to Dolores by way of Caborca.

CHAPTER THIRTY-SIX

Mission Dolores
March 1694

With a mission presence at Caborca and Altar River access to the Sea of California, we saw clear route to mission in California. I turned attention to shipbuilding, enlisting the good offices of Lieutenant Manje to assist in these endeavors. He joined me in the parlor of our modest rectory to discuss preparations to further our cause.

"A barca? Padre, I am a soldado. I have no naval experience."

"We'll not ask you to sail her, my son. We will find a seaman to captain her. We only need you to assist us in gathering wood sufficient to make a ship and transport it to Caborca."

"Is that all? Oh, that is much different."

"Sí."

"Padre, do you know how much lumber you will need to construct such a vessel?"

I drew out my sketches and measurement calculations and spread them on the table before us.

"See here. If we lay a keel of one-hundred-thirty-five cubits at a draft of thirty cubits and a beam of twenty cubits, I calculate it at ten thousand eight hundred cubits. We would do best to provision eleven thousand five hundred, not counting masts and spars."

Disbelief is the only way to describe the good lieutenant's response.

"Where do you propose to gather so much lumber?"

"That is a problem. We know the reaches from here to the coast to be desert, barren of trees suited to shipbuilding. We shall have to look east to solve our problem."

"East?"

"Sí. The Sierra Madre. Apache pine at higher altitudes will prove serviceable masts and spars. Oak suitable for keel, ribbing, and hull making is plentiful at lower altitudes."

Manje looked off to the peaks in the east. "*Apache* pine. Apache no less. How do you propose to transport so much lumber to Caborca?"

"Mule carts for the lumber, mule teams for masts and spars. How many men can you spare, Mateo?"

Our adventure in shipbuilding began with a logging expedition in the Sierra Madre.

Journal Entry

We established base camp in the foothills to support our logging work. Trees were felled, stripped, and hewn into planks for shipment. We climbed the timberline to find Apache pine suitable to serve as masts and spars. Two lofty pine were felled for masts. A third would yield the needed spars.

All the mules and carts used in freighting trade goods were employed to transport loads of lumber down the mountain. Arrangements were made to procure canvas suitable to sailmaking and the additional carts and stock needed to convey shipbuilding materials to the river port at Caborca. Preparations continued throughout the summer as we prepared to depart soon after harvest.

October 1694

We departed Mission Dolores escorted by Lieutenant Manje and a company of His Majesty's dragoons. Twenty trained carpenters of the Cosari Pima would assist in building our barca. Seventy-five mule carts loaded with lumber and supplies wound its way westward. Abel rode with us to serve interpretation should we find it needful. We reached Mission San Ignacio the first night where we were welcomed by Padre Augustin.

We arrived in time to pray vespers before taking our evening meal. The vast quantity of lumber and fittings for our barca proved a great curiosity to the Indio at San Ignacio. Abel became much in demand to explain the purpose of so much building materials.

Over dinner I begged Augustin his indulgence to ride the circuit of our four missions in my absence.

"Eusebio, I understand your affection for a mission to California, but is this wise? We have only the two of us to serve all of eastern Pimeria Alta. We already extend ourselves west to Caborca. Five missions. Two priests. We need laborers in the vineyard. Where are our brothers to come from?"

"As in Acts, we are sent two by two. We are here. For California, God will provide."

"Of this, I am sure. The question beyond us is when? Why build a barca now when we could wait for some sign of our Lord's time?"

"If the Lord should see we are prepared, perhaps it might encourage him to put forward His providence."

"With you there is always room for more. A barca for California, indeed."

"Of course, we shall also need a shipyard."

"A shipyard?" Augustin's eyes widened. "At Caborca?"

"Sí. A shipyard and somewhat more."

"More?"

"La Concepcion del Caborca is ideally placed to port a supply ship, serving a new California mission."

"And we are to provision it?"

Now it was my turn to be incredulous at the question.

"With our help, of course, my friend."

Augustin and Manje exchanged glances. I knew I could count on them.

We passed a pleasant evening, departing early the following morning to continue our journey west.

We traveled west to Magdalena and on- ward to El Tupo through high desert hill country, watered by scattered streams and river tributaries. These we put to good use with so many men, horses, and mules to water. Over the course of our journey, I oc- cupied my evenings making detailed draw- ings of plans for constructing our barca. Mateo had among his company escorting our party, a man of engineering abilities.

He studied the plans with interest, posing questions in matters requiring greater clarity.

On the sixth day of our journey, we were met by a party of Pima under the leadership of El Soba, cacique at Tubutama. He greeted us as old friends full of excitement at the progress of building their mission under Padre Augustin's spiritual direction. They guided us the rest of the way to Caborca where we were warmly welcomed to mission La Concepcion.

We rested a few days explaining our intended purpose. El Soba listened intently as I described the small shipyard we wished to establish on the river.

Within a fortnight, we established a base for the shipyard and commenced preparations to begin construction of our vessel. El Soba's people assisted in constructing shelters for the men and an open-air pavilion with a thatched roof to serve the engineering and management needs of the enterprise.

With preparations underway, Mateo appointed his engineer to base commander and charged him with completing the barca within the coming year. He left sufficient troops to garrison the camp and undertake the work of building our ship.

■ ■ ■ ■

Sea of California

Mateo and I took advantage of the opportunity to again journey twenty leagues further west through harsh desert conditions, this time reaching the shores of the Sea of California. The journey served to confirm the importance of Caborca as the base from which California missions might be supported. We camped on the beach with California a visible shadow hugging the western horizon.

I stood on the shore at sunset, surf lapping gently at my sandals. I watched the sun sink over souls I prayed one day to serve. With work undertaken to advance a California mission the goal seemed well-more within reach.

"It summons you still does it not, Padre?" Mateo appeared at my elbow. I nodded.

"It does, my son."

"Why does it? You've so much before you in Pimeria Alta."

"I wish I knew. Who can explain hearing a call? Most blessed San Francisco Xavier heard his call to Cathay. For me California symbolizes mission."

"Cathay proved unattainable to San Francisco."

"It did. I pray California may be opened to me."

"For your sake, Padre, I hope your dream is realized. It will have to overcome the resistance of royal and ecclesiastical misgivings arrayed against you."

"The barca is a start. It begs to be employed. By God's grace we shall see it to fruition."

I said it as the last spars of light slipped below the horizon.

We returned to Caborca the following day and inspected the progress underway. Satisfied, we bid El Soba farewell. In company of Abel and our escort we departed on our return to Mission Dolores.

Whispers

Ambition. Kino dreams grandiose visions of California. He seeks westward expansion of his mission, while needful work remains to be done among souls already entrusted to his care. He gallivants hither, thither, and yon, blown like a wind wherever whim leads. He fancies himself a statesman, forging peace treaties and building alliances. He builds a boat as though he were Noah on mission from

God. Is this the work of Holy Mother Church or the quest of a strutting grande born of personal ambition? Who cannot see him for what he truly is? Must I alone be the one to say it so?

M.

Chapter Thirty-Seven

Mission Dolores

On our return journey I composed a letter, reporting our progress in the west to Father Provincial and requesting appointment of a missionary to establish a mission in California. I confess, I offered my services to that appointment if a suitable replacement were available to continue my work at Dolores. Upon our arrival, I dispatched it with Mateo's next courier bound for Guadalajara.

It felt good to be home. The prospect of establishing a mission in California excited me, though I felt myself torn by affections for our flock at Cosari. Our return was warmly greeted by the people, especially the children who had as much affection for Damascus as they did for me, perhaps more for a few of the older boys who wished to join Abel's vaqueros. We sat at table following our first evening meal with Abel and I regaling Coxi with tales of our travels.

Coxi for his part too offered news. He reported heavy fighting in the east, defending against Apache raiders. Coro's people fought the Apache alongside Spanish troops, stationed at Bacanuche. I found the news both troubling and encouraging. Fighting on its face is troublesome. Our Pima people proving a reliable ally to the Spanish bode well for the peaceful well-being of colonists and their Indio neighbors. Such sobering thoughts came to a happier close.

"We have visitors," Abel announced. "Come in, come in."

We were joined by Young Hawk's mother, Rain, and Fawn's mother, Sweet Grass. "What is it you wish?" I asked.

"Fawn has come into her womanhood," Sweet Grass said. "Soon she will dance in celebration. With that she will receive suitors."

"Hawk will be among them," Rain said.

Sweet Grass nodded. "Fawn will choose no one, but Hawk. We wish to have them married."

We knew this was coming. How best to respect custom with the sacrament became the question. I'd given the matter some thought after consulting Francis on customs. "When Fawn has chosen, I will come to Yellow Feather's lodge. There I will give them their marriage instruction. On the fourth day, the day of marriage, they must come to the mission where we will celebrate the Sacrament of Matrimony with the Holy Sacrifice of the Mass. Will that please you?"

We were rewarded with broad smiles.

It came to pass as we proposed. The rite of the sacrament interwoven with tribal custom to everyone's satisfaction.

Mission Dolores
November 1694

We were pleased to greet the arrival of Father Francisco Saeta soon after concluding the harvest. Father Francisco informed me of his assignment to Caborca. Padre Augustin would be relieved to return to minister full-time in our rectorate at San Ignacio. We set about immediate preparations to escort Reverend Father to his new mission. I welcomed Padre Saeta's arrival, though privately I wondered, what of a California mission?

Departing on the nineteenth accompanied by Francis Pintor, Lieutenant Manje, servants and officials of this Pimeria. Abel and a vaquero crew sufficient to manage one hundred mares and colts along with herds of cattle, sheep, and goats brought up the rear of our party. We traveled by way of Mission San Ignacio where the hospitality of mission extended to weary travelers.

From San Ignacio we continued another thirty leagues inland, delivering Father Saeta to Mission La Concepcion and the loving embrace of Cacique Soba and his flock. There the people proudly showed us their new chapel awaiting the arrival of their new pastor. We concelebrated Padre Saeta's first mass in his new mission church.

Having seen Padre Saeta to his new appointment, Father Augustin related rumors of unrest among villagers north and east of Caborca, brought about once again by reports of forced labor and excessive crop levies. These disturbing reports brought to mind the abuses we confronted six years earlier emanating from the presidio at Bacanuche then under the command of Lieutenant Solis. This time the reported troubles would not be so easily quelled. Discontent festered below the tranquil surface of our missions in Pimeria Alta.

We were pleased to find our barca nearly assembled; soon she would be seaworthy and ready for launch to California should permission for such a venture ever be granted. I recalled the crude drawings I'd made by campfire light to serve as plans for the ship and marveled at the result. The

Holy Spirit I acknowledged must truly have guided my hand. I congratulated Manje's engineer on having achieved the intended purpose with such limited guidance. I lifted my eyes to the small cross atop the barca main mast. Sunrays rendered it in shadow. I felt the call, tugging me to mission in a land, golden in possibilities. I prayed permission soon would be granted. Footsteps approached from the village behind me. A presence paused at my shoulder.

"What is it, Francis?"

"I came for your instructions."

"Instructions?"

"For our departure."

I smiled to myself. "You know me too well, my son."

"How could I not after all these years. When do we depart?"

"It occurs to me perhaps you should not."

"Should not? Depart? But why?"

"Your catechetical service to my mission is responsible for so much of what we have achieved. The need here, to assist Padre Francisco, is the greater need now. I cannot order you to do anything. I can only ask you to consider it. The Lord knows I will miss your companionship and ministry, but I feel the Holy Spirit calling you to ministry here. Should you find it in your heart, my son?"

"I have never found it in my heart to question the Holy Spirit. If you hear such a call, I am here to serve. I shall miss your guidance, Padre."

"Not as much as I shall miss your assistance and dedication to our flock at Dolores."

He turned to go. "One last thing, my son."

"Sí?"

"Does she have a name?"

"The ship?"

"Sí."

He shrugged. "I think not."

"Then she shall have one. We shall christen her *Resurrection* and pray our California mission finds life."

Mission San Ignacio
Holy Tuesday
March 29, 1695

Word reached San Ignacio. An overseer at Tubutama, seventeen leagues north of Caborca, beat a young boy conscripted to forced labor farming. Other impressed laborers rose up, against the bonds of forced labor. Soldados, overseeing the labor party, were overcome. These paid dearly for their misdeeds. Warriors secured weapons in greater numbers and hostilities spread across the Altar Valley. As Padre de Aguilar told it, uprising outrage enflamed the impressed laborers. Tools of planting and building became weapons. Padre escaped into the hills where he was sheltered by some faithful of his flock. The rumored angers of which we recently heard, boiled over.

The mission and church at Tubutama were sacked and burned. By the time reinforcements arrived from the presidio, it was too late to do more than bury the dead. Padre Augustin made his way to Mission Dolores, arriving on Holy Thursday. We took him into the safety of our fortified mountain position. He reported the tribal medicine men seized on the spontaneous revolt, agitating the war leaders to rise up and drive out the Spanish invaders and their black robes. The hue and cry spread, giving us all grave concern for the fate of further outlying missions. We agreed among ourselves these developments needed reporting to our provincial superiors in Guadalajara. With nothing further to be done for his mission it was decided Padre Augustin should carry the message, departing with a small military escort the following Easter Monday.

■ ■ ■ ■

Mission Concepcion
Caborca
Holy Saturday
April 2, 1695

Padre Saeta watched beside the mission well. Forty armed warriors approached the mission compound from the hills, specters shimmering in bright sunlight. He did not recognize them as members of El Soba's tribal community. None among them were known to him to be baptized. A shadow of uncertainty tremored in the good father's breast. He dismissed it with a prayer, opening his house with a warm smile of greeting and welcome.

Believing they had come in peace, Reverend Father showed them to the church. Apprehensive, they paused at the doorway, peering into the dim light within. Father made his way to the altar, gesturing invitation for his visitors to follow. Two entered, glanced around, and exchanged a nod. Satisfied they cautiously made their way up the aisle. Others followed. When they were assembled before the altar, Padre blessed them with the sign of the cross.

"Our Father who art in heaven . . ."

At that the leader nocked an arrow. Others followed.

Padre held up the cross he wore at his breast. "Peace be with you . . ."

The first arrow pierced his breast. He studied it for a moment. "Forgive them, Father, they know not . . ." He slumped to his knees, embracing the cross and crown of martyrdom. Other arrows followed.

The war party sacked and burned the mission and church. Francis Pintor, too, earned a martyr's crown that day.

CHAPTER THIRTY-EIGHT

Mission Dolores
April 5, 1695

We received word of the tragic fates of Padre Saeta and Francis by runner. I sent Abel to summon Mateo and took the news and my tears to the chapel to pray. Padre Saeta embraced the possibility of martyrdom when he accepted his mission, as do we all. For Francis I felt personal responsibility. He was an innocent, serving the Lord in spreading new faith. It was by my invitation he fell victim to the attack. I cried and prayed for forgiveness. Consolation came in knowing the heavenly crown he earned by the sacrifice of his life.

After commending Padre Saeta's and Francis's souls to eternal rest, I greeted Abel's return with Lieutenant Manje. He questioned the runner, but got little more than reports of Padre's death and the sacking of the mission.

"What do you make of it, Mateo?" I asked.

"We must take defensive precautions. It would appear the rising at Tubutama is spreading. The mission here is more defensible than the presidio. With your permission, Padre, I would move my garrison here for our mutual security as we await developments."

It seemed a reasonable plan. Not so among Mateo's company of soldados. They argued the greatest assurance of safety would be attained by withdrawal to the presidio at Bacanuche, itself the likely source of many of these troubles. The mutinous tone of protest Manje faced harkened back to Don Isidro's decision to abandon San Bruno at the behest of his men.

Mateo stood, eyes cast down, helm in hand. "Padre, for the good and safety of all we must withdraw to Bacanuche."

I consulted Abel with my eyes before speaking. He knew my mind as I knew his. "Mateo, I cannot leave my flock."

"But Padre, the risks . . . I cannot protect you. You must come with me."

"I cannot. My place is here."

"Is your place to follow Padre Saeta?"

"If it is God's will."

He turned imploring eyes to Abel.

"Abel?"

The boy looked to me.

"Go with Mateo, you will be safer," I said.

He smiled and shook his head. He would stay. He would not lose a second father.

Pained Mateo donned his helm. "Vaya con Dios, Padre."

"And you also, my son." I offered my blessing.

With the departure of our garrison much remained to be done. We stripped the altar and church of sacramental vestments, sacred vessels, and statuary of devotion. As much as we could carry, including the precious fresco of Our Lady of Guadalupe and the crucifix hung over the altar. These we secreted in a cave on the mountain above the mission. From there, we returned to the chapel and took up our vigil in prayer.

Days turned into weeks. The flames of bloodlust cooled. Mission Dolores was spared. We took account of our situation with the courage to accept God's plan for the future.

May 1695

The uprising and sacking of the mission at Caborca along with the murders of Padre Saeta and Francis sent waves of shock and fear through the ecclesiastical hierarchy and

307

His Majesty's authorities. Coronel Zevallos called out the army to track down the perpetrators and exact capital justice. This I feared risked punishing the innocent along with the guilty, if the guilty were even to be found. The response of Holy Mother Church's hierarchy proved even more alarming. The bishops came to openly question our ability to sustain missionary presence on the frontier. I felt the need to do something, only to be struck down by illness and fever.

As I lay sick abed, my fevered brain grappled with what could be done. I reckoned the military threat the imminent danger to our flock. If that could be put to right, I prayed the archbishop's hand might be stayed. With Don Isidro Atondo now installed as viceroy, I felt I had a place to start. I roused myself to put shaking hand to pen and parchment.

Excellency,
I hope you will forgive the impertinence of your humble servant who turns to you for help in this hour of grave need. I know you are well acquainted with the unfortunate events recently to befall our brother Padre Francisco Xavier Saeta and his mission at

Caborca. As I am sure you are aware, Coronel Zevallos has called out His Majesty's royal forces to make right this matter. I write to beg your indulgence and mercy for some time to allow the caciques of our peaceful Christian flock to bring forward the guilty, thereby sparing the risk unjust punishment might befall the innocent. Acting with military restraint in this matter may be placed to your credit, as it is wholly in keeping with the spirit of His Majesty, King Philip's royal cédula. With all trust in the judgement of your good offices I make this plea.

As ever your humble servant,
Eusebio Kino S.J.

I summoned Mateo before the ink dried on the parchment and returned to my pallet.

"Padre, you are ill."

I waved concern away. "It is nothing, my son. Old men are given to ill humors."

"You are not that old, Padre."

"Tell that to these bones. I need your help, Mateo."

"Anything, Padre. You know this."

I handed him the letter. "I need this to reach the viceroy in Mexico City as quickly as possible."

He read the letter. "I understand. I will

send my swiftest messenger. I will also send the presidio surgeon to see about these humors of yours."

"Thank you, my son."

I next summoned Coxi who knelt beside my pallet, listening to my instructions.

"I need you to find El Soba. Tell him I have taken steps to have the army stand down in their search for those responsible for sacking their mission and killing Padre Saeta. In exchange, he must find those responsible and turn them over to the army, lest innocents be mistakenly caught up in the punishments meted out."

Coxi took my request as a solemn obligation and set out that day.

Weeks later Manje returned word the viceroy ordered Zevallos to stand down and await word from us on handing over the guilty. I breathed a prayerful sigh of relief. Soon after Coxi returned with word El Soba had leaders of the uprising under guard awaiting instructions. In consultation with Mateo we sent a message to Coronel Zevallos at Guadalajara, the guilty would be turned over at El Tupo in a week's time. Coxi dispatched a runner to El Soba with instructions to turn the guilty over to the soldados who would meet them at El Tupo. Mateo agreed to attend the El Tupo meeting in my stead. With this I began to recover, thinking matters well in hand for the moment.

El Tupo
June 6, 1695

Mateo attended the events at El Tupo, reporting them to me on his return. El Soba arrived with fifty mostly unarmed men escorting twelve leaders of the uprising all as agreed. A company of soldados arrived under the command of Lieutenant Solis. An unfortunate choice as events would unfold. The guilty were handed over without incident. Two of the prisoners, knowing their fate and likely out of revenge for their capture, began shouting accusations: Cacique El Soba should be numbered among the guilty. El Soba stepped forward to confront the liars, where upon Solis, thinking El Soba perpetrator of treachery, drew his sword and severed the cacique's head. In panic El Soba's Pima followers attempted to flee. Solis ordered his men to fire. Many were killed. A few escaped, burning with the tale of Spanish treachery.

Mission Dolores
An uneasy peace prevailed for a time after the confrontation at El Tupo. The garrison

at Bacanuche was soon called to Apache mischief in the east. With the soldados away, Pima outrage over the treachery at El Tupo boiled over. The remains of the mission at Caborca were sacked and burned, along with the barca still awaiting orders to launch. Missions at Imuris, and Magdalena too, were sacked and burned. For a mercy Ignacio, Remedios, and Dolores were spared. Why, one could only conjecture. Some said these were viewed to be mine and that I held the last measure of faith for the flock.

Once again, the army was called out against the Pima for fear rebellion might spread to all of Sonora. The military campaign swept through the mission ruins to our north and west. They found no hostile opposition, only scattered remnants of once peaceful people. I knew fears of rebellion were unfounded, but this did nothing to lessen concerns as far away as Mexico City. His Majesty's authorities became defensive and distrustful of the Pima, who were now cast in the same light as warlike Apache. Ecclesiastical authorities too became fearful anew for the future of missions on the frontier. My written plea to the offices of the viceroy won restraint for a time only to have trust destroyed on both sides by rash acts of overzealous violence. I saw but one course of action to take for the temporal welfare of my flock. It led to palace halls four hundred leagues south and east.

CHAPTER THIRTY-NINE

Mexico City
November 1695

Accompanied by Abel, Black Thorn, and Hawk, we pressed our journey to seven weeks out of an abiding sense of urgency. On reaching the city, we found lodging in the Company of Jesus provincial house, Casa Profesa. The following day I called on the offices of the archbishop, requesting an audience at his earliest convenience. I also sent a note to Don Isidro, advising him of my presence in the city and my desire to meet with him should he be so kind. With these requests little remained for us to do but wait. I thought to put the time to good purpose. I felt drawn from the moment we entered the city.

On a cool autumn morning, Damascus and I retraced the short pilgrimage to the shrine at the mount of Our Lady of Guadalupe. There I knelt before her beautiful likeness, silent and soothed in gentle light with scents of candles and past offerings of incense. I poured out the troubles besetting her children. I prayed for guidance. How best to preserve the faith and devotion she so personally claimed for her people? She sent a peasant boy to a bishop with an unlikely message. I felt very much the peasant boy for the message I must take to another bishop and a viceroy no less. In prayer she encouraged my thoughts. Words came to mind. More would follow. The sun turned golden over the lake toward the mountains by the time I left her chapel.

Invitation to audience with the archbishop arrived a few days later. I presented myself at offices adjoining the basilica at the appointed hour and was shown into the archbishop's beautifully furnished apartments. We took comfortable seats beside a massive fireplace not yet put to purpose of heating the room.

"Welcome, Eusebio. You've come a long way."

"Thank you for seeing me, Eminence. I thought the matter of some urgency."

"I concur. Word of the situation on the frontier that reaches us sounds dire. I am eager to hear from someone whose eyes and ears know the circumstances precisely."

"What is it you hear, Reverend Archbishop?"

"The viceroy informs me from military dispatches he receives. They speak of a Pima rebellion, the sacking of missions, and the killing of Father Saeta and his catechist at Caborca, God rest their souls. I fear for the safety of your missionaries and the future of your mission in the face of such hostilities on the frontier."

"It is much as I feared."

"Am I misinformed?"

"To some degree, but only for the information Don Atondo receives. The Pima are not in rebellion. If they were, my missions at Dolores and Remedios would have been sacked as well and I should wear a martyr's crown along with Padre Saeta. Rogue elements of the people are responsible for the actions reported to the viceroy. These actions were taken in reprisal for abuses inflicted on the people by the very military who report the Pima in revolt. The beating of a boy forced into labor by the army in violation of His Majesty's royal cédula caused the tragedy at Caborca. The incident at El Tupo, observed on my behalf by Lieutenant Mateo Manje, stemmed from the actions of one Lieutenant Solis. He wrongly beheaded Cacique El Soba in the act of giving up those responsible for Padre Saeta's death as agreed. When El Soba's unarmed men took flight, Solis ordered his men to fire on them. The incident at El Tupo led to the sacking of missions at Magdalena and Imuris. Military injustice and provocation, Eminence, not rebellion by our people, are responsible for reprisal and bloodshed at our missions. The military reports to the viceroy tell the story as the military would have it told."

"What would you have me do, Eusebio?"

"We need to inform Don Isidro of the events as they actually occurred. We need the military to respect His Majesty's royal cédula. We must not waver in our commitment to mission, Eminence. The future of our flock in Pimeria Alta and beyond depends on it."

"I cannot speak for his Excellency Don Atondo; but if he can root out the risks of provocations you describe, it seems our missions on the frontier are called to go forward. I will ask the viceroy for an audience."

"I already have, but your request will add the weight of authority to the matter."

I left the archbishop encouraged by his

willingness to objectively view the situation on the frontier. Still risk to our purpose remained should Don Isidro not take appropriate action to stop military provocations. The future rested in God's hands, encouraged I prayed by the patroness of one special lady. As peasant boy padre, I could do little more than deliver her message.

On entering the gates at Casa Profesa, I stopped short at a hailed greeting.

"Eusebio! I heard you were in the city."

I turned to a smiling, Juan Salvatierra. We embraced.

"What are you doing here?" I asked.

"Doing what is necessary to await appointment to a mission. I have an idea I know what brings you on such a long errand."

"Word has spread."

"Rebellion fears often do."

"There is no rebellion, Juan."

"Missions sacked and burned. A brother's blood spilled in martyrdom. Sounds like rebellion to me."

"Reprisal for military abuse and provocation, yes. Committed rebellion, no."

"How did the archbishop see it?"

"He is willing to be circumspect for the moment. All will depend on the viceroy's judgment."

"And California?"

"California awaits. First we must save the good works of our Pimeria."

"For that I will pray. Come, let us see if the refectory offers some of that wonderful beef from one of your rancherias."

"Are you sure? We have caterpillars left from our trail provisions."

Within two days of the archbishop's request, we were summoned to audience with the viceroy, once again at the ancient Aztec Palacio Real, now seat of royal authority in New Spain. We sat again at the long table, the archbishop and I on opposite sides at one end with the seat at the head awaiting his Excellency.

Don Isidro arrived, looking much as I remembered him, showing only traces of gray in his beard to mark the passage of years. We rose from our seats.

"Padre," he took my hand in greeting. "So good to see you after all these years. Would it were under more pleasant circumstances."

"It is good to see you too, Excellency."

He inclined his head. "Please, Don Isidro to my traveling companion."

"As you wish, Don Isidro."

"And you, Reverend Archbishop, good to see you again as well. I meant no impertinence it is only Padre Kino and I traveled together on our early explorations of California."

"I understand, your Excellency."

"Please, be seated."

We took our seats.

"Now to the business at hand. Given your presence here, Padre, and the archbishop's request I assume we are here to discuss the Pima rebellion among the frontier missions."

"We are, Excellency," the archbishop said. "Padre Kino has come a great distance to describe a situation . . . somewhat at odds with the one you and I have heard."

Diplomatically put. I waited.

"How so, Padre?"

"If I may be frank, Don Isidro?"

"Please."

"We have had incidents affecting the frontier missions, some of them bloody and violent; but the Pima are not in purposeful revolt, or rebellion as some have called it. In each case the violence came about in response to provocation. In the tragic death of Padre Saeta at Caborca, the violence started in response to an overseer beating of a young boy, put to forced labor in violation of His Majesty's royal cédula."

"I did not hear that, though certainly you

can't mean it to excuse murder?"

"I do not mean to excuse it. In fact, as you know, the cacique of our people promised to turn over those responsible for the violence at Caborca, which they did. This was arranged to take place at El Tupo. A company of soldados was sent out from the presidio at Bacanuche to take charge of the prisoners. When the prisoners were handed over, one of them, in the spirit of revenge, falsely accused Cacique El Soba of complicity in the murders. At that the officer in command struck El Soba with his sword, cutting off his head. When El Soba's unarmed escort ran, they were fired upon. Many were killed. That is what lead to the reprisals at Imuris and Magdelena."

"The reports I received from Coronel Zevallos contained none of this. Are you certain of this, Padre?"

"I was not there to see it myself as I was ill at the time. I asked Lieutenant Manje to attend in my stead. He reported these events to me as I have described them to you. He can confirm everything I have told you."

"I see."

Don Isidro drummed his fingers on the table in thought.

"Did Lieutenant Manje name the commander at El Tupo."

"He did. A Lieutenant Solis."

"Very well. It seems I have an inquiry to make. If all is confirmed as you have stated, Padre, and I have no reason to doubt you, I assure you and you, Archbishop, changes will be made. Can peace be restored, Padre?"

"I believe it can, if I am given opportunity to try."

The archbishop nodded his approval.

Before departing Mexico City, Padre Salvatierra and I made further effort to convince the archbishop to allow us to open a mission in California. In this we failed. He withheld his permission out of an abundance of caution, given remaining uncertainty over our ability to restore peace and order to the frontier missions. We were left to return to Pimeria Alta to take up the work of peacemaking.

CHAPTER FORTY

Dolores
March 1696

Winter gave way to calving and planting the following spring. I enjoyed my time working in the herds or helping sow the fields. Our mission rancherias thrived on cattle and sheep. The introduction of wheat as a staple crop benefitted our agricultural villages. Both provided food for the people and trade goods for other necessities.

Abel had grown into a stockman capable of managing large herds. Mounted on Azucar he recruited young men attracted to working herds on horseback. These became skilled in horsemanship and use of the riata. Herdsmen, known as vaqueros, became an honored profession among men and boys, second only to warrior status in the rights of passage to manhood. While some men provided for their olas kih by hunting, vaqueros provided by working rancheria

323

herds. In this way mission herds were protected against marauding Apache by skilled warriors whose work was volunteered without resorting to abusive practices of impressed labor.

The herds also provided a source of supply for extending our missionary explorations. Exploration parties would number fifty horses to serve as mounts for the vaqueros to drive herds of cattle or manage flocks of sheep to stock new rancherias. One hundred fifty head of cattle with a bull or bull calf would be driven to establish a new rancheria as foundation for some new mission. Missions and rancheria flourished together. The military were free to establish presidio according to the needs of the crown and settlement by whatever mission best suited their purpose.

Our efforts at peacemaking continued with the onset of summer. With the cessation of hostilities, now Capitán Manje returned with a small garrison. He reported a General Petris de Cruzate Jironza in command of the presidio at Bacanuche, Coronel Zevallos having been recalled to Mexico City along with Lieutenant Antonio Solis whose ruthless disregard for the Indio had twice provoked hostility and violence. Mateo made General Jironza aware of the abuses responsible for the uprisings as he had confirmed our reports to the viceroy. The general sent us his assurances he would countenance no further mistreatment of our people. He requested we take these assurances to people in the region so recently the scene of bloodshed and violence.

Tubutama

Mateo and I, accompanied by Coxi, rode west to Caborca to assure the Soba they were under no threat of military reprisal for it was now known and understood, they had no part in the uprising. From Caborca we rode north to Tubutama where we found Padre Augustin de Campos in company of General Juan Fernandez de La Fuente and a delegation of Pima ambassadors. We said mass at El Tupo to begin a conference of peace.

The Pima ambassadors condemned violence and bloodshed. They pledged once again to bring those responsible to justice. Agustin and I gave assurance missions would be restored as soon as replacement could be found for our martyred brother Padre Francisco Xavier Saeta. I couched the assurance in the blood of our brother to emphasize the consequence of the uprising. With agreements given and received on both sides, General de La Fuente pronounced the peace satisfactory to the Spanish crown. With that, the ambassadors departed to the fulfillment of their covenants. It was then the general approached Mateo and me with another subject.

"A word if I might, Padre?"

"Of course. How may I assist?"

"Unrest among the Pima distracts us from the far more serious threat posed by the Apache. The Apache threaten Spanish settlements. They also threaten the Pima. You enjoy the confidence of the Pima. You are in the best position to forge an alliance between the Pima and the crown. Would you be willing to undertake such a purpose?"

I thought. "I see the opportunity. I shall consider the possibility on our return to Dolores."

"Gracias, Padre."

Whispers

Peacemaker! He neglects his flock, posing as a diplomat. He grasps at authority to curry favor with the crown, the viceroy, the military, should the king himself be next? Is this the work of the church? Is this the work of mission? He sets himself apart to speak for the Pima, a people who have proven themselves untrustworthy. He deals in illusion and lies. Cannot his superiors see through these pretentions? Must we be the source to see reason in this?

Z.

Dolores
May 1697

We were pleased to receive joyous news, my prayers at last answered. The archbishop, satisfied of his reservations concerning peace in Pimeria Alta, was prepared to authorize a mission to California, led by Reverend Juan Salvatierra and me, pending affirmation of the appointments by Father Provincial of the Company of Jesus. I began preparations at once, to receive my replacement and depart as soon as Juan could reach the frontier. My joy proved short-lived.

Further word followed even before Juan arrived. I was not to be relieved for ministry in California. On hearing of the plan, the viceroy raised objection to my part in it. Atondo argued I was personally responsible for making peace among the Pima and my presence in the region was essential to keeping it. I had no opportunity to plead my cause. The die was cast in the highest offices of royal and ecclesiastical authority, likely in an exchange of favors unknown to any but those party to the bargain. Further to my "essential" presence in the region, I was given instruction to make explorations for purposes of mapping northern and western reaches along the San Pedro and Hila Rio Grande valleys. All of it came with a curiously familiar secular odor.

Juan Mateo took the news with a mixture of sympathy for my disappointment and wry amusement at the machinations of power to which we found ourselves subject. For that we had no choice but to commence preparations to depart on a mission west, following spring planting. A journey to further our field of mission and advance the cause of a Pima alliance with the crown. Explorer, diplomat, and, time permitting, priest. I took the assignment with resignation. I heard the cry of souls in California, while pushed to purposes beyond my control.

Journal Entry
June 1697
San Pedro River Valley
With spring planting complete we prepared to depart on a mission of peacemaking along the San Pedro River Valley in company with Capitán Manje, Cacique Coro, and

thirty warriors, including Black Thorn and Yellow Feather. Abel and a crew of vaqueros handled a herd of sixty horses and mules, along with one-hundred-fifty head of cattle and a yearling bull; they would accompany us as far as Cocospora. We traveled north through Remedios thirty leagues to Cocospora.

Ndolkah Sid watched from the shadow of a rocky outcropping high in a butte overlooking a lush river valley. Sun shimmered in the distance as a black robe appeared accompanied by a small company of Spanish soldados clad in red and gold pantaloons, armor and helms agleam. Mounted Pima herded cattle and horses strung out in a long file up the dusty trail to the north. Ndolkah Sid's dark eyes narrowed at the corners in thought.

Rancherias added grazing land to the fields cultivated by the Sobaipuris. These grew up around the missions the black robes built, often followed by soldados and a presidio. Here they encroached on Apache land. The mission they could deal with. Soldados with fire sticks posed a different problem. For now, Ndolkah Sid remained content to watch. When the soldados withdrew it would be time to deal with the Sobaipuris.

From Cocospora we traveled onward at a faster pace with no further need to drive a plodding herd. We traveled arid desert, passing through Huachuca five leagues southwest of Quiburi. From Huachuca we followed the cottonwood-lined banks of San Pedro River to Santa Cruz. There we encountered a Capitán Bernal on patrol along the western reaches of Apacheria with twenty-two heavily armed soldados. Our party went lightly armed in the spirit of our diplomatic purposes. Bernal and his men accompanied us to Quiburi where Cacique Coro and his Sobaipuris people greeted us with great hospitality.

Quiburi was a village of some one hundred lodges set on a mesquite-dotted hill overlooking the river valley below. This high ground they deemed helpful defense against the threat of Apache raids. We arrived at a time celebratory of a great victory, having recently vanquished an Apache raiding party.

I approached Capitán Bernal. "Our Pima people too are threatened by the Apache."

He nodded.

"As you can see, they make effective opposition."

"Sí, Padre. What do you make of it?"

"There is a natural alliance to be made here. Pima and Spanish interests are aligned against the Apache. If you agree, I urge you to bring this opportunity to General Jironza's attention. Can I count on you, Capitán?"

"Sí, Padre."

Departing Quiburi, Capitán Bernal continued his patrol, while we tarried to preach the gospel and offer baptism to those who wished to embrace the faith.

On leaving Quiburi, Cacique Coro accompanied us with thirty of his warriors to guard us against Apache attack. We traveled twenty leagues north along the San Pedro to the village of Cusac. We were met on the trail by Cacique Humari, adorned in all trappings of his office and accompanied by thirty of his warriors. He presented himself so to embrace us in hospitable petition for mission and to impress Coro by a show of force. Clan frictions between them having persisted for generations.

Humari led us to his village at Ojio, where we were welcomed with dancing and a fine feast. We presented the people with gifts of simple tools, needles, and knives along with the small wooden crosses we introduced to the faith. We listened to petitions for mission, promising to convey their request to the proper authorities who might one day honor their wishes.

In the spirit of hospitality, we endeavored to mediate peace between the clans, with talks extending through the whole of the night. Caciques and leaders of both clans spoke at length. I blessed prospects for peace on behalf of Holy Mother Church. Juan Mateo assured both clans His Royal Majesty King Philip would preserve peace among his people. Following mass, the morning after this parley we were pleased to see Humari and Coro embrace in agreement to end the ancient feud.

With peace made among the Upper Pima, we followed Hila Rio Grande west by way of ancient ruins at Casa Grande. Casa Grande remained massive at four stories in height. Long abandoned by those who inhabited it, the deserted ruin was thought to be haunted. We dispelled the superstition by celebrating the Holy Sacrifice of the Mass for the benefit of Coxi, Coro, and their people.

We continued west to San Andres on the Santa Cruz River. Here we turned south, beginning our return to Dolores. We followed the Santa Cruz to San Augustin, a large village of some eight hundred souls and two hundred lodges. Here we rested, taking advantage of the hospitality and good wishes of the people.

From San Augustin we traveled southeast along the river to San Xavier del Baac where we paused to rest among our Sobaipuris friends. With the danger of Apache attack greatly reduced, Cacique Coro and his warriors set out to return to Quiburi. We presented Coro with a fine horse in gratitude for his service in seeing to our safe passage. Continuing our journey, we returned to Dolores in time for the observance of Advent and celebration of Christmas. We made our return journey not knowing trouble brewed closer to home.

Chapter Forty-One

Mission Cocospora

The mission community at Cocospora prospered. The Sobaipuris cultivated rich river bottom with maize and wheat as staple crops; fruits and vegetables added variety to the harvest. A small herd of cattle along with a few horses and mules played their part in the beginnings of what would become a prosperous rancheria.

Abel and his vaqueros spent several weeks settling the new herd to grazing lands. Sobaipuris vaqueros learned skills needed to care for the cattle and horses. By late summer with the herd well established, Abel and his vaqueros returned to Cosari in time for harvest.

February 25, 1698

Ndolkah Sid and his war party crept down the rock-strewn hillside toward the sleeping village in the gray light of predawn. Dark shadows moved silently, seeping over the land as the passing of shadows. Weakened winter grip chilled the night air. This time the prize would be more than a few horses. This time the Sobaipuris would feel Apache war medicine.

Spears of bright sunlight pierced the gloom above the eastern horizon. The Apache struck with a fury. Sobaipuris warriors scrambled from their sleeping blankets to their weapons in a futile effort to defend their women and children. Apache arrows rained on many as they crawled from their olas kih. Those who found their kawad and clubs engaged the attackers only to be overwhelmed by superior numbers. Women who chose to join their men in combat too were cut down, raped, and mutilated. Others were not so fortunate. These were taken captive to slavery. Children were captured or killed according to their value as slaves.

The fighting lasted but a short time. The Apache torched the village. They rounded up the Sobaipuris horses and drove their cattle, sheep, and goats from the village. By full sun the raiders rode south with stolen cattle and captives, setting a false trail toward Los Remedios in Pimeria Alta.

One young boy escaped his family lodge at the edge of the village to take shelter in

335

the river bottom. He watched with tear-filled eyes as all he knew of life was destroyed.

Santa Cruz
March 30, 1698
Ndolkah Sid attacked the sleeping village with a large war party. Alerted by camp dogs, the Pima escaped; taking shelter they suffered minor losses. Emboldened, the Apache occupied the village. They slaughtered some cattle, preparing a feast.

Word of the attack reached Cacique Coro at Quiburi two leagues to the north. He led his warriors south, attacking the Apache by surprise as they celebrated their victory. Warriors of the Santa Cruz clan rallied to aid Coro and his warriors. The Apache fled into the hills. Coro mounted relentless pursuit. His warriors, inflicting heavy losses by use of deadly poison arrows.

Whispers
Quiburi Pima are known to have had a hand in the raids plaguing the north these past months. Much blood has been spilled among their clans. The Pima are untrustworthy. They cannot be relied upon as allies to secure Spanish settlements. The black robe Kino makes them out to be

something they are not. They enrich themselves by raiding even as mission rancheria grow wealthy, monopolizing the choicest land while Spanish settlers are left to the margins. Royal authority must be made to see these things as they are and not be fooled by myths told by the old priest. Reports must be made. Justice must be done.

Z.

Mission Dolores
July 1698
Raids and uprisings in the north that spring gave us cause for concern and reason to pray for all those who suffered, but these troubles seemed far removed from the peace and tranquility at Mission Dolores and our village of Cosari. Still the long shadow of suspicion fell across our fields that summer.

I tended the mission garden one bright morning. I must confess I found contemplative comfort indulging in menial tasks. Capitán Manje arrived accompanied by a visiting officer. I remembered Capitán Bernal from our visit to Quiburi. Abel summoned me to join our visitors in the mission plaza.

"Mateo, my son and Capitán Bernal, to what do we owe the honor of your visit?"

The tall officer of proud bearing bowed. "Padre, I am afraid the Quiburi Pima have been implicated in hostilities at Cocospora and Santa Cruz. I have orders to arrest Cacique Coro and the senior warriors of his clan. Capitán Manje suggested I speak with you before my men carry out our orders."

"Our people, implicated? This is not possible. What makes you believe our people are involved?"

"In raid after raid the trails lead toward Pimeria Alta. Some reports say the Quiburi Pima are responsible."

"Who makes these reports?"

"I have not received any directly. I have been told of them."

"Rumors then."

"Possibly, but persistent."

"Rumors of Pima treachery are always persistent. They are also most often proven false. And these trails, do they lead to Quiburi?"

"The raiders are clever. Eventually they cover their tracks."

"You lose the trail is what you are saying."

The capitán furrowed his brow, uncomfortable with my conclusion.

"Sí, Padre."

Abel made the sign for Apache.

"You lose the trails at the point where the

Apache backtrack to the north. We have seen this trickery before, have we not, Mateo?"

"Sí, Padre. That is why I asked Capitán Bernal to bring his allegations to you."

"Capitán, do you know the times and places of these raids?"

"Sí, Padre."

"Bueno. Come let us ride to Quiburi. Abel, summon Coxi. Ask him to come with Black Thorn and Yellow Feather. I believe we can resolve this aspect of your investigation quickly."

Quiburi

We departed at once, reaching Quiburi late afternoon of the third day where we were greeted by Cacique Coro.

"Welcome, Padre. How may we be of service?" he said in his language.

I inclined my head toward Capitán Bernal.

"What does this soldado want?"

"They investigate raids among the Sobaipuris in the north."

"What has this to do with Quiburi Pima? We too have been raided by Ndolkah Sid and his marauders."

"Capitán Bernal follows the raider's trails. They lead here."

"The capitán is mistaken. No raiders come from here."

"What is he saying?" Bernal asked.

"He says you are mistaken. No raiders come from here."

"Ask him where he and his warriors were in February and March."

"No need to ask, Coro and his men were here in the time of spring planting."

"Ask him, Padre," Bernal said again.

"The capitán wishes to know where you and your men were in the time of spring planting."

Coro looked to Coxi, Black Thorn, and Yellow Feather. All nodded. "Padre knows, we were here as we should be, defending Santa Cruz from the very raiders you speak of in the month of planting."

"What did he say?"

"All say they were here at spring planting as I said. Further they repulsed Apache raiders at Santa Cruz."

Capitán Bernal questioned the Pima whereabouts at the times of other raids. Coro and our witnesses were able to account for all of them.

"Then how do you account for the trails leading here?"

"Apache," Abel spoke up. "We have seen this trick before. They set a false trail south

340

before doubling back to the north."

"It is true, Capitán." Mateo spoke up. "I have seen it with my own eyes."

"So it is the Apache we must find," Bernal said. "Apache are like mist in the morning, gone before day becomes light."

"You will need help to find them, Capitán. Pima can help." I turned to Coro and Coxi.

"Could you join your warriors to exact justice on the Apache?"

The cacique exchanged nods of agreement. "It must be so," Coro said.

"Capitán, let us see what our Pima brothers can make of Apache crimes."

Bernal grudgingly agreed and returned to Bacanuche. In truth he had not much choice. It would be easier to capture mist in darkness than find Apache in their hidden mountain lair.

Chapter Forty-Two

Apacheria
August 1698

Coro encamped with a band of forty warriors in the foothills leading to the mountain strongholds of Apacheria. Coxi joined him at his fire. They smoked to the four winds, considering how they might proceed.

"How many wolves must we send out to find Ndolkah Sid and his band?" Coxi asked.

Coro clenched his jaw, his features a mask etched in firelight and shadow. He gazed beyond the circle of firelight into darkness. "We do not send wolves. Tomorrow we send smoke sign. Ndolkah Sid will find us. He must face us to save face with his people."

Coxi nodded. "My brother is wise."

Ndolkah Sid read smoke sign against a cloudless blue sky. *Pima seek a parley of honor.* His tribal council read the sign too.

Capotcari, a war leader with a strong voice at council, spoke for the others.

"What means this parley of honor?"

Ndolkah Sid scowled. "Ask the Sobaipuris or the Pima Spanish masters."

"What brings them to us?"

"The Spanish we fool. The Pima, it seems not."

"The Pima make it a matter of honor. How do the Apache respond?"

"We meet the toothless Pima dogs. I speak no more of it." He stood and left the headmen to ready their warriors.

They appeared in the hills above the Pima camp in first light the following day. Coro and Coxi climbed a short distance beyond their camp. Arms folded they waited. Ndolkah Sid and Capotcari descended to meet them.

"What matter brings Pima to challenge Apache honor?"

"Apache leave false trails of blame for their raids to the Pima."

Ndolkah Sid laughed. "So the Pima nation now does the bidding of their Spanish masters, calling it a matter of honor." He spit a rotted taste to his words.

"Pima defend our honor. Do Apache have honor to defend?"

"Apache honor is not a matter to question."

"Good. Then the Apache are prepared to defend it."

"What do the Pima propose?"

"We settle a matter of honor by champions, ten Pima, ten Apache, battle to the death."

"Where?"

"There," Coro pointed. "In the valley below."

"When?"

"When sun is full high."

"Done."

The sun reached its zenith. The Apache led by Captocari spread an irregular line along the north end of the valley out of bow shot. Pima under Coro similarly faced their adversaries from the south. Yellow Feather and Black Thorn were numbered among the Pima champions along with Hawk, grown to a warrior of twenty summers. Coxi and the remainder of the Pima observed from the west valley wall. Ndolkah Sid and his Apache held the east valley wall. The contest commenced with a yelp.

The Apache began a stealthy advance across a broad uneven front. Low and crouching they came darting from rock to scrub, taking natural cover where it could be found. The Pima moved forward on both flanks, Black Thorn leading the left with Hawk, Yellow Feather leading the right, each warrior tucked behind his kawad. Coro held the center of the Pima line with five warriors in the rear, presenting the Apache few targets of opportunity.

The first Apache arrows arched, testing their range. These fell short, inviting the Apache to continue their advance. Black Thorn and Yellow Feather halted their advances on the flanks, drawing little in the way of Apache arrows and defending those they did with kawad. To the south Coro and his men withdrew a short distance.

Sensing weakness, Captocari quickened the pace of his advance, leaving two warriors, one to each flank, to cover Black Thorn and Yellow Feather's advances. Yellow Feather judged the Apache advance from the right, biding his time. His dove call signaled Black Thorn. Arrows let fly. The Apache rear guard on the west went down. The first arrow on the guard to the east missed. A second, long shot from the west took him down. Black Thorn and Yellow Feather turned on the rear of the Apache advance. They crouched low, moving in a zigzag pattern, positioning for shots at good targets.

Warrior pride filled Hawk's heart as they closed on the hated Apache. He nocked an arrow, reckoning the length of his shot, drop, and windage. He drew careful aim and let fly. The arrow flew true, arcing to bury in the back of the neck of an unsuspecting target. Hawk followed his flight with a triumphal whoop.

Captocari recognized his peril the moment the warrior beside him fell, round-eyed at the arrowhead struck through his throat. In an instant he sensed danger on two sides. He ordered two warriors to attack the rear.

Coro and his men struck from the center, closing the trap. Pima arrows rained on the Apache, unable to staunch attacks, entrapped on three sides. Kawad did their work in traditional Pima defense. Apache fell. Their numbers dwindled, five to four, three to two, and one. Captocari dropped his weapons and stood. Coxi sent his men forward. Stones did their work. Battered and blooded the Apache war leader died.

Ndolkah Sid and his band abandoned the east valley wall, running north to safety in the mountains. Coro and his band gave chase, joined by his victorious champions. More Apache were taken in flight. Twelve warriors were added to the vanquished ten, twenty-two killed and counted by notching a lance. This they would present to the soldado capitán as proof of Pima retribution. They tracked the Apache to Ndolkah Sid's mountain village. This they overran, though Scar escaped along with a few of his warriors and wives. The victorious Pima liberated Sobaipuris captives for return to Cocospora. Coro sent a runner with the notched lance to bring word of great victory.

Mission Dolores

The runner brought the notched lance and word of Pima victory. We mourned the loss of life though accepted it as necessary to exonerate our people. Manje sent the lance to Capitán Bernal at Bacanuche. Within days Coxi and the Cosari warriors returned. Coro and his people along with the rescued Sobaipuris returned to their village. Early in September we were visited once again by Capitán Bernal. We summoned Coxi, Black Thorn, and Yellow Feather to the mission plaza.

"What is it now, Padre?" Coxi asked.

"The capitán has questions concerning your defeat of the Apache."

Coxi shrugged. "What does he wish to know?"

I translated for the capitán.

"Am I to believe the Apache were defeated because of notches on a lance?"

"Coxi, tell the capitán of your battle with the Apache."

Coxi retold the events of the battle of champions, pursuit of the vanquished, and liberation of the Sobaipuris captives. Bernal listened as I translated.

"We have all this on Coxi's word? He tells us Coro and his warriors are innocent of these crimes by telling us they exacted retribution on Apache who are guilty. His word and this spear are all we have."

"Coxi is an honorable man. I trust him at his word."

"I must tell you, Padre, I do not share your belief in mere words."

"What then might convince you?"

"More witnesses and evidence."

"Then, Capitán, you shall have both in due course. Join us in Remedios the end of the month. We are dedicating a new statue there for their chapel. You can join the festivities and receive ample proof all in one joyous occasion."

Capitán Bernal's stubborn disbelief of our Pima troubled me. The Pima embraced our teaching the faith. Why would royal authority fail to acknowledge goodness in that? I broached the subject with Mateo soon after the capitán's departure.

"It is the nature of military men to be distrustful, Padre. We are trained to deal with treachery and so we come to expect it."

"How do we persuade the capitán our people speak the truth?"

"Proof. We must show him proof."

"Very well then, with your help we shall show him proof."

Coxi sent a runner to Coro inviting him to fiesta de los Remedios and requesting he bring any booty or spoils taken from the Apache as proof of their victory for the Spanish capitán. Similar invitations were sent to surrounding dignitaries and headmen including the liberated Cocospora captives.

Accompanied by Black Thorn and Yellow Feather, Coxi guided Mateo, Abel, and me north to the scene of the battle. We searched the grassy river valley for the remains of the fallen. Scavengers had done their work, though weapons and relics found there attested to the battle of champions Coxi described.

We rode on following the Apache trail fleeing into the mountains, finding evidence of pursuit. Mateo drew us to a halt.

"I have seen enough, Padre. I can tell Capitán Bernal the fighting took place as Coxi described."

"There is more," Coxi said.

Manje shook his head. "There is no need to climb further into these mountains. This is Apacheria. They were defeated, not vanquished. We are unprepared to meet them in force should they seek reprisal against us."

"Mateo speaks wisely," I said.

With that we returned to Mission Dolores. There we found Coro arrived with Apache scalps. A Sobaipuris girl arrived a few days later. She spoke of her Apache captivity and the Pima sacking of the Apache village to free her. With all in readiness we departed for fiesta.

Remedios
September 30, 1698
Dignitaries gathered from across Pimeria Alta. Caciques Coro and Coxi were joined by Humari of Ojio and Cola de Pato come from San Xavier del Baac. Capitán Bernal came for proof of Pima victory over the Apache, accompanied by none other than General Jironza himself. Capitán Manje saw to it Spanish officials too were present to

witness our Pima exonerated of Apache misdeeds. Coro and Coxi were most pleased to show them plunder taken in battle. Mateo made his report on inspecting the battlefield and evidence of pursuit. The Sobaipuris girl, shy in the presence of so auspicious an assembly, managed to convey enough of her story to satisfy the general. There being then no need to further convince our skeptical capitán.

We dedicated and blessed a magnificent statue of Saint Joseph by celebration of the Holy Sacrifice of the Mass. The afternoon and evening passed in joyous fellowship where the peaceful friendship among the people of Pimeria Alta were on full display for all authorities to see. In an atmosphere of fiesta, much goodwill was exchanged on all sides, furthering the cause of peace between our clans and their Spanish neighbors.

CHAPTER FORTY-THREE

Dolores
October 1698
While at the celebration of dedication at de los Remedios, I received instruction from General Jironza, encouraging me to further exploration west to the lower reaches of Rio Colorado and Sea of California coastal regions. With California mission now opened by the heroic ministry of my compadre Juan Maria Salvatierra, may God assist him in his holy work, it was time to determine at last a land route to California should there be one. Upon our return, Mateo and I engaged in planning for just such an exploration. By the end of the month, we were ready to depart.

Journal Entry
November 1698
We departed Dolores with the coming of November, in company with Capitán Manje

and Coxi with Black Thorn, Yellow Feather, and Hawk acting as scouts. We traveled north from Remedios, taking respites of hospitality among friends at Cocospora, Quiburi, and Ojio, following the San Pedro River to confluence with Hila Rio Grande. There we turned west on the longest westward exploration of this region. We did this in the belief this river emptied into the Sea of California. Along the way we passed through Cocomaricopa lands where we were greeted with good grace and hospitality. What we came to was yet another confluence. Hila Rio Grande joined Rio Colorado flowing south.

We traveled south to the village of Sonita. From there we rode west a few leagues further to an inactive volcano we were able to climb. There we observed Rio Colorado empty into Sea of California in the distance. The sea appeared to narrow there, though no land route to California could be seen from the vantage we held. I made our position to be somewhere between thirty-two and thirty-three degrees, north latitude. Having mapped our journey and recorded our findings we turned east by way of return.

We crossed vast desert, harsh road we would come to know as Camino del Diablo,

Devils Road. We reached Adid, great village of the Papago people, where we were happily received. We continued east, pausing to rest and resupply at Caborca. We returned to Cosari by way of Tubutama, Magdalena, and San Ignacio in time to celebrate Christmas.

Dolores
January 1699
I invited the good Capitán Manje to sup of a winter's evening. Later we spread my maps of Pimeria Alta on the rough-hewn table, serving all my simple purposes. By the warmth and light of a fragrant mesquite fire, we discussed exploration and mission building plans for the coming season. As always California begged my attention. Attention yes, but the island itself, unattainable to me it seemed. It was Mateo who suggested a new course.

"Padre, I know your passion for California. The difficulties there are a frustration. Yet we know there is much to be gained west and north of Rio Colorado to the Hila Rio Grande. Still further exploration remains to the Sea of California shore. Territory and riches are there for the crown with a bountiful harvest of souls for Holy Mother Church."

I prayerfully pondered his recommendation. Perhaps my yearning for California was little more than the need of new challenge. Mission Dolores prospered. The people of Cosari embraced the faith. I was their pastor; but another could fulfill these needs. I heard my calling to open new mission fields for Christ. I had been blessed to discover ways to align the faith with the customs of new flocks. These blessings, I felt, called to use for the ever-widening propagation of the faith.

"What do you suggest, my son?"

"We have visited Papago and Cocomaricopa people in the west. I hear reports of Yuma further south. Such a mission would extend the reach of our holy faith with an exploration to please the viceroy and your humble servant's superiors."

I smiled. Mateo too mastered the art of aligning ecclesiastical and royal purposes. "You have thought this through well, Mateo. I shall pray over it the more. With God's blessing it may please him to see this as you do."

And so, Mateo and I determined to extend our exploration to the shores of the Sea of California. This time we would take advantage of cooler winter season to cross Camino del Diablo to the sea and return by northerly route along Rio Colorado and Hila Rio Grande.

Journal Entry
February 7, 1699
Mateo and I departed on an exploration of more than two hundred leagues accompanied by Pima scouts Black Thorn and Yellow Feather. Abel sent vaqueros to manage our remount remuda and packtrain. We crossed the sierra to San Ignacio to spend a pleasant evening.

Whispers
He goes again. The Grande, gallivanting hither, thither, and yon. He leaves his flock to draw maps and gaze at the stars. All in the name of a dream called California. A dream given to others. He has no part in it, yet he justifies all this to mission, baptizing infants and those infirmed by illness. Catechesis to the faith? Faith has little time or place in this journeying. The prize here can only be seen for opportunity to personal glory. What of poverty and obedience? Once vows.

M.

Days passed pleasantly, sunny and cool save for the occasional shower to freshen the air and send the desert into bloom. As we traveled, we encountered villages of various sizes and clans. These welcomed us with hospitality ever curious over our horses and mules. We were treated to the fruits of their produce; in return, we offered instruction in the Good News of Jesus Christ. Many souls came forward to seek baptism.

In the evening, Mateo and I shared a campfire. We passed peaceful evenings around the fire, he with a favored book of poetry, me with the psalms and seasonal reflections of my daily Holy Office. It was on one such evening two days' west of Magdalena, the remuda became restless, stomping, nickering, straining picket ropes, eyes wide, ears laid back.

One of the vaqueros galloped into our circle of firelight. His mount danced an agitated circle, wide eyed.

"Capitán, lion!" He pointed to the darkness in the direction of the herd.

Mateo leaped to his feet; priming his arquebus, he followed the vaquero into the night. I followed concerned the vaqueros in as much peril as the stock.

Along the picket line vaqueros sought in vain to calm frightened animals. A thick cloud of dust rose from so many hooves, hanging in the air, to draw a curtain over starlight and moonrise. Mateo moved in dark shadow beneath a rock outcropping and cottonwood canopy overhead. I followed, breath caught in my throat.

The prowling cat's shriek clawed raw fear at my breast. I said a short prayer for Mateo and listened. He moved cautiously. The cat lurked unseen, its presence only a sense of foreboding. I imagined it crouched, ready to spring on the unwary. Later I could not recall why, my eyes were drawn up to a dark ledge above. Starlight peeked through the trees here and there. There. There I caught light, two eyes.

"Mateo!"

"Sí, Padre," hushed out of the darkness.

I pointed up. "Look."

"There! I see."

Soft light betrayed a shadow out of place. Mateo took aim. One shot. The arquebus flared powder flash and charge. The great cat shrieked a death throe, falling heavily through the branches of a tree. It staggered to its paws, lunged clumsily, collapsed, and lay still. I crossed myself in thanksgiving.

In time horses and mules quieted. Mateo and I returned to our fire.

"How did you see him, Padre?"

I shrugged. "I looked up. Starlight lit his eyes."

"What made you think to look up?"

"I can't say."

"Fortunate. A cat that size might kill a man with but the strike of one paw."

"Fortune or providence, my son?"

"Sí, Padre. For you, providence."

"And for you also, my son. A single shot."

We reached Tubutama without further incident. Rested there and traveled onward to Caborca. Here again we took respite before undertaking Camino del Diablo for the desert crossing to Sonita. Crossing in winter, though still difficult, proved less so for man and beast alike. We were able to make the crossing at a faster pace than that permitted by desert heat. Still Sonita offered welcome respite on our arrival there.

We paused once again to refresh ourselves of the rigors of desert crossing. A devil's road to salvation. The irony would be amusing were conditions not so harsh. We did not tarry long before continuing southwest to the banks of Rio Colorado.

Nearing the river, we were met by giants, five in number. The largest Indio I had ever encountered. Black Thorn stepped forward anticipating the need of an interpreter. I gave him an inquiring look.

"Yuma," he said.

"Bid them welcome."

He did to my welcoming smile. We dismounted, inviting them to join us. I presented them with the small wooden crosses, symbolic of mission, assuring them we came in peace. This they expected having heard much of the work of the black robes. They invited us to visit their village in the valley of the Rio Colorado.

We followed our guides, two leagues to the village, where we were greeted with a joy and affection. A feast was held in our honor at which gifts were exchanged. For our part, we received beautiful blue shells of the sort I remembered finding in California on the shore of the great western sea. Curious to find them here, I inquired through Black Thorn if they might be found along the banks of the river. In reply our hosts only laughed.

The next day Yuma guides led us south along the river to a marshy delta at the mouth of the Sea of California. There Mateo and I saw California on the horizon, though nearer than previous observations.

We returned to the village that night. The following morning with pledges of friendship and promises to return, we departed north along Rio Colorado. We reached the

Cocomaricopa village of San Andres near the confluence of the Hila Rio Grande, and there, spent a pleasant few days with our friends, offering instruction in the faith and baptism to infants and those suffering illness. After a long evening of instruction Mateo and I retired to our blankets for much needed rest.

"Padre, I am curious."

"How so, my son?"

"Why I never asked this before I don't know; out here on the frontier, you give instruction, but baptize only infants and those in danger of death. Why?"

"We have no ministry to offer these faithful. They have no mass, no sacraments with which to practice the faith. It is my prayer the infants will have ministry in time. Those at death's door deserve all we can give of salvation."

"Ah, now I see. Good night, Padre."

"Good night, Mateo."

Before departing, I showed the Cocomaricopa blue shells given us by the Yuma. I inquired as to where they might come from. They greeted my query with a shrug. The shells pecked at my thoughts, like specks on a map not yet drawn complete.

In the days that followed we retraced our first journey, stopping at San Xavier del

Baac before turning south along the Rio San Pedro to Ojio, Quiburi, Remedios, and at long last Dolores.

CHAPTER FORTY-FOUR

Cosari
April 1699

Hawk returned from Apacheria a respected warrior in the full vigor of manhood. His return was greeted by yet another measure of manhood. Fawn announced she carried his son. Joy filled their olas kih with warmth through the long moons of winter that followed. Early spring found her great with child. Sweet Grass made ready to assist when her daughter's time drew near.

At the appointed time, Hawk left birthing work to the women and climbed into the hills in quest of a name for his son much as his father once sought his name. He retraced the trail he remembered from the earliest days of his warrior training with sling and bow. At the trail summit he sat on a large flat rock at the mouth of a cave where he might observe the valley and hills below. Warm sun washed a soft breeze over his skin, drying the droplets of perspiration there. He waited for a spirit to speak a name for his son. Hours passed. The sun drifted toward shadowed peaks in the west.

Something moved through sage and creosote bushes below. Slowly, cautiously, testing the breeze for any scent of danger. She poked her head out, nose and eyes alert. A red fox. A good omen. Satisfied the way was safe she trotted off to a cistern hidden in the rocks. Five, young kit scampered and tumbled after her. Red Fox Kit for a milk name, Red Fox for a warrior. Hawk smiled. He watched mother drink her fill and nurse her young beside the pool. The sun touched the tallest peak in the west wind. Time to return to the village.

Sweet Grass smiled as he trotted into the village.

"You have son, Hawk."

"And Fawn?"

"She rests. Birthing was hard as first births often are. She does well, though she is tired. It will cheer her eyes to see you. Go to her."

The olas kih was warm with scent of sweat and blood and sweet with the sight of a tiny round bundle at Fawn's breast. She smiled.

"You have a strong son."

He knelt beside her. "You have done well."

"Did your spirit search find a name?"

"Red Fox Kit is his milk name," he said with a nod. "Red Fox his warrior name."

"Kit, I like it. Padre will want a baptism name for him. Did the spirit speak to you of this?"

"No. What do you think?"

"I think Padre can help."

Mission Dolores

Three days later Hawk and Fawn presented little Red Fox Kit at the mission. We discussed the need of a Christian name and prayed over it. We listened. I heard, Joseph.

"What would you say to Joseph?"

Hawk looked to Fawn. She nodded.

"It is a strong name."

Hawk nodded.

We baptized the babe Joseph Red Fox. He would be known thereafter as Kit, until the days warrior training conferred manhood on him.

Baptism, the rite of Christian initiation, never failed to impress its power upon me. Baptism joins the faithful to Christ in death to sin and a share in his resurrection. In this baptism, as in all the baptisms since we first withdrew our mission to California, the souls of all those there to be saved cried out to me with every sunset. The difficulty of sustaining meaningful California mission continued to thwart us even with the support of new barca. We believed the barca to be the answer. The vagaries of weather and sea remained difficult. Yet I believed in my heart and in my prayers, there must be a way. Once again, I was to be reminded, the Lord works, we are but instruments he chooses when it suits his purpose. His messenger would find us with the answer in his own good time.

Remedios
March 20, 1700
On one of my scheduled circuit rides to Remedios I received an emissary from the Cocomaricopa cacique we visited the previous year. He came bearing yet another request for mission at San Andres along with a gift of blue shells. Curious. An unknowing shrug becomes a gift in the span of but a year. Another speck to pick at my thoughts. What could possibly connect the western California great seashore with those who inhabited the valleys of Rio Colorado? Were the shells common to other regions? Did they travel by sea in trade among the Indio? Or could there be . . . I wondered. The mystery sang its siren song in my thoughts and in my prayers, hoping against hope we might find

some sustainable passage to mission in California. Find it too in time to support Juan Maria's continued mission there.

Dolores

On my return from Remedios, I took quill in hand, laying out the puzzle of the blue shells in letters to Father Visitor Padre Antonio Lael, my brother Juan Maria Salvatierra, and General Jironza at Bacanuche. To each I posed the question of the blue shell's origin and the mysterious connection that may exist to the great western Sea of California. Replies were promptly received from Father Visitor and our provincial governor general. Both urged continued exploration for the possibility of discovering a land passage to California. I had no need to wait for Juan Maria's response. I could have written it for him.

San Xavier del Baac
April 21, 1700

More than three thousand Sobaipuris souls welcomed us to San Xavier del Baac. In the days that followed we busied ourselves, laying foundation for a capacious church with the help of our Sobaipuris brothers and sisters. Abel and his vaqueros bedded a herd in new pastures, acclimating Sobaipuris vaqueros to care for the herd. I must say here, I developed deep affection for the people at Baac. If California were not to be given to my ministry, I prayed over the possibility of moving here to a field more in need of conversion.

During these days of laying foundation for mission, I dispatched messengers to the north, south along the San Pedro River Valley village, and west to villages along the Hila Rio Grande as far west as Casa Grande, making inquiry as to the origin of the blue shells. In ensuing days, word returned from these messengers. All agreed the blue shells were unknown to them. This left me to conclude they must be found in the more southerly regions of Rio Colorado, inhabited by the mighty Yuma. This Mateo and I discussed at length.

"For all our explorations of the Sea of California, Padre, we saw no evidence of shells such as we observed on the western coast of California. It is clear from the reports we have received these blue shells are most uncommon."

"Sí, my son. And yet by some means they have come into the possession of people in the southern regions of Rio Colorado."

"Do you suppose they are to be found along Rio Colorado?"

I pondered this possibility. "I think not. How do you explain such vivid color attained in fresh water? We have no evidence of them being found anywhere but the shores of the great salt sea. Intuitively their origin argues for the source where we first found them."

"If that is so, they can only have traveled by trade."

"Which begs the question, how did the traders travel, by sea or by land?"

"Then if we are to reward the viceroy and your superiors with a land passage to California, the blue shells point to an exploration west and south from Rio Colorado."

I nodded. "It would seem so, my son. It would seem so."

Here I was again torn by the tug of mapmaking and exploration pulling me away from my mission. I wanted the church built at San Xavier del Baac. I had come to believe Mission Dolores served the spiritual needs of the Cosari Pima. The time had come for new pastoral leadership there. I planned to petition Father Provincial to assign someone to Mission Dolores and allow me to move here with our Sobaipuris flock. Having a church built could only strengthen my petition. Exploration served to further delay continuation of my ministry. Still, I knew California for a harvest of souls worthy the price. A land route, should the Lord so favor us, would make it sustainable.

"When might we undertake such an exploration, Padre?"

Mateo, ever the pragmatist. "Perhaps in the fall, my son. First I must return to Mission Dolores and report our progress here to Father Provincial."

Mateo cocked an eye, as though he might be reading my thoughts. I could only smile.

Mission Dolores

Upon our return in May, I set quill to vellum once again to report progress of our mission at San Xavier del Baac.

Most Excellent Reverence Father Provincial,

Greetings from Mission Dolores and your most humble servant.

It is in the joy of our Most Holy Savior, Jesus Christ, I bring you news of our mission at San Xavier del Baac. We serve there three thousand Sobaipuris souls, many of whom have embraced the baptism of our faith. Foundations have been laid for a church to serve the spiritual needs of our flock. They have only need of a priest to guide the people in finishing construction. I shall return to the subject in due course.

We have introduced cattle, horses, sheep, and wheat cultivation to augment the produce of farming for food. As in our other missions all these provide for the temporal needs of our children, giving them food, trade goods, and domestics to lighten the burden of their labors.

You have no doubt taken notice of the beautiful and most unusual blue shells that accompany this letter. These were given me as a gift from Cocomaricopa people known to inhabit the western reaches of Rio Colorado. We have also seen them in the possession of Yuma people in the southern reaches of Rio Colorado. Capitán Juan Mateo Manje and I have seen shells like these before. Sixteen years ago, we found similar shells on the western sea-coast of California. We have seen nothing like them anywhere else, even along the coasts of the Sea of California. It leads us to wonder if a land route to California might exist further to the west and south. With your blessing, Capitán Manje and I propose to undertake such an exploration. It may by God's grace open sustainable roadway to our California missions.

By your leave, I pray one final matter of a personal nature before I close. Mission Dolores and these Cosari Pima are filled with the Holy Spirit. They are ready for new pastoral leadership. If it be with your blessing, Most Reverend Father Provincial, I pray a replacement might be assigned for me here. I wish to go to San Xavier del Baac to finish the work of mission begun there.

In this I remain your most
obedient servant in Christ,
Eusebio Francisco Kino S.J.

CHAPTER FORTY-FIVE

Journal Entry
September 24, 1700
We began our explorations in search of an overland route to California in earnest that fall. We departed Mission Dolores by a northwesterly route to the Papago village of Merced. Black Thorn and Hawk accompanied me, Black Thorn to act as scout and interpreter with Hawk to manage a small string of pack mules and remounts. From Merced we continued northwest to visit the Cocomaricopa, from whom we recently received the gift of blue shell, giving purpose to this journey. We arrived at the Village of San Pedro October 6th.

We were gratified by the warmth, generosity, and joy with which our children there greeted us. It called for celebration. We were feted to a feast of fish and fresh viands to slack our hunger and thirst. In turn, we preached the word of God to them, baptizing infants and those suffering illness.

We were next joined by visiting Yuma, who by appearance and customs evoked resemblance of the Didius people we remembered from San Bruno so many years ago. Knowing the purpose of our exploration, they offered to guide us further south and west the following day. Their generous gesture and assistance would prove immensely useful to our purpose.

October 7, 1700

The day dawned clear and bright. We set off soon after first light. Our guides led us two leagues west before turning south three leagues. Sparse desert vegetation of the species we observed in California dotted the landscape. At midday we reached a mount we were able to climb. There we took sightings visual, telescopic, and by use of the astrolabe. At thirty-two degrees north latitude we found our position not far north of the position where we first encountered blue shells on the shore of the great western sea. We searched for sign of the California Sea. We saw none. Continuous land mass stretched south and west as far as horizon could be seen.

Never has sighting so little revealed a discovery of such momentous import.

There, before our very eyes, lay no less than the long-sought road to California. I gave my thanksgiving in prayer. By the vision of that road, one day we would drive herds, produce, and material to sustain California missions. I savored the moment. So long no more than a hope, a dream now seen, come to be true.

We took our midday meal and rest, though I confess I rested little, preferring to drink the vistas as long as I might. News of this discovery descended with an urgency to hasten our return to Dolores. We returned to San Pedro and provisioned for our return by way of Camino del Diablo.

Over the course of our return journey, I began sketching and noting the significant changes our discovery would make to our mapped understanding of the land called California. One of the first practical insights captured the importance of Sonita to the future of a California road. Sonita must be developed as a mission rancheria to serve as an oasis on Camino del Diablo. Such an important road cast in the name of the devil gave me pause. It struck me, aptly named for the perils of passage. Yet a road to mission named for Satan seemed albeit sacrilegious. Then, on the chance it should irritate old Beelzebub, I found amusement in it.

We traveled swiftly after Sonita through Tubutama to San Ignacio.

San Ignacio

We were warmly welcomed by Padre Augustin de Campos, who greeted news of a California road with great joy.

"Eusebio, I know how long you have dreamed of this possibility. I could not be happier for you and the future it portends for the Lord's work."

"It is all of that, though my part may be no more than finding the way."

He smiled. "Still in your blood, is it?"

"I confess, though I am reconciled it is not a field to be given me."

"We can pray then for your California intentions and celebrate opening the way."

"What news have you from Dolores?"

"All is well. You have accomplished much both there and at Remedios."

"So much remains to be done. Too much to indulge contentment."

"You have been tireless in your work. What more could anyone ask?"

"As a friend, Augustin, I am ready for a new challenge even if it is not to be California."

"Oh, and where might that be?"

"Our mission at San Xavier del Baac needs me."

"Have you petitioned Father Provincial?"

I nodded. "I've heard nothing."

"You know Eusebio, you have done so much for the Cosari Pima at Dolores; not to mention your tireless service to the crown in your many explorations. I wonder, is it time for a new beginning so large as del Baac? Could it be Father Provincial's silence begs a similar question?"

I let his question hang on the desert breeze. I felt it in my bones. We ignore the passage of time until we can no longer. Augustin held up my reflection in his words. Still there is much to do. I may be an old champion of the faith, but I remain a champion still.

"Age is my constant companion, Augustin. I know this. Still, I see so much more to be done."

"The harvest is bountiful, Eusebio. It will always be so."

"But the laborers are few."

"Regrettably, but a laborer who might replace you might also find his fields and flock in a new undertaking."

"A laborer who is younger."

"A laborer who has much to achieve to reach the half-measure of all you have accomplished."

"You are too kind. I only hope Father Provincial will prayerfully consider my request. I feel I belong to work we have only just begun."

"I'm sure Father Provincial prayerfully considers every request."

Augustin's assurance along with Father Provincial's lack of response, perhaps provided all the response I should require.

Mission Dolores

Upon my return I again wrote his Most Reverend Father Provincial to report our successful exploration and discovery, by providential favor, evidence of a land route to California. I wrote similar letters to Father Leal, Juan Maria Salvtierra, Mateo, and General Jironza. In Reverend Father Provincial's letter, I presumed to inquire again concerning prospects for my assignment to the Sobaipuris at San Xavier del Baac. In this I was not rewarded by the letter I received from Father Provincial the following February.

CHAPTER FORTY-SIX

Whispers

Triumphant he returns! All hail the con-
quering hero! Explorer, discoverer of El
Camino de California. All accolades be
showered upon him. He wanders the
continent far and wide, neglecting the flock
given to his care. And what comes of it?
Encouragement to still further exploration.
Who could possibly compare? Whose
shadow, could be cast so long? None.

M.

Dolores

As my sixtieth year approached, I was
forced to admit the strain of these last
explorations. Much of the vigor of my
younger years long since spent. Even Damascus advanced in years beyond this most
recent exploration. He needed a quiet
pasture even if I denied a similar need of
my own. It was a bittersweet moment when

I led him to a lush green pasture. He seemed to sense it when I released him of his halter. He nuzzled me as I stroked his nose. We traveled countless leagues together on the road to conversion. How many souls had his strong back borne me to? He was my constant companion in all my journeying these past seventeen years. Seventeen years. Hard to believe. Where have they gone?

"It is time, old friend."

He tossed his head, flared his nostrils the way he did whenever we were to depart on some new adventure. He picked up his familiar gait to well-deserved rest. I wiped something moist from my eye, wondering what might become of my halter.

Retiring Damascus presented an immediate need. My circuit rides would continue and so would the prospect of further California exploration. I consulted Abel, who by his work with the herds had become expert as stockman. He smiled as I approached, having guessed my purpose, I suspect.

"Good morning, Padre. How may I be of service?"

I returned his smile. "I suspect you already know."

"Sí. But first I must tell you, there is only

one Damascus."

"This I know. I was a younger man when I claimed him. We've grown old together."

"Good. You still need a sturdy mount, reliable with endurance to travel great distance."

I nodded.

"I think then I have just what you need. Come."

He led the way to a corral where working stock browsed hay in a manger. He took a halter from a fence post at the gate and entered. He crossed the corral, rounding the manger out of sight. I waited. He reemerged, leading a buckskin mule with four black stockings, black mane and tail, through the gate.

"A mule? Am I that old, my son?"

"She is the sweetest jenny, gifted an easy gait under saddle."

I stroked her velvet muzzle. She regarded me with large brown eyes, ears twitching.

"You will not be disappointed, Padre. Let me saddle her so you may get acquainted."

He did, handing me the reins.

"How is she called?"

"Willow."

"It suits her, though if she is to undertake me as a burden, I shall call her Elizabeth."

"Elizabeth?"

"She bore a Baptist late in life." I stepped into the saddle, squeezing her into an easy trot west.

Responses to my letters announcing El Camino de California were of one accord. Reverend Father Provincial, Juan Maria, Mateo, and General Jironza all stated further exploration was needed to map a route serving Salvatierra's mission at Loreto. Juan Maria saw this as of such importance, he would personally join the exploration.

Dolores
February 1701
Juan Maria reached us in February to a celebratory welcome. Preparations for new exploration complicated when Apache raiders descended on Pimeria Alta. Mateo and his garrison responded to an attack at Cucurpe. I took precaution to visit Remedios and Cocospora to inspect defensive preparations against the risk of attack. Salvatierra rode west, crossing the sierra to San Ignacio where he was welcomed by Augustin. Manje joined him there for the journey to Tubutama. They descended the Altar River to Caborca, there to await my arrival.

■ ■ ■ ■

Journal Entry
March 9, 1701

We departed Caborca for Sonita, a distance of some thirty-three leagues. Spring arrives early in the desert. Rains bring the desert into bloom. A riot of colorful floral display flavored the air with a sweetness to refresh the taste of dust.

Our second day on the trail we were approached by an Indio offering a calabash of water in trade. We traded for some beads. We asked where the water came from. A spring he claimed, far away. I offered more beads for more. He ran off, returning too soon for far away. Mateo followed his trail to a nearby spring where water was plentiful. We replenished our water supply and watered our animals, marking an important oasis on the road to Sonita.

Sonita

We reached this important way station three days later. Crossing here we faced the difficult test. North led to the Cocomaricopa before turning south. Camino del Diablo led west to the Yuma. South skirted the ancient volcano Cerro de Santa Clara, from

383

which I made observation on my earlier exploration. We debated the choices, settling on the southerly route of my experience.

Journal Entry

We departed Sonita ten leagues south along the Sonita River to an impoverished village where baptism was given to a dying old woman. Southwest another five leagues brought us to a village served ample water by a natural cistern. Again, the village was marked for promise of a mission rancheria, an important stop on Camino de California.

We celebrated Palm Sunday the following day, departing west along the southern foot of the old volcano. Jagged, rocky terrain traversed black remains of long-ago lava flows devoid of meaningful vegetation. Six leagues west of Cerro de Santa Clara we came upon a rainwater cistern in a boulder strewn arroyo we christened El Tupo. There I climbed a low ridge to a vantage with vistas south and west. The way ahead rolled in windswept sand dunes.

I expressed concern for the difficulty of the passage before us. At Mateo's suggestion, we left the packtrain in the safety of ample water. We made a crossing of eight leagues on March twenty-first, reaching the confluence of three streams with browse for the horses and my Elizabeth, who was proving on the trail to be all Abel promised. There we camped for the night.

Judging distance to the sierra visible in the west and convinced we had entered California, we explored southeasterly expecting to reach the seashore. We searched the beach for blue shells and were rewarded to find none, affirming belief they came from the shores of the great western sea beyond the sierra.

At dawn the next day, Holy Thursday, Juan Maria and I took our morning prayers to the seashore. There we witnessed the sun rise in the east over the sea. We embraced at the celestial blessing. The Sea of California is but a gulf.

Energized by discovery, we continued south along the shore ten leagues. In the onset of a golden twilight, we saw smoke sign rising from the beach.

Sunrise Good Friday revealed a curious crowd of Indio come down to the beach to observe the intruders. Mateo and your most humble servant, recognizing them as Yuma, were minded of the people we encountered on our earlier California explorations. I recalled the gentle souls we encountered at San Isidro on our second mission to California. Juan Maria too confirmed them for Californians.

Canoes lay overturned on the shore, drying nets and baskets serviceable to fishermen. Men clad in woven breechclouts awaited us armed with bows and arrows, spears and stone clubs. The absence of women and children bespoke uncertainty and caution.

Juan Maria spoke peace in a tongue close enough to their own native language for comprehension. The headman, Otter, stepped forward. Juan Maria introduced himself, Mateo, and me. With all peaceful intentions established we were greeted warmly. The headman invited us to visit their village.

We were led to a small village in the hills not far from the shore. There we found thatched lodges, similar to Pima olas kih. People of simple souls, as have haunted my call to mission since first I set foot in California, awaited us there. Naked children paused at their play to gape in wide-eyed curiosity at the black-robed strangers come into their midst. Women, quiet and shy, clothed in woven skirts and soft smiles waited to see what might come of these strange intruders. Otter invited us to his lodge fire for an evening meal of dried fish, corn cakes, and beans. We spoke, with Juan Maria translating in a dialect sufficiently comprehensible.

"Why does the black robe come to California?"

"To bring the good news of the Most High's Son to the Yuma people with his blessings and assistance in living."

He puzzled at this. "Yuma do not know this Most High or his Son."

"That is the good news we shall speak of in due course."

I took a bite of fish. "This fish is very good. Did you catch it today?"

Otter shook his head. "Fishing is very bad. We are able to gather and grow some of our food needs, but fish are very important. For some time now, fishing has been poor. We fear some sea demon may have enchanted the schools away."

"Then perhaps that is why we are here."

"You can bring back the fish?"

"The Son of the Most High had friends who were fishermen. Peter, Andrew, James, and John too were discouraged by poor fishing. Jesus, he is the Son of the Most High, helped them catch fish and made them fishers of men. Perhaps that is why we are here. Tomorrow, Jesus will fish with you."

Juan Maria hesitated to translate, his

glance asking, *Are you sure, Eusebio?*
"He will. You shall see."

CHAPTER FORTY-SEVEN

Holy Saturday we woke to a leaden sky. I offered my morning prayers, chastened by the impertinence of my supplication. I didn't ask for fish so plentiful nets might burst or risk boats sinking as Jesus blessed Peter and Andrew in the Gospel story. That catch so bountiful James and John were needed come to their aid. I merely asked for a catch, I thought it reasonable, in Jesus's name.

We made our way down to the beach with the fishermen, who put out to sea in their canoes. Mateo, Juan Maria, and I followed in a canoe provided for our use. I stationed myself in the bow. When the fishermen lowered their nets, I stretched my arms over the sea, holding a cross for all to see. Otter and his men gazed at me with undisguised curiosity.

The moment passed in a blink as the nets called their attention. My prayer turned to one of thanksgiving as the nets were drawn up with the catch. They lowered the nets again and again. Three catches filled the canoes. The exhausted fishermen turned to me open-mouthed. I offered a blessing and took up my paddle, returning to shore.

There on the beach, I opened the Holy Bible to Luke chapter five and read the story of the fishermen's catch. All listened as Juan Maria translated. At the point in the story where their nets were filled to bursting the men began to exchange glances, hearing their own story come forth from the pages of this mysterious black book. I took the moment to conclude.

"Brother fishermen, invite all your people to embrace faith in Jesus Christ by the holy sacrament of baptism."

Otter stepped forward to speak with Juan Maria.

"He wishes this baptism," Juan Maria said.

That night we feasted on a bountiful catch. I offered my prayers in thanksgiving. That day the fishermen caught fish and the fishers of men caught souls. I felt the Lord's blessing on the work of a California mission. With the help of Mateo and his men we built a small chapel to celebrate Easter with the Holy Sacrifice of the Mass.

For the next several days we gave instruction to Otter and all those who sought baptism. With the headman and the men of the clan leading the way the harvest of souls drew women and children, matching the bounty of our first catch of fish.

During these days with our new flock, we made two discoveries that would serve us well in our further explorations. Several of the women and a few of the men wore amulets and adornments made from blue shells like those we found on our exploration to the great sea. The people spoke of neighbors to the south and west. The coincidence seemed to further confirm California a peninsula reaching the sea from the mainland.

Further to our belief we had indeed found a land route to California, we came upon trees and other vegetation mindful of those observed in our earlier California explorations. In this exploration, we descended a few leagues south of thirty-one degrees north latitude by my sightings of the astrolabe, reaching an area south of the northern gulf coast.

Thus, encouraged to our purpose, we returned to Mission Dolores by way of our missions, arriving after a fruitful year of exploration, rewarded for our holy quest with a land road to California mission.

Our return to El Tupo once again made difficult for crossing a sea of sand. We rested there making further observations before returning to Sonita. There we separated, Juan Maria returning south by way of Caborca. It was a moment of shared triumph and sorrow. Triumph at having the long-awaited celestial favor of a land route to California. Sorrow at the parting of dear friends. Juan Maria would return to continue the work of mission in California, while I returned to Pimeria Alta. I could not deny the part of me wishing I might join Juan Maria.

I tarried a few days, building a chapel and rudiments of mission, befitting Sonita's prominence to the future of El Camino de California. We departed northeast in early April through Papago, arriving at Dolores by way of San Xavier del Baac nine days later.

Mission Dolores

We received congratulatory letters and accolades from every level of royal and ecclesiastical authority. All were overjoyed at confirmed discovery of a land route to

California. For my part, I paid little attention to the notoriety, concentrating rather on documenting our discovery by drawing a new map and drafting a detailed report of observations in support of the peninsular confirmation of California.

The map and report were not without controversy. Many remained skeptical of findings in disagreement with prevailing belief, including even my friend Mateo Manje who pointed out significant unexplored reaches remained between thirty-one degrees north latitude and twenty-six degrees north latitude, the site of Juan Maria's mission at Loreto. This led Juan Maria to suggest yet another exploration would be needed. The vision for such an exploration would travel down the gulf coast all the way to Salvatierra's mission at Loreto.

Despite my burning desire to prove the naysayers wrong and our zeal to further mission for Holy Mother Church, support for the exploration fell victim to circumstances proven beyond our control. Laborers needed to harvest new mission fields were denied passage to New Spain by the winds of war.

CHAPTER FORTY-EIGHT

Remedios
1702

With westward exploration and expansion embargoed we turned our attentions to completion of churches at Remedios and Cocospora. With cattle and produce as trade goods, we were able to acquire needed material in addition to feeding and clothing the needs of our laborers. Willing workers came from as far as San Xavier del Baac, those led by no less than Cacique Coro himself.

Both churches were spacious, made of adobe brick, with chapels on either end of the transept. Both were finished with wooden floors and cupolas topping the roofs. Finished in time for Christmas we dedicated both the following January.

Whispers
Pima treachery again. Cola de Pato,

Cacique at San Xavier del Baac, and Coro plot to regain manhood as a warrior. Winds of rebellion foul the air. We should fear for the fate of Spanish settlements as well as the missions. The blood of Padre Saeta, God rest his soul, cries out in warning from the grave.

Z.

Mission Dolores
These rumors alarmed Father Visitor Antonio Leal, who wrote of his concern for our safety with a request for information. I saw no cause for alarm, past irritation with those who persisted in spreading calumnies against our people. I summoned Cacique Cola de Pato, who came at once with his sons. Together we rode to Cucurpe that all might be addressed to Father Visitor's satisfaction and the discredit of those wagging tongues.

Mission Dolores
May 1703
Father Provincial arrived for a visit in spring. He stayed with us a fortnight. It was then he offered answer to my requested relief in this ministry to the Cosari Pima.

"Eusebio, I am reminded I have not answered your request for assignment to

San Xavier del Baac. We needed the right time to have this discussion."

I knew his decision before he uttered it. It whispered to me ever after my discussion with Juan Maria on the trail to Sonita.

"As Paul has written in second Timothy, you have 'Poured out yourself like a libation' in this mission. You have accomplished more than any of us might have imagined possible. Your heavenly reward will be great and justly deserved.

"I will send you an assistant to succeed you here in this ministry, but it will not be to reassign you to San Xavier. It is time for you to enjoy the fruits of your labors. Care for your flock without the rigors of explorations and mappings and ranching. Do you see wisdom in this?"

I bowed my head in prayerful contemplation for a moment. "It matters less this old missionary sees wisdom in your words. It matters more he feel wisdom in them, and I do. Time passes. Age claims us all." I looked at my hands once more. Gnarled and spotted with age, they bore witness to all of it. "I understand."

March 1704
True to his word Reverend Father Provincial sent my replacement early the following

year. Reverend Father Louis Velarde, a Spaniard and member of our Company of Jesus, arrived to relieve me of the heavy burdens of ministry. I used the time following our return from California exploration to decide my future. We built a small home, a room really, off the church opposite the sacristy adjoining the sanctuary. Here I could spend my days in prayer and contemplation. Free of temporal obligations, I turned my life to the Spirit.

I was most pleased on meeting Padre Velarde. A kind man, warm and gentle, he would make a fine pastor to my Cosari Pima and a valued confessor to me. We spent the first month following his arrival visiting the surrounding missions to acquaint him with this Pimeria. With that accomplished, I retired to my refuge.

I furnished my room with a sleeping mat, one chair with a table and oil lamp for reading the holy office and scripture along with writing reflections on my ministerial journey. A small wooden kneeler stood beside the door to the sanctuary, always in the presence of the Blessed Sacrament. Meals I took in the rectory in company with Padre Velarde with whom I came to true friendship and affection. Here I passed my days in prayer and meditation, some of which I chose to record in a journal following all the entries made over the years of my priesthood.

Journal Entry
A Reflection

As I pass my days in meditation and prayer, I reflect on the journey that has led me here. I see it now marked out as paving stones on a path, uneven, irregular in shape. Stones laid in general direction, seldom a straight line. Stones paving a path we can't see, setting the course of our journey. As one attuned to plotting courses with great precision, I am minded the Lord's ways are not our ways. His paths are not our straight lines. We have only to follow where we are led.

In Hebrews 1:1 Paul tells us God speaks to us in "partial and various ways." Curious I find this insight in Paul. Still the paving stones of my journey have indeed come to me in partial and various ways. From illness to shipwreck, from continent to continent, from blue shells of discovery to this Pimeria and a road to further mission. We hear the word of God in partial and various ways. We hear the word by seeking, by searching and listening. Listening, that most excellent form of prayer. Listening to the Lord is true prayer. Prayer is not limited to recitation and petition. In listening we invite the Lord to speak to us. In listening we hear. In seeking we find.

Further to the paving stones of this journey, they lead to discipleship. They lead to the purposes God has set out for us on our journey. In fulfilling those purposes, we follow our Lord and Savior Jesus Christ. We know not where he might lead. We follow and accept the works entrusted to our care. In fulfilling God's purpose, we achieve the true measure of discipleship.

As I know the journey of blessed San Francisco Xavier, I see parallel opposites in my own. He journeyed to the east and ancient worlds. I to the west and new worlds. Always the word of God spreads. Much has been accomplished. Much remains to be done. San Francisco did not see his desired work completed in Cathay. I am not to taste fruits of the harvest of souls in California. Fittingly that mission passes to Juan Maria Salvatierri, may God speed him in his purpose. Like our patron, San Francisco who led those who followed to Cathay, I was given only to show the way others might follow to the dream that is California. I take comfort in knowing I have fulfilled the purpose for which I was called to become the instrument. That is enough.

Pimeria Alta
The Year of Our Lord 1711
I closed the journal. Contemplation and prayer. I supposed it true by some measure, but still work remained. There were two more journeys to the Gulf of California in 1706, building foundations for missions to the Cocomaricopa and Yuma people for whom we found great affection. For these journeys, Damascus gave way to a sweet-tempered, buckskin jenny mule, christened Elizabeth for John, a burden she bore well past her childbearing years. Another of Eusebio's biblical names sprinkled with a bit of irony.

In those years we married Abel to a Sobaipuris maiden he fell in love with while tending the herds at San Xavier del Baac. They live there now with a young girl child we baptized five years ago already. Hardly seems possible. Hawk succeeded Abel as head vaquero at Cosari. We said Requiem masses for Black Thorn, Rain, and Yellow Feather. Sweet Grass now lives in the olas kih of Hawk with Fawn and young Kit. Old Coxi remains Cacique, though in time many expect Hawk to follow him.

Tensions between ecclesiastical and royal authority did not abate with the passage of time. Always we found need to come to the defense of our flock. Away at the time, we suffered a rogue military raid at Cosari with the loss of stock and impressed servitude for some in our flock. Later we felt further distress from an unlikely source. Our companion and friend Juan Mateo Manje, now general, became an advocate for Spanish settlement by redistribution of mission lands. The missions, he argued, served only small Indio populations, while occupying the choicest farm and ranch lands needed for Spanish settlement. What may have been well-intentioned seemed to us an act of betrayal. Painful at the last. Though mended by the passing of time.

Padre Eusebio Francisco Kino left the solitude of his chamber to consecrate a new chapel to his beloved patron San Francisco Xavier at the village Santa Magdalena. There he took ill and joined his patron in eternal reward.

Eternal rest grant unto him oh Lord and let perpetual light shine upon him.

We laid him to rest in the shadow of a statue of his patron, San Francisco Xavier.

Requiescat in Pace.

—Louis Velarde, S.J.

AUTHOR'S NOTES

This is a biographical novel. The events of Padre Kino's life guide us, though as we note here, literary license has been taken in some aspects of the story. Locations and events seen through the lens of four centuries invite discrepancies. The best research sources we found are at times in conflict. Where inconsistencies appeared, we relied on what seemed to be the best indications. It is entirely possible a knowledgeable reader may find reason to dispute an account here or there. In any such case, our purpose is to entertain and inform a general audience.

Characters who play major roles in the story have a basis in historical fact, though some roles have been expanded to limit the number of characters the reader encounters in a work of broad scope. Father Goni's part in the seminary years is among them. Manje's role along with that of Atondo have been expanded to provide continuity to tensions between royal and ecclesiastical authorities and purposes. Manje enters the story for early California explorations he did not participate in. Atondo is "promoted" to viceroy in later chapters of the story. Father Augustin de Campos was a major figure in Pimeria Alta along with Father Kino. He enters the story early and serves as a proxy for the many missionaries who came and went over the years of Father Kino's ministry. Most tribal characters are fictional with the exception of prominent caciques who are based in historical fact. Minor characters incidental to the story are fictional.

Much is known about Father Kino's work in New Spain from his journal and personal writing along with those of Manje. Less is known of his journey there. We took some literary license to add adventure and human interest to that part of the story for the reader's enjoyment. The storm delay did occur and encounters with pirates were not uncommon at the time.

Other fictional elements in the story include dramatization of actual events as well as inclusion of fictional events consistent with Father Kino's ministry. Raising the hummingbird, for example, is fiction, though I have witnessed the phenomenon. His visits to the shrine of Our Lady of Guadalupe are speculation, though she did play an important part in connecting the faith to his tribal flock. Though he was tireless in his travels by horseback, Damascus is a fictional character. He did sleep on the ground or the floor with his saddle for a pillow as a matter of habit. He did make use of a rubber ball, magnifying glass, compass, and sundial to impress some of those he evangelized. He made multiple explorations to California once having established land passage possible. We have not included all of them for the sake of repetition. He is not known to have summoned schools of fish as in the gospel story.

Presuming to write about tribal culture without personal heritage or training as an ethnologist is difficult. When it comes to customs, beliefs, habits, values, and history, research only goes so far. Nuance and oral tradition, not reflected in source material, is significant. There is much we cannot know. Pima people are protective of their customs and traditions. Little is revealed to those not affiliated with the people. We can only hope to give the reader some appreciation for tribal perspective by fair and respectful portrayal.

We refer to the various tribes depicted in this work, using the anglicized names by which they are commonly known. "Pima" people, for example, encompass a number of clans depending on the region they inhabit and the structure of their communities. Pima refer to themselves as O'odham, phonetically pronounced "Authm," according to my ear. I do not claim my hearing is correct. See what we mean about nuance?

We have attempted to present the story as it unfolded in the seventeenth century to give the reader a clearer picture of the history. Examples include present day Gila River, then known as Hila Rio Grande, the Gulf of California, then thought to be the Sea of California, as California was believed to be an island. Similarly, the mission near modern day Tucson we know as San Xavier del Bac, is recorded in Padre Kino's journal as "Baac."

Today some disfavor the term *conversion,* in referring to evangelization. Conversion may imply some level of coercion. While a more enlightened view is certainly possible, it is a twenty-first-century perspective taken four centuries after the events of the story. Kino's evangelization was in no way coercive. Conversion is the term used by the black robes of the time and that is the one we use in the story. In a similar way, *Native American* is a term preferred by contemporary non-Native Americans, not necessarily preferred by tribal members themselves. We do not use the term out of respect, instead preferring the period term *Indio.*

Over the course of my writing journey, I have taken on some complex chapters in history. The Punitive Expedition, the Kansas-Missouri border prequel to the Civil War, and the Lincoln County War in New Mexico are examples. This story may be the most complex of all. Research, writing, and publication took more than four years. The project could not have been completed to the level we achieved without the advice and critique of generous supporters with expert knowledge of Father Kino and his ministry.

We owe special thanks to: Mark O'Hare, Father Greg Adolf, and Clague Van Slyke III, distinguished experts in the history of Padre Kino's ministry one and all. Each of them gave generously of his time to read and comment on our manuscript, helping shape its final form and keeping our story consistent with the facts and spirit of Father Kino's life. We cannot thank them enough.

Thanks are also due cartographer Matthew Hampton for his renderings of the maps, illustrating Padre Kino's mission fields. This is the second time we've turned to Matthew for his cartographic talents and once again he has come through in splendid form.

Still, with all this support, a work of this scope involves tradeoffs and considerations for the sake of the reader. I have attempted to note them here, though it is likely I neglected to mention one or more; historical nuances may have been overlooked and it is entirely possible discrepancies remain that are inconsistent with some aspect of the historical record. Wherever any of these occur, our intent is to present a fictional account for the enjoyment of a general audience.

As we prepare this manuscript for publication, Padre Kino's cause for canonization has been advanced by Pope Francis. His candidacy is now two steps away from sainthood.

—Paul Colt

SELECTED SOURCES

Kino's Historical Memoir of Pimeria Alta by Eusebio Francisco Kino. Applewood Books, 1919.

Eusebio Kino, S.J. Not Counting the Cost by John J. Martinez, S.J.

Rim of Christendom by Herbert Eugene Bolton. Macmillan Company, 1936.

The Padre on Horseback by Herbert Eugene Bolton. Loyola University Press, 1986.

A Pima Past by Anna Moore Shaw. The University of Arizona Press, 1974.

Catholic Public Domain Bible; electronic book edition, V.0.6.0.k.

ABOUT THE AUTHOR

Paul Colt's critically acclaimed historical fiction crackles with authenticity. His analytical insight, investigative research, and genuine horse sense bring history to life. His characters walk off the pages of history with a blend of Jeff Shaara's historical dramatizations and Robert B. Parker's gritty dialogue. Paul Colt History entertains and informs. Paul's *Grasshoppers in Summer,* and *Friends Call Me Bat* are Western Writers of America Spur Award honorees. *Boots and Saddles: A Call to Glory* received the Marilyn Brown Novel Award, presented by Utah Valley University. Reviewers recognize Paul's lively, fast-paced style, complex plots, and touches of humor. Readers say,

"Pick up a Paul Colt book,
you can't put it down."

Paul lives in Wisconsin with his wife and

high school sweetheart, Trish. To learn more visit Facebook @paulcoltauthor.

Printed in the USA
CPSIA information can be obtained
at www.ICGtesting.com
JSHW021116041023
49568JS00004B/4